Payton Edgar's Portrait

M. J. T. Seal

To Bootle

PROLOGUE

Payton's Plate,
The London Evening Clarion,
July 19th, 1962

Why would any self-respecting diner wish to attend La Maison Sebastien in the heart of dear old Knightsbridge?

This was the question I posed to myself as I entered the establishment for what we were promised would be a most delicious evening of cuisine classique par excellence. There are many obvious answers to this query as, for a few years now, we have been force-fed juicy lies from the culinary grapevine hailing Sebastien Ferrier's premier concern 'Chez Sebastien' as a tour-de-force of fashionable food, ambience and style. Given the unfathomable success of what has become one of London's "*most hippest joints*", to quote Harwell's derisory Guidebook (one should not, however, expect too much from our transatlantic cousins), it was only a matter of time before the Grande-dame of French cuisine spawned en enfant terrible.

Monsieur Ferrier's second restaurant considers itself to be a cut above other London eateries, and certainly makes something of an impression upon entering. The faux-french decor with its brightly coloured pillars, chalk boards and hanging vegetables makes for a jarring contrast from the grey city streets outside.

While my dining companion, Mr Spence, was impressed by the elaborate furnishings, I could not fail to be distracted by the stench of the proprietor's unnecessarily raised self-opinion. Those who are acquainted with Monsieur Ferrier cannot help but draw comparisons between the owner and his establishments. This new venture is sure to be similarly over-rated.

When dining in a highly regarded establishment, one does not expect to be horrified by the tablecloths. While Monsieur Ferrier may con-

1

sider white paper coverings to be authentically French, they are, in fact, cheap, unappealing to the eye and somewhat harsh on the elbows. If a proprietor cannot find the funds in his pocket to obtain decent linens then what similar cut backs are we to expect of his food?

This question was soon to be answered.

Our waiter, Henry (although one imagines in this role one would spell it Henri) was about as French as Buckingham Palace, but nevertheless demonstrated a shocking Gallic drawl, Hollywood-style. This was most embarrassing as his French vocabulary did not even seem to cover the words contained on the menu. On top of this, the young man was clearly set to local French time with his service being around an hour behind.

And so to the menu - a typically English view of France's offerings it has to be said, with an equally predictable wine list. It is difficult to go wrong with French wines, but La Maison do their very best and so to accompany our meal we settled for a basic, tolerable Cotes de Rhone. To begin with Mr Spence rather bravely opted for the soupe de poissons and I played safe with the oeufs en cocotte, after having witnessed a neighbouring diner noisily gagging over his unusually lumpy foie gras.

My appetiser arrived in a rather vulgar ramekin but was pleasant enough, although I was shocked to find a few delicate asparagus tips under the eggs which should surely have been mentioned on the menu. Mr Spence's watery fish soup was a resounding failure that I refused to sample, and I am certain that any self respecting alley cat would do the same.

Our entrees carried with them the feeling of deja vu in the quality department. My tiny foie de veau was disappointing in the extreme, containing the smallest, toughest pieces of meat I have ever tasted which were hiding within far too generous a portion of parsley au naturel. Mr Spence was comparatively pleased with his confit de canard au figues but was too polite to point out the stringy meat's slightly sour aftertaste. One should always be suspicious of figs when out of season, not to mention far from their country of origin, and with good reason considering the over-sweet mush my companion had been served.

Our palate was so jaded following this that I avoided entremets and accepted a suspiciously watery port before hastily departing.

To use an appropriate term, our experience at La Maison was something of a faux pas. And so I return to my original question - why would any self respecting diner wish to attend La Maison Sebastien? To which I have only one answer.

Je ne sais pas.

Payton Edgar

PART 1

Chapter I

In which Payton Edgar suffers an abysmal day

Payton Edgar studied himself in the mirror by the hatstand.

Despite one or two wrinkles and that slowly receding hairline, he didn't look half bad: the shirt immaculately ironed and fully buttoned, the encasing waistcoat holding in the navy tie which had been knotted with precision, the duck-egg tweed suit freshly pressed and without a mark, and finally the piece-de-resistance - a cyan neckerchief folded in a reverse puff in the top pocket.

With eyes still on the mirror, Payton Edgar took up his hat and stick and allowed himself a wry smile.

You've done yourself proud this morning, Mr Edgar.

And with that, Payton Edgar left the house.

Had he known that he was going to have such an unsavoury day then poor Payton Edgar would perhaps have stayed in bed.

Life is full of days that roll on by - uneventful and bland - each just like the one before it. Life is only very occasionally spattered with those all-too-rare days that are stimulating and life-affirming. And some days (and one hopes that these are of the rarer kind) are just abysmal.

Unfortunately, this Tuesday in July was to be one of those days.

It began with a disappointingly below-par breakfast at Mario's. Although the cuisine was, on the whole, fairly average, I had long enjoyed Mario's Café for it's atmosphere and it's heart. I had eventually got used to the bustle of the place and, at times, had even found myself enjoying the hum and swing of a busy city eatery. Mario himself was a rotund Spaniard with an unconvincing working-class bent and a tendency towards over-familiarity, but despite this I quite liked the place. It captured the spirit of the traditional English Tearoom, and never more so than at breakfast time.

Unfortunately, this Tuesday the place was more creche than café.

My peaceful contemplation of the charred hash browns were repeatedly interrupted by the squabbling of an inept mother and her small child, the likes of which should surely have been behind a desk at school and not causing chaos on a tea-room floor. The woman could barely lift a sugar lump to her cup without a great deal of concentration so how she managed the care of a young tearaway was beyond me.

Mario, pasty-faced and dripping in sweat, had failed to receive his delivery of the papers that morning and so I was forced to browse through an old coffee-ringed edition of 'Good Housekeeping'. The prices some girls would pay out for the latest in wedding fashions was appalling. To my left, a rhythmic tinkling sound caught my ear. A scruffy gentleman with thick, straw-like hair was stooped over a steaming cup, the handle of a teaspoon clamped between thumb and forefinger, stirring the brew. He continued to stir.

Any sugar within would have long dissipated, and yet he continued to stir.

And stir and stir and stir.

I tried to block out the tinkling, to focus my mind elsewhere, but it was all I could hear. Tinkle, tinkle, tinkle. It was a kind of torture, and yet he continued. He was in danger of wearing away the cup.

Soon, unable to tolerate the happy chirping of the frenzied urchin nearby and the tinkling of the scarecrow's teaspoon, I departed the establishment in a huff, and with only a cursory farewell to Mario.

For the umpteenth day in a row it was humid and uncomfortable, and it was with an unsettled heart that I made my way through the miserable throng of London Town as it cooked slowly in the heat. The recent smog had lifted, yet the air felt no clearer.

After purchasing a Clarion from the vendor outside Pimlico tube station (today's predictable headline, *'Britain Bakes'*), I made my way through town. The summer sun was a little hazier than it had been, but the heat on the ground was unbearable and I found myself in the unusual position of experiencing some unwanted perspiration within my suit.

I rather regretted wearing the waistcoat.

Town was fairly quiet that morning and I was glad of it. People always seem to get in the way.

I found myself mindlessly sucking my way through a quart of lemon sherbets in the looming shadow of Westminster Abbey. Although I had purchased The Clarion I was not of a mind to read it and the thing was to stay posted under my arm for some time. I was expecting to enjoy a lengthy pause for silent contemplation, however within minutes a small gang of filthy men in overalls appeared from nowhere and proceeded to clatter dustbins together, hollering and cursing in a most unap-

4

pealing manner. The stench of old fish and rotting vegetables was suddenly wafted into the warm air and I moved on, my stomach churning.

I headed towards St James's Park.

For me, London's parks have always been places of great peace and contemplation. My breakfast sat heavy in my gut and I felt the familiar acid heat rising in my stomach, a discomfort that could only be quelled by peaceful deliberation in one of our capital's nicest parks.

Unfortunately, my thirst for peaceful deliberation was not to be quenched.

It was a little busier in the park than out on the street, but the air was still. It was almost alarming to see how everybody was subdued by the sweltering sun. The ducks were gathered together in the shade like old women at a bus stop. Even the dogs were ambling about languidly rather than sprinting, panting and drooling in an extremely unappealing manner as they went. There were, thank goodness, very few children out in the small open spaces of the park, and I soon found a pleasant deckchair that had been erected in the shade of a huge oak as if especially for me.

I had only been resting there for a small number of minutes before my peace was rudely broken by a young couple who chose to frolic in the grass not more than a few feet from where I sat. I shuddered at the young lady's shrill giggles. A camera was produced, and the young man began to take snaps of his young companion. Her highly irritating outcries burst into my peaceful contemplation like tiny explosions. The young man was no better, grunting like some mindless idiot and ordering her about in some unfathomable northern accent. He grabbed her waist and swung her around in a number of circles. One cannot comment on how this affected her, but it certainly made me a little nauseous as I sat and scrutinised from my deckchair.

As she began snapping photographs of him in ridiculous poses I realised it was only a matter of time before they saw me and asked the inevitable. I was to be proved right.

'Excuse me, Sir?'

I looked up to the young woman who was holding out the camera to me, albeit with a sweet smile.

'Would you mind?'

She barely waited for a reply, and within the proverbial flash the camera was in my hands and they were snuggling up together and grinning like fools in my direction. Controlling my displeasure with a record-breaking calm, I merely smiled and lifted the camera to my eye. Once the picture was taken they trotted away and I lay back in the deckchair smiling to myself in silent victory, picturing the moment when they leafed through their ridiculous snapshots to find the one I had taken. I had been careful to cut out almost the entirety of their bodies, merely snapping the very tips of their foreheads and the hanging trees above, which were most surely the best feature in shot.

Their lesson - never cross Payton Edgar while he is relaxing in a deckchair.

I was granted five minutes rest and I drifted in silent concord until a polite cough brought me out of my thoughts. A young man in casuals was standing over me, around his neck hung a metal ticket contraption.

'Tuppence for the deck chair, sir,' he said with a squeak.

'How much?' I blustered, in genuine surprise. I was aware of the recent addition of charges for what I considered to be a public seat, however had not had an opportunity to assess the cost.

'Tuppence, sir.'

I made to get out of my chair.

'Well, I will not fork out a fortune, urgh!' I was having a little difficulty getting up. 'I will not fork out for just sitting in a public place, grr!'

Placing his arm through mine the young man helped me up. He was surprisingly strong, his arms probably strengthened by lugging deckchairs around day in, day out.

I uttered a meek *'thank you'* and then straightened myself, posted my newspaper back under the arm and then produced a coin out of my pocket. I held it high.

'Here is tuppence for you, for your help in getting me on my feet, young man. That is all. Payton Edgar will not pay for the privilege of merely sitting!'

After making a point of handing him the coin I stomped off, feeling a little better in myself for having taken a stern stance against deckchair extortion. I soon found that many of my preferred benches were taken by layabouts and gossiping fishwives, and was forced to retire to an empty bench which was, unfortunately, only partially shaded. I was soon gazing out across the green, my eyelids heavy.

I dozed.

I do not know how long I sat there, but it was certainly long enough for the sun to move and the shade to slide away, for when I did stir my nose and forehead certainly felt a little hotter, stiffer and drier than before. The rustle of the newspaper falling to my feet brought me back to my senses. I snatched it up, shuffled along the bench back into the shade and began to browse mechanically over the pages. I rubbed my cheek gently, aware that it had also reddened somewhat in the lazy sun.

The news itself that day was unremarkable and made for a grim read. More politicians getting their knickers in a twist over international trivialities, some unimportant drivel about a new rock and roll band and yet more discussion on the recent smog.

And then to the letters page.

I have never taken any particular interest in the letters page. The general public's opinions are, more often than not, wholly disagreeable and very poorly written, often focusing on frustratingly trivial matters such as domestic waste removal or tavern opening hours, their pointless ranting always spattered with horrendous grammatical errors. However two words on this particular letters page caught my eye. A name.

My Name!

Payton Edgar.

I felt a flutter of a thrill. A letter - about me! This had been a long time coming, much, much too long. I had been writing my restaurant columns now for well over a year with nothing more than a vague reference in the editor's summary, and yet now, finally, I was getting returns. My eyes shot to the name at the foot of the letter.

Fabien Pouche, Bayswater.

There was no address, just the name and area, and I have to say that I was a little relieved that it was entirely unfamiliar. A fan? The unusual name had a ring of sophistication about it, that of foreign mystique - surely a man of erudition. However, as I sat back and took in the letter, my opinion changed rather dramatically.

I read and re-read the vile letter in absolute horror.

Chapter II

In which Payton Edgar stands unjustly accused

Your Letters
The London Clarion, July 1962

I write in response to the review by Payton Edgar of La Maison Sebastien (July 19th). Does Mr Edgar himself have any experience of running a successful eatery? One can only assume that he doesn't. I have attended the aforementioned restaurant on a number of occasions and have been consistently surprised, not only by the simple quality of the food but also of the service itself. Please could The Clarion request a little education in its correspondents, as surely even the most naive Gallophile is aware that the country sets its clock an hour ahead of GMT and not behind as Mr Edgar states in his piece. In response to Mr Edgar's particularly fastidious comments about the paper tablecloths I would say that if he finds such materials symbolic then I would like to point out that his review will now be nowhere better but covering today's greasy fish and chips, which is in my opinion exactly where it belongs.

If the Clarion cannot find a fair and - more importantly - educated restaurant critic then I suggest they disband this column and extend the more entertaining (not to mention altogether more accurate) horoscopes column opposite.

Fabien Pouche, Bayswater

I could barely draw breath.
I read the letter a number of times in disbelief, each time my heart

pounding a little faster in anger. Rage blinded me for a good few minutes before the questions flowed. Just who was this Fabien Pouche chappie, anyway? How dare he question my experience? How dare he imply that my reviews are inaccurate? How dare he call my comments fastidious?

In the main, *how dare he*?

I nearly tore the newspaper to pieces there and then, but instead forced myself to carefully fold it and place it beside me on the bench. I primed my chest with a deep inhalation before scowling for a while out over the miserable yellow-green of the Summer grass. I heard Irving's soothing voice in my ear, telling me to keep calm; to breathe slowly and keep calm. Unfortunately, even the thought of this gentle order only served to stoke my irritation. Irving was often irritatingly nonchalant about such things.

Folding my arms in closely to my chest I began to reason with myself. One single negative letter was all it was, compared to the hundreds of positive, awestruck reports I would receive if only people were not so busy in their lives to put pen to paper. Of course, this made sense - the man Pouche had been free to bother writing such a pointless letter to the paper, and therefore he must have an excess of time on his hands, and surely be unemployed. And why would he be without employ? Because he was lazy. And probably entirely unemployable come to that. Fabian Pouche; unemployable, lazy, angry and irritable. The man must spend his life finding things to complain about, his only satisfaction being to pick upon perfect pieces of journalism and to write endless inane letters of complaint.

Fabien Pouche - clearly a very lonely, stupid and unhappy man.

And what sort of a name was Pouche anyway? French or Spanish perhaps?

My eyes focused on a slightly Mediterranean-looking bowler-hatted gentleman who was fast approaching with great strides, and for a ridiculous moment I wondered if this could be him - if this could indeed be Fabien Pouche passing by?

Steady yourself, Payton, I told myself. Random speculation was a path I must avoid. I tried to compose myself as I watched the striding businessman move on. This was a respectable City gent, and could not have been Pouche.

My man Fabien would have no hat.

A moment later a hatless young man passed by on a bike. With slight continental features he looked the spitting image of Fabien Pouche. I had to restrain myself from trotting on in his wake and shouting obscenities. I felt the well of anger stirring in my stomach once more, my wrinkled brow dry and burning, and realised that I had to move, to walk away and walk quickly.

I stood and set off, my fists clenched.

I was a good few strides along the path before I realised that in my haste I had set off without the blasted newspaper, leaving the ludicrous letter on the bench for any passing stranger to read. I turned sharply back towards the seat where a short, plump lady in a prim green dress suit was approaching the bench from the other direction. A stiff, grey-looking man followed in her wake. In his hand was a lead which connected very close to the ground to a small hairy creature that sat yapping.

As the woman went to sit I stooped quickly and reached out for the paper, rescuing it from being pressed underneath her ample rump by pulling it away just in time. At my swift action the lady gave a loud shriek akin to an opera singer warming up for the opening night and we all started. Even the dog stopped yapping at this deafening emission.

'Heavens!' She panted, clutching her bosom. 'You touched me!'

I forced a gentlemanly smile. 'I do beg your pardon, madam. I was merely retrieving my newspaper-'

'Mortimer! He touched me!' She continued to shriek, yapping like the dog at our feet. Her eyes were wide and frenzied, her jaw firm. She was a curious, horse-faced woman. Her companion's expression remained inanimate.

'He... ' she ran her hand down her hip as if wiping away filth, '- touched me!'

'I was merely-'

'How dare you!' she hollered, as if she were the Queen of England and I had tweaked her nose on Coronation day. Her eyes ran up and down from my feet to my head as she appraised her assailant with distaste. I squared up and returned her glare, realising how preposterous the ageing lady was in her neat pressed suit and garish headscarf. She was caked in make-up akin to household plaster, her hair stretched tightly up over her crown and fastened with a shining jewelled clip. Horse-face may have presented herself as a shrieking lunatic, but she was clearly a moneyed shrieking lunatic at that.

In normal circumstances I may have been appalled that my actions had been misunderstood and caused a lady such distress. I would have most humbly apologised for any unintentional upset caused, possibly even doffing my hat in respect, had I being wearing one. However on that particular abysmal morning, and after reading that rotten letter nothing else mattered, and certainly not the squealing of an over-privileged harpy.

Horse-face continued to shriek. 'Mortimer! The man... touched me!'

'I was merely picking up my newspaper,' I said through gritted teeth before turning to leave.

'How dare you touch me like that!'

My bubbling anger reached a critical point and I turned back to face her. 'I did not touch you, in any way! My newspaper may have brushed past you, for which I am sorry-'

'Ugh!' she clamped a painted hand to her throat. 'I feel nauseous.'

'Madam, I-'

'I mean it! I'm going to be sick!'

'If I could just-'

'I knew we should avoid the park!' She ignored me, addressing the lap dog of a man who accompanied her. 'You see! Two minutes stroll and I get attacked - by a pervert!'

'Excuse me!'

Incensed, I moved in closer - perhaps too close because the be-jewelled crone shrunk back a little, her eyes wide. 'Madam, if you would be so kind as to stop your carping for just a minute, I could explain, but as you won't listen to anyone but yourself I shan't bother, only to say that I wouldn't touch any part of your corpulent, repellent old body if you were the last human being on Earth!'

And with that I left her, clucking and simpering to her aide. As I walked away seething I rolled the newspaper tightly in both hands, my mind beset with thoughts of Fabien Pouche.

Lucille was no comfort whatsoever.

I returned home with a slam of the door and some rather satisfying huffing but still she did not appear. I thwacked the newspaper on the kitchen table with considerable gusto, taking deep breaths through my nose, and even then she did not come. The house sat still and silent. Miss Kemp, our live-in nursemaid, was in town shopping for my aunt's sundries. I breezed through the lounge and into the hallway. The door to Aunt Elizabeth's room was closed, as usual, and I softened my footsteps instinctively. The last thing I wanted was another pointless confrontation with the old woman. She had been especially galling of late.

Once I was at my bedroom, where my heavy curtains remained drawn against the sun, I flicked on the light sharply.

Lucille had been enjoying one of her regular epic naps, and even with the room suddenly illuminated she did nothing to acknowledge my presence save to open one eyelid lazily, her head nuzzled into my plump bedspread which sat folded on the ottoman. I stood in the doorway for a moment waiting for her to move in acknowledgment of my presence, to slide over to me or, at the very least, to sit up. Anything to show that she wished to sooth my seething rage. And still, nothing.

The eyelid closed once more and she continued to dream her feline dreams.

Snapping off the light noisily I strode back along the hallway, infuriated further by her nonchalance. At times like this, I cursed the cat. Why was it that when, on the odd occasion that I returned home needing peace and quiet, I was consistently dogged by Lucille and her attention-seeking mewing, and yet when I returned needing support and somebody to talk to she was nowhere to be seen? I would at least have thought that she would have come to me guided by her stomach. I glanced at my watch. Surely she must be hungry again by now?

An answer of sorts came when I noted the blood-stained remains of a rat's hind quarters on the mat besides the back door. My stomach churned. Lucille had already dined well at lunchtime. Disgusted, I left the corpse, hoping that it would be finished off later, otherwise I would have to instruct Grace to don her marigolds and dispose of the fetid thing.

I returned to the kitchen where I grabbed the newspaper and headed around to number twenty-nine Clarendon Street.

Number twenty-nine Clarendon Street; home to Mr Irving Spence, my dear friend and companion.

At times the man can be the irritatingly vacant and distracted, for he is an artist. Indeed he is the most prolific artist I have ever known, when he puts his mind to it. The year had started badly for my friend, for he had suffered a prolonged period of, for want of a better phrase, painter's-block. However, after some prime meddling by *yours truly* he had recently shaken this off and turned into an avid and talented portrait painter. It had been quite a turnaround, and most welcome. He even had a major exhibition on the horizon.

As I approached the house I had been dismayed to see that a bird had left it's message on his lower front window and that Irving hadn't bothered to clean this away. It took four sharp knocks before the door was opened, and even then only with a distracted click of the lock. I retrieved the warm pint of milk which had sat on the doorstep for heaven knows how long, pushed the heavy door open and moved on in. Irving was already disappearing back into his studio.

'You should at the very least see who it is at the door!' I called after him.

No reply.

'And you do know that there is a sizeable amount of bird dirt on your front window?' I persisted to no avail. I edged slowly along the hallway.

Irving's house is very similar to mine in construction, however it could not be any more different when it comes to furnishings. I am exceedingly proud of my abode. There are not many houses in central

London that can boast an antique Tibetan singing bowl in the living room and pottery slates from ancient Mesopotamia mounted in the hallway. I believe that one's accoutrements must be both functional and appealing to the eye. I have worked hard over the years to make the rooms in my gorgeous townhouse spacious by clever use of such furnishings. Asked to sum up my abode in one word, the word *deluxe* springs readily to mind.

At first impressions, Irving's hovel appears more cramped, its dark hallways winding.

Where I have opted for a Regency air, with sweeping curtains, plastered columns and discreet palm motifs, Irving's place has an unfinished, rustic feel with - if one is looking for it - the odd corner of wallpaper peeling off and furniture that is durable and practical rather than enjoyable. I am keen to ensure that my abode carries the scent of dried roses through its rooms, where upon entering Irving's place one is usually assaulted by the stench of oil paints. At Irving's place, my eyes are always on the lookout for those first signs of rising damp that must surely only be a winter or two away.

With this in mind, a short time ago I had bought him a gift - the gift of Mrs Montgomery.

I have had Mrs Montgomery in to do what needs to be done once a week ever since my divorce and have always found her to be an exceedingly efficient domestic. She is quiet, unremarkable and happy to do the household jobs which I find gruelling. Her duties include the dusting, the polishing, the cleaning of cupboards and the refrigerator, using the unfathomable vacuum cleaner, the washing of windows inside and out, the pulling of weeds from the cobbles outside the front door, and handwashing my clothes and pressing my trousers. She can also be called upon to repaint scuffing on the skirting boards and has shown skill with upholstering small items of furniture, at my direction, of course.

The dear woman had also agreed to maintain the stock of my refrigerator and larder, as light food shopping is (without wishing to sound haughty or supercilious) a duty which I consider to be far beneath a person of my social stature. Unlike many helps that I have come across she is also discreet and unconcerned with the details of my personal life. She is, in short, a domestic angel. Providing an angel is permitted to have a scrubber's stoop and hands drier than a desert carcass, that is.

The disarray of domestic anarchy in Irving's place had finally proved too much for me to witness and, not entirely unselfishly, I had presented him with Mrs Montgomery as a birthday gift, paying her a fair raise on her regular rates to keep his troubled house in order. All rooms except the studio that is, as was his rule. The woman was a godsend, and had done a sterling job, given the circumstances.

I deposited the milk on the formica work surface of Irving's gloomy kitchen and took one cautious step into the studio. Irving's studio was what would have been a pleasant living room had a normal person dwelt within. Instead, features such as the fireplace and windows had been hidden from sight by countless canvasses. I was always careful not to sit or to brush against anything, as moist paint smears were abundant.

Irving, in his usual painting uniform of loose flannel trousers and a white linen shirt, was drying a couple of brushes on a messy rag that had once been curtains, and I ordered him to the front room immediately.

Miss Kemp had once described Irving to me as *"the Laurel to your Hardy"*, a simile that had enraged me at the time but had given me cause to smile a little whenever it came to mind. My Mr Laurel was soon perched on the arm of his moth-eaten recliner and peering at me over his little round spectacles.

'Good Lord, Payton, you are positively glowing!'

'What?'

'It's barely lunchtime and you have the skin of a lobster!'

'Yes, well-' I stammered, running my fingers a little over my face unhappily. I had not come to discuss the condition of my skin, although from the minute that he had pointed it out I felt the soreness with every facial movement I made.

'I have had a dreadful morning, Irving, and I have to tell you about it. I have been assaulted in the park,' I began. 'I was-'

'Goodness!' he said swiftly, 'by a dog?'

I stopped at this interruption and looked him in the eye. 'No, not by a dog. Whatever gave you that idea? It was a woman, but that is not the point-'

'A woman assaulted you?'

'Yes, but-'

'Why on earth would a woman assault you?'

I sighed. 'The horse-faced misery sat on my newspaper. It's a long story, and not what I intended-'

'This is what you need to see me about, so urgently? A lady in the park sat on your newspaper?' Irving groaned, his face a little stern. If I hadn't known better I would think that my interruption to his work had been unwelcome.

'Irving, if you'd just stop butting in all the time I could explain it to you. The assault was merely the cherry on the rancid Bakewell that has been my morning. *This* is the problem!' I pushed the newspaper towards him dramatically.

'Read this. Page nine, letters to the editor.'

He did as instructed while I paced the room, the words of that vile letter running through my head like a particularly nasty poem. *No experience? Fastidious! Fish and Chips!* To question one's review of an establishment may be fair enough, but this was an attack. A very personal attack.

An attack against the very name of Payton Edgar!

What happened next was more than a little unfortunate, but Irving could not help himself. As his eyes scanned the page a thin smile had appeared and I caught him struggling to keep his lips together and not reveal teeth, desperately trying to avoid turning the wry smile into a laugh. My heart lurched with indignation.

'Irving! How dare you smile!' I said with force, my brow burning once more. As he finished the letter he had the audacity to allow a chuckle burst from his lips. I snatched the newspaper back and moved to the window.

'I have had the most dreadful morning - and you laugh!'

'Payton, be calm, be calm!' He outstretched his fingers and lowered his palms in a noticeably patronising plea for silence. I found myself breathing in deeply through my nose. He took a step forwards and I made sure to keep my back to him.

'You are a journalist Payton, your work is in print. You are out in the public eye, and will have to get used to that. You are going to get this kind of thing. Besides, you've had the odd comment before over Margaret Blythe-'

'That may be true, Irving, but that was Dr Blythe and Dr Blythe's column, and not Payton Edgar. Do you see? Dr Blythe invites debate. Payton Edgar's piece is...gospel.' I swallowed hard before continuing. 'This denigration is aimed entirely at me! And you can stop smiling! It is not amusing. Not amusing at all. Where are the praises, the plaudits? I know for a fact that my restaurant column is enjoyed by thousands of Londoners all over the city and yet the one letter printed is this – this - contemptible attack!'

Irving was still smiling, albeit lightly.

'People don't write in to a newspaper with praise, Payton. Or at least if they do the editor doesn't bother to print it. Where is the interest in an *"oh, that was really nice"* letter? Readers want conflict, anger, damnation!' He pointed to the newspaper with a paint spattered finger. 'I'm sorry but I think this is great!'

'I beg your pardon?'

'It is free speech! The right to reply. As it should be.'

I was now fighting a fresh fury in my chest. 'You agree? You agree with this... this... idiot?'

'I am not saying that, Payton, not at all. All I'm saying is that you have had the freedom to write your opinion, and then he should have the freedom to write his.'

'It is a personal attack!' I shook the paper firmly in the air briefly. 'He questions my education, he implies that I am the idiot!'

Irving shrugged. 'Perhaps, but I say it's a good thing. It's good for the paper, and, believe it or not, I think that it might even be good for your column.'

For a moment I was stunned into silence. I fiddled with my cravat thoughtfully, but it was no good. Irving was wrong, pure and simple, and I could not quell the feelings of frustration, not to mention betrayal. It was easy for him to say these things from the outside, when it wasn't happening to him. It was easy for him to shrug it all off as it wasn't he who was being questioned, his very persona assassinated in the London press. I said as much, struggling to keep my voice from slipping into an anguished squeak. However, Irving simply stood and looked at me calmly, waiting for me to finish.

'Look, let's not get knickers in twists, Payton. Why don't we head out to Harvey's tonight for a really nice meal? That'll put things in perspective.'

A nice try! I raised my chin.

'No. I have a better idea. There's something I have to do. I have an itch to scratch.'

'An itch?'

'Yes,' I replied, 'an itch.' A thought had occurred to me about the Fabien Pouche letter, a niggle of a suspicion that had grown and grown. This vague sense of suspicion had now matured to become a simple truth. 'I have to return to Chez Sebastien's tonight-' I continued with bravado, '-and you are coming with me.'

Irving shook his head stubbornly. 'Out of the question! What on earth would drag you back there? You loathed it, and I'm not sure I can take another night of you moaning and sneering at the place. Payton, you said yourself that our first visit would also be the last. The review was dreadful even by your standards. And besides,' his face darkened, 'Sebastien Ferrier may be there...'

'My point exactly!' I flung the newspaper to the carpet with admirable dramatic flare. 'I think that cretin Ferrier is behind the letter!'

'What?'

'Who else would write such a venomous piece? It's no coincidence! I give his restaurant a bad review and then what happens? Suddenly this letter appears! This is how he responds, a childish attack on the letters page!' I nudged the toe of my brogue into the newspaper and gave it a sharp little kick to the corner of the room. 'I bet that Mr Fabien Pouche doesn't even exist. Or if he does, I bet he is something to do with that fool of a chef. The whole thing smells of the snide Monsieur Ferrier! Fishy!'

You may have guessed that there is some difficult history between myself and the faux-French restaurateur, however the details of this are too complicated and, quite frankly, too unimportant to go into at this point in time.

Irving was looking at me wearily and yet did not reply. He merely shook his head and made for the door.

'You go where you like, I will not go back there with you, Payton.'

'Fine!' I declared, more than a little hurt. 'I will go alone.'

I had absolutely no intention of going alone.

Chapter III

In which Payton Edgar scratches his itch

Dear Mr Spence,
You are cordially invited to dine with The Raqs Sharqi Club on Wednesday 25th at the Follett Gallery, Kensington. 9pm sharp. This invitation is extended to Mr Payton Edgar of the London Evening Clarion. Please do not R.S.V.P. We look forward to seeing you both.
Lord and Lady Charles Follett

Of course Irving accompanied me to La Maison Sebastien that night, for I had him over a barrel.

After declaring that I would dine alone and making overtures to depart, Irving had spoken slowly and quietly, as I knew he would.

'I'll see you tomorrow then, Payton.'

I froze abruptly and then turned smoothly on my heel, fixing him with a quizzical look. 'You haven't forgotten?' he continued. 'Tomorrow night is the Raqs Sharqi Club meal. I'll call on you at half past eight.'

It had not slipped my mind.

Poor Irving had been working like a trouper in the lead up to his second major exhibition which was due to open at the Follett Gallery which sat on the outer edges of Tower Hamlets. Word of his unique style of portraiture had spread and Irving had found himself commissioned by a certain Lord Charles Follett to paint not only his portrait, but that of his wife and to display these amongst other work at their gallery.

He had also invited us to dinner on the 25th.

It was to be a meeting of the Raqs Sharqi Club, an elite group formed by the Folletts themselves and known only to those who move among the upper echelon of high society, in particular those who are the pivotal players in London's art scene. By this I do not mean the disheveled and unsavoury artists themselves, but those who pay the highest price for the expensive trinkets, sculptures and canvasses produced by such people. Those that swing from auction house to art house with a mere flutter of the wallet.

I had heard many titbits of interest about the Raqs Sharqi Club over the years. They were, by all accounts, an extremely select group. I had learned from the society pages of the Clarion that they congregate monthly in a wing of the Follett gallery for good food, fine wine and intellectual conversation. It was rumoured that The Raqs Sharqi Club contained persons known for their creativity in the arts, and renowned medics or scientists who may be pioneers in their field. It had been suggested many, many times that only the greatest names and individuals of note are called upon to join the group.

Somebody who moved in such circles had clearly heard of my acquaintance with Irving, as they had specified in the invitation that I should accompany him to dinner. My restaurant reviews had been well received from day one, and it was not a surprise that word of my celebrity had got around town. As I had suspected, I was destined to move in higher social circles now that I was *a name*.

The club's members were reportedly hand-picked by the Folletts, and it seemed that I was to be one of them. At first Irving had been reluctant to attend, but I had soon persuaded him that to go would be in his professional interests. An invitation to such an event is one of the greatest honours of elite London society that I can imagine, and I had been thrilled at the thought.

Of course, I could never have let such an appointment slip my mind, but I let my face go blank and feigned ignorance.

'I beg your pardon?' I asked Irving coldly, and not without malice. 'What about tomorrow night?'

'You can't have forgotten, Payton! Dinner at Tower Hamlets?'

Irving glared at me indignantly. I bit my lip and arched an eyebrow.

'Oh, that. I can't come. Sorry.'

'What?'

'I can't come,' I said simply, calling a bluff like I had never called a bluff before.

Irving gritted his perfectly white teeth. 'But we have to attend now, Payton. You insisted, and it is too short notice to cancel-'

'Then you will have to go alone.'

'Payton! You know I need you there.'

I allowed a faint smile to pass my lips.

'And I need you tonight, at Sebastien's.'

There was a long pause, holding something of a stony silence. I could see Irving marvelling a little at how childish I could be and I have to admit I had even impressed myself. Finally, he spoke, and this time quietly and with care.

'Okay, you win. I will come to Sebastien's tonight,' he said and raised a finger, 'but on one condition. No hysterics, no creating a scene. I want a nice, quiet meal.'

Ignoring his ill-chosen words, I nodded, but promised nothing.

'Call for me at seven. And wear the mustard yellow suit.'

Irving looked puzzled. 'You told me to wear that tomorrow night, with the Raqs Sharqi lot.'

I had indeed insisted that he wear his neat mustard suit, my particular favourite, to the meal at the Follett gallery.

'Okay, the pistachio green will do for tonight. Mustard tomorrow.'

And with that, I closed the front door behind me.

Walking the few steps back to my flat I felt the warm glow of a personal victory settle over me. I had a plan - to investigate the origins of the mysterious Fabien Pouche, and with the added bonus of having Irving at my side. And I still got to dine with the Raqs Sharqi Club in to the bargain.

Once inside the comfort of my town house I moved over to my beautiful Rococo mirror and spent some time studying my alarmingly red face.

La Maison Sebastien, yet again.

The irritating maitre d' welcomed us in the same smug manner that he had only a fortnight before, issuing an unnecessary and overloud "*bonsoir!*" upon our arrival. If he recognised us from our previous visit he gave no sign of it, merely nodding at the name, taking my hat, my stick and Irving's jacket and then shuffling us along to our table. He was, thankfully, too professional in manner to ogle my deep red blazing forehead and nose. As the day had progressed my mildly scorched face had dried and cracked into a mask of relentless discomfort.

We were shown past the rather over-exposed table in the centre of the room in which we had been positioned before and moved over to a pleasant little booth at the back, where we were seated and presented with the familiar flimsy cardboard menus I had disapproved of so strongly on our last visit. Wasting no time I caught the white-haired attendant before he glided away with a pointed finger and a sharp question.

'Sir, is Mr Pouche here tonight?'

He stopped for a moment and I was convinced that I caught a

flicker of recognition sweep across the man's face. I may, however, have been mistaken.

'I'm sorry sir, the name is not familiar to me,' he said dismissively. 'Do excuse me. As you can see, we are very busy tonight.' With that he slid away rather sharpish. Very busy? I counted six empty tables as I examined the restaurant floor. Irving was fidgeting uncomfortably in his seat and I watched him for a moment.

He had knocked on my door at precisely seven o'clock, looking fairly natty in the mustard yellow suit. I was vexed in the extreme.

'I said to wear the pistachio suit tonight! The mustard was for to-morrow!'

His brow had furrowed and he had protested rather assertively that I had requested the yellow suit for the evening and I, not wanting to antagonise his sensitivity more than I already had that day, had gracefully conceded. The second-rate pistachio would have to do for the Raqs Sharqi Club. I also chose not to mention my displeasure at his choice of tie; a somewhat clownish red bow tie that would not be amiss at a child's birthday party.

We were both on our best behaviour and humouring each other somewhat as we set off on the short walk to La Maison Sebastien.

It was a beautiful summer evening and the day trippers had fled the city leaving its streets littered and baron, awaiting the night time crowd of diners and drinkers. The sun was low in the sky, sending golden blocks of light across the roads ahead of us, and I was glad that a gentle evening breeze had stirred in the wake of another blistering day.

As we strolled along, Irving and I talked a little about my work and the various hats I wore, for not only was I the Clarion's restaurant critic, I had also been working on the agony piece for some time.

Peggy's postbag had once been an unimpressively fluffy affair, an assembly in print for the illiterate and the idiotic. The very fatuousness of the agony column had made it even more surprising that I had been commissioned to take over the piece earlier in the year. This was, on reflection, a considerably wise and shrewd move by the powers-that-be at the London Clarion. I had reinvented the piece, creating a forum for the social philosopher.

The column had proved to be a huge success, threatening to outdo even my restaurant review. Dr Margaret Blythe took no prisoners, and was on a crusade to right the Capital's wrongs.

The fact that I was indeed Dr Margaret Blythe was a closely guarded secret.

It had been some months since I had taken on this double life, and the secret thrill of it had lost none of its sting, and it was nice to chat with my friend about the peculiarities of my correspondents.

It was Irving who started the quarrel.

It was as we passed by Victoria Station that he made his absurd statement.

'I can't believe we are bothering to do this,' he said, 'all to scratch an itch.'

I was quick to reply.

'What better to do with an itch but to scratch it, Irving?'

A stern silence accompanied by a sharp upward glance was worse than any reply he could have made. I went on, reminding him of various times when past itches of mine had proved fruitful, and even though I may have flowered my language a little he accused me of altering facts in the stories just to fit my theory. I knew without a doubt, however, that my intuition was second-to-none, and said as much. It all got fairly heated and I soon grew sick of the word "itch".

As is so very often the case on such occasions, I was pleased to be the one to have the last word.

'And anyway, Irving,' I had said with an air of finality, 'my feelings about the origin of that vile letter are no longer down to a mere itch. It is now a *conviction*. Ferrier has something to do with it, you mark my words.'

It was a touch too warm within the restaurant with all the hot food and perspiring bodies crammed inside, but still I kept my light summer jacket on. One would never wish to appear in public in just a mere shirt and tie. Opposite me, Irving was squirming a little. I could see why he was finding it difficult to get comfortable on the red leather upholstery. Like the rest of the establishment it was brand new and, as well as feeling stiff to one's seat, was sprung rather generously with what felt like sharpened iron springs. These springs poked at the buttocks when in certain positions.

Perhaps Monsieur Ferrier considered discomfort to be a detail particular to the traditional French restaurant.

I found myself frowning as I fingered the corner of the crisp white paper tablecloth in silent disapproval. Irving caught this act of condemnation and gave a discreet shake of the head to remind me I was not here as a critic tonight. As if I could ever truly be anything else!

'Irving, my dear, you seem to think that I am able to remove the mantle of critic as easily as one removes a hat, and at any available opportunity. I am afraid that you are wrong.' I glared at him from under my brow, instantly regretting the move as it merely tore at the leathery sunburn on my forehead. I stopped myself from going on. Had I been a tad too harsh? Perhaps. And so I amended my statement.

'I will, however, endeavour to doctor my *modus operandi* and avoid my natural urge to act as a detractor for the purposes of this evening if you wish, Irving.'

He had the temerity to roll his eyes, and I forced myself to study the carte de jour with a faux innocent curiosity. We sat in silence for a while as we considered our selections. I browsed the menu, lips pursed, and was a little surprised to see a rather interesting selection of special dishes paper-clipped to the page. I muttered idly as I perused my options.

'We shall order, and I shall enquire once more about Pouche!' Irving spoke out with a measure of irritation in his voice.

'If you have to Payton. As far as I'm concerned we are here to put to bed the ridiculous idea that that letter is all a part of a Sebastien Ferrier conspiracy.' He waved a hand around as if shooing off a bluebottle. 'Please just go ahead and ask whatever questions you have to and then we can enjoy our meal.'

'Enjoy?' I whispered dismissively, but then allowed myself to give a short snort. 'I will do my very best. But I beg of you, Irving, please don't have that fish soup abomination again.' At this my companion said nothing.

The young boy Henry (*"Henri"*) sloped over to our table and, unlike the maitre d', this worker recognised Irving and I at once. He proceeded to greet us with a little too much familiarity for my liking. Also unlike the maître-de, the young man was most certainly not too professional to ogle my sunburn, and he grimaced in mock sympathy before continuing to stare in amusement at my delicate visage.

'Gentlemen, bonsoir!' he had chimed. 'Vous returnez!'

I did not answer this piece of poorly executed pidgin French, but Irving did and they exchanged a few friendly words. As they spoke I told myself that to get to the bottom of the Pouche mystery I would have to change tack and butter up the boy somewhat.

'Have you chosen your vin for this evening, gentlemen?'

Irving, holding out the more-than-disappointing wine list, went to speak but I interrupted with a smile.

'We will have a red. Not the house red, but a red of your recommendation, Henri. Whatever region and grape that you currently advocate.' I ignored Irving who was now looking at me in surprise.

The boy shrugged. 'It depends on what you are eating.'

'Well, I feel in the mood for a succulent red meat dish tonight, perhaps one of your delightful specials. So whatever you think would go well with that shall be superb, I am sure.'

Irving was now looking at me as if I had sprouted rabbit ears, well aware that my usual tack was to grill the unsuspecting server on their knowledge of vintages and dimensions of olfaction. But that night Henry was lucky to be sheltered from such demands, owing to my ulterior motive. It was not long before he returned to us with a fairly acceptable Cahors and took our orders.

Throughout this I was biding my time for the right moment to strike, and did so just as he was about to leave.

'Oh! Just before you go, young man, I have a question,' I said, sensing Irving shrinking back in his seat. Henry looked down at me, blank faced.

'Is Mr Fabien Pouche here tonight?' I asked.

'Fabien?' said Henry with some cheer, 'not tonight, no. But he should be in tomorrow.'

My heart gave a leap. My itch was well and truly scratched!

Chapter IV

In which Payton Edgar hunts down a man

Dear Margaret,
I have fallen in love with our milkman. My husband works dawn shifts at a car factory, and so I have plenty of time to get myself made up in the morning. I so enjoy our chats, and it has become the most important part of my day. I have found myself requesting extra cream just to start up a conversation. I am sure that he likes me too. Sometimes he even brings me custard. He has no wedding ring, and I make sure to take mine off once my husband has left for work. I want to tell him how I feel, but it seems so silly.
What shall I do?
Housewife, Streatham

Margaret replies; Thank you for your very honest letter. However, you do not appear to be aware of the extreme sluttishness of your behaviour. While your husband is out working hard to provide for you, you reward him by spending his hard earned cash on unwanted cream, simply so you can toy with the delivery boy. This is deplorable behaviour. Buy a cow for the garden if you have to, but cancel your milk order at the earliest opportunity. Remember your wedding vows, put your ring back on and go without custard immediately.*

And so, yet again, Payton Edgar had been proven correct!
Our waiter Henry scurried away, leaving me dizzy with glee. My heart pounded in my chest and I raised a clutched fist in the air front of me, rather like a sportsman who has just slashed a record.

'I knew it!' I exclaimed pointedly to Irving who looked fairly taken aback himself. 'I was right - the man is here! Pouche is here! I was right! The letter was personal, after all!'

'Payton-'

'He is back tomorrow, and so we have to come back here tomorrow. I must see this Fabien-'

'I am certainly not coming back tomorrow,' said Irving sternly. 'We have the Raqs Sharqi meal.'

'Bother!'

Half-heartedly I chinked my glass against Irving's and took in some wine without so much as a swill of assessment, such was my distraction. The drink, a smidgeon too cold, was only just tolerable, yet I said nothing. After this exciting development I was barely in the mood for challenging our waiter.

If I have to be honest, the meal that night was a considerable improvement on our previous visit. My duck liver pate was surprisingly flavoursome and well accompanied with warm rustic toast, and even Irving's tomato salad was considerably tastier and well-dressed than most limp English salads. I was less impressed with my main course; a run-of-the-mill slab of pepper steak which edged too far under my requested *"a point"* for a man like me who really does not like to see blood on his plate.

I was also a little envious of Irving's chicken and sausage cassoulet.

All in all it was a satisfactory dining experience, and I was relieved that I was not there to review the meal. It would choke me to give any compliments to the noxious and underhand Sebastien Ferrier. As usual when not reviewing a dining experience, we skipped dessert.

It was not that long before we were all paid up. Our meal had been over a little too quickly and left me wanting more, which I always say is a sign of a good dining experience. We would have left the restaurant and avoided all the trauma and danger that was to come, had Henry not returned with a skip, just after we had settled our bill.

The boy caught us as Irving was pulling on his jacket.

'You asked about Fabien?' he said without the merest hint of a french accent. 'I am afraid I got it wrong, what I said earlier. He won't be back here for a week or so. Don't know what that's about. Therese says he has taken some leave, last minute. Sorry 'bout that.'

I was, of course, considerably disheartened by this news. I could not wait seven days to face my foe, I would simply explode! I enquired about Therese.

'Oh,' said Henry, 'Our Chef de Partie. She works in the kitchens with Fabien.' He gestured over his shoulder to the kitchens where, from where I stood, I could see a number of white cotton clad bodies dashing about through the steam.

'May I have a quick word with her?' I asked.

Irving cleared his throat. 'Payton-'

I sent him a flick of my hand dismissively before turning back to the waiter. 'Please, if I could? It is extremely important.'

For the first time Henry showed a glimmer of interest in my enquires. A perplexed expression crept onto his boyish young face and his bottom lip protruded slightly before he nodded and shuffled away to the kitchens. I shot Irving a soothing glance and followed after the young waiter to linger outside the double doors through which he had vanished.

A minute later they opened and a slight young girl stepped out. She was the picture of Southern Gallic beauty despite her food-spattered overalls. Her olive skin was devoid of wrinkles, her eyes dark and wide. Her brown locks had been swept up underneath a netted cap, and she did not smile. I tried to guess her age, which is always difficult with Europeans as their dark smoothness often denies their years, but it was a pretty safe guess that this young lady could not be that far into her thirties.

'Therese?' I asked.

'Is me,' she said, sharply, almost rudely, and then gave a small twitch of a smile as an after-thought. Her voice was in contrast to her appearance in that it was deep and almost masculine. It was clear that English was not the girl's first language. Her eyes were piercing, almost alarmingly so.

'I understand that you are acquainted with Fabien Pouche?'

Even as I said the words I was aware that I sounded like a policeman. She gave a short nod. 'I have to speak with him,' I said quickly.

'He is on holiday,' she said, slowly and carefully. I caught the beginnings of suspicion creep into her eyes.

'Yes, so I hear. Unfortunately I can't wait until he gets back. It's very important. Does he live near here?'

'Maybe-' she began, with an air of caution '-now I have to go, I tres, tres busy.'

'Please, I have to see him!' I said.

She had turned a little, but then stopped herself and eyed me suspiciously. 'Who are you?'

I made sure to smile as I proffered a fib. 'It is a long story, but I am a friend.'

'A friend?' she said.

'Yes.'

'But you are not knowing where he lives?'

'No,' I replied hesitantly. 'He never got around to telling me. But I must speak with him. It is important. Very, very important.'

There was a pause and then I noticed the change in her, as she relaxed her knitted brow and she decided not to worry. I was sure that she still didn't trust me, but she spoke with a tone of resignation.

'He live in Hyde Park Square, above the post office, number six, flat three. You go through the park-'

'Ah, yes, I know the area. Thank you. Thank you very much.'

'But you will not see him. I think Fabien… en vacances. He is away.'

'Never mind,' I said, stepping backwards. 'Then I can leave a note. Thank you.' I smiled to myself as I went back over to join Irving.

I had absolutely no intention of leaving a note.

It was a dark night with a mere toenail-clipping of a moon.

Irving had refused to accompany me, and I found myself braving Hyde Park in the shadows on my own. At first I had protested a little at his obstinacy, but then withdrew my pleas. I was actually secretly pleased that he had opted out, and was quite happy to go alone. I could do without him bleating morality at whatever I said or did. He had completed his part of our deal, and I allowed him to head for home.

I cannot pretend that I had any idea what I was going to say to the man, Fabien Pouche, but knew that whatever it was, I would do it better alone.

We parted on the corner of South Carriage Drive and I plunged into the darkness of Hyde Park, determined not to let the shadows unnerve me. I could have gone around the park, but my aching feet didn't fancy the detour. Soon I was surrounded by great open plains and then the odd towering tree, where all city life seemed miles away. It was only the clang of a distant siren that betrayed the peace and stillness. The occasional shuffling noise from within the shadows of the park reminded me that I was not alone, but I focused directly ahead and ploughed onwards through the darkness.

It was not long before I was out of the black open space and slowly perusing Hyde Park Square for number six. The post office was unlit and heavily bordered by an iron grate but it was easy to spot, being signposted by the fat barrel of a pillar box on the pavement. Sure enough there were flats above the shop and a number of lights were on in the windows. The door to number six was just to the right of the post office door, and it was open. Not wide open, but ajar, just enough to catch the unmistakable - not to mention unpleasant - scent of rotting fish coming from within.

A disheveled panel on the wall held no names but was clearly labelled with flat numbers and I gingerly pressed number three. Hearing nothing, I couldn't be certain that a bell had rung inside. As I waited I sensed movement further along the street and saw two figures bustling out of a tavern on the far corner. These were the first two people I had seen since leaving Irving. How quiet the night was. Their footsteps and merry chatter trailed off into the night.

After pressing the button once more I really should have departed, but, feeling somewhat aggrieved at having walked so far with no welcome at my destination, I took a quick glance up and down the empty road and then pushed through the door into the darkness within. I was immediately assaulted by the stench of rancid fish, much stronger than one could bear. I automatically fumbled along the wall to my right and found a light switch that illuminated the source of the odour. The door of the ground floor flat was closed but the flickers of a far off television could be seen through the frosted glass. By the doormat sat a couple of cat bowls with the remains of bones and flecks of white flesh within.

I clutched my handkerchief to my nose like a posy and stomped up the poorly-carpeted staircase, passing by another door until I found a small landing and an identical frosted door with a hand painted 'three' on the wall beside it. This door was also ajar.

How unusual. It was as though someone had been expecting me to come along, snooping under cover of darkness, and had made my job a littler easier.

A growing sense of alarm gave me pause, and then without asking myself what I intended upon doing, I knocked lightly on the glass panel. Nothing stirred from within, but I could see a light from a distant room cast along the floor between the shadows.

'Mr Pouche?' I called rather weakly. There was no noise from inside. I took in a deep breath, and entered.

The light from the far room travelled enough for me to see that the living room into which I had stepped was empty. Disorderly and musty-aired, and devoid of life. Still reeling from the stench of fish, I caught the unmistakable heady aroma of rising damp and looked up to see dark moist shadows creeping up the far wall to the ceiling. This second revolting stench churned my stomach, and I found myself wondering what kind of human could live in such malodorous squalor.

Whoever he was, Fabien Pouche was no millionaire.

I moved slowly through to the far doorway and found myself in a brightly lit but poorly-furnished kitchen. There was a curious noise coming from somewhere in the recesses of the flat, a noise which was impossible to identify - rather like a hammer clashing onto iron and the rush of the sea. Two pieces of burnt toast littered the filthy floor, and on the work surface above a knife smeared with runny butter stuck to the tiling.

It was only then that I noticed I was not alone. A scrawny black and white cat was crouched on the counter, licking at the knife with a tiny tongue. It was unaware of my presence until I took a step further into the room, and even then it merely glanced up momentarily before returning to its feast. Besides the animal a quarter-full pint of milk and a number of filthy plates sat amongst the clutter.

I shook my head in silent disapproval at the squalor before me.

The curious whooshing noise was coming from behind an open door to my right, although there was no illumination from within. Was someone moving in the darkness?

'Mr Pouche?' I said, a little louder so that he could hear me over the sound of iron pipes clanking. Cracked white tiles on the floor of the room confirmed that it was a bathroom. Had I caught the man shaving?

Perhaps I should have been apprehensive, scared even, but I was not. It was plain and simple fury that led me on. I simply had to see the man who had written that letter to the Clarion. I stepped into the room where the noise was louder.

'Mr Pouche?'

As I entered, the toe of my shoe knocked against something in the doorway, sending it spinning to a stop a few steps away. It was what looked like a rolling pin, caked in some sort of sticky substance. It was difficult to see clearly as the white-tiled bathroom looked grey in the light from the kitchen, and my trunk cast a fair shadow. My eyes flickered over a lavatory next to a sink unit as I moved around the open door.

I clutched at my chest with a start!

The rusty pipes were jolting as water shot through them in forceful pulses, the water then spraying out in sharp bursts from the shower head. The long metal piping of the shower was wrapped twice around the neck of a young man who was hunched sideways within the bathtub, fully clothed. A large deep red bloodstain started halfway up the tiled wall and slid down to meet the back of his head. The water spurted from the shower head and spattered against his chest, sending rose coloured water down the plug hole.

My heart lurched. The man was clearly dead.

His eyes were wide and fixed upwards to the ceiling in something of a scream. His jaw hung loose revealing surprisingly white, well-kept teeth. Although pale in death, I could see that he had had a healthy tan in life and what some would assess as rather handsome features. Looking back, it was curious that at this time I felt no panic, only a deep sadness for the boy, and, if I have to be honest, a wretched frustration that I would never get to confront my letter-writing foe.

After standing still in the doorway for a moment I was overcome by a need to stop the noise and the flow of the water as it ran from his shoulder down his body. I moved tentatively closer and felt my resolve crumble a little.

I have seen a small number of corpses over the years, but will never, ever get used to the chilling presence of death. The very *finality* of it.

Reaching out my right hand past the young man's cheek I twisted the tap head. It squealed noisily in my grasp. The water flow steadied and then halted, the tired pipes resting a moment later.

I was only to get a second of sweet silence however, as there came a noise from the other room. It was at that moment that I glanced down and saw that it was blood and dark hairs that caked the rolling pin at my feet.

'Mr Pouche? Mr Pouche, do you have Connie with you again? I can't find her anywhere! May I come through?'

The voice had the growl of a school mistress, and was followed by a sharp gasp. I straightened and turned. In the doorway stood a greying, hunched lady in a crumpled brown pinny. She was holding one hand to her bosom and glaring at me with wide eyes. I went to speak, taking one step forward, which sent the rolling pin spinning across the floor and scattering bloody droplets as it went. Her wide eyes watched it spin for a moment, and then caught sight of the corpse.

I have heard some screams in my time, but never like this. That such a shrill emission could resonate from such a tiny, bent frame was unbelievable. The woman's scream caused me to jolt back violently, as if hit by the sound. Her eyes danced fitfully back and forth from the bath-tub to myself, a veiny hand clutching at her throat in terror.

The shock of finding the body released its hold. My fight-or-flight response kicked in, and I am somewhat ashamed to say that I fled.

In the corridor I encountered the blasted cat - Connie - and we pelted down the stairs together. I could still hear the screams in the flat behind as I bolted through the pungent, fishy air of the hallway and out onto the empty street where I collided with a roar against the thick red pillar box outside. Pushing away from it, I had to hold on to my hat as I trotted back towards the safe darkness of the park.

Once inside, I ran for some time before catching sight of the first bench I could find in its shadows. I collapsed upon it, entirely out of breath.

Chapter V

In which Payton Edgar dines out as if nothing untoward had happened

MURDER IN HYDE PARK FLAT
Man caught fleeing from scene!

The body of an unnamed man was found last night in a flat in Hyde Park Square. Police have reported that a witness observed a man fleeing the scene. The gentleman, thought to be a vagrant, was seen running into Hyde Park and was soon caught. He is as yet unnamed and is being held for questioning. The victim's landlady, Mrs Peasgood, 62, claims that the perpetrator also attempted to murder her cat. She is currently being treated for shock at St Thomas's Hospital.

I spent most of that Saturday in hiding.

The events of the previous evening felt like a strange and horrible dream, as if they had happened to somebody else and not to me, poor guiltless old Payton Edgar.

Once again the day was blisteringly humid and I was all too happy to rest in the shade of my house, allowing the skin of my face to calm in the cool dim light. Nobody called around and the telephone did not ring once. My aunt's door remained closed and I managed to avoid Grace Kemp as she busied herself about the house.

I imagined many times the scene that would have played out in that smelly flat in Hyde Park Square after I had fled. I could picture the hysterical landlady, having been calmed by a snifter of sherry, telling the police about the mysterious stranger she had encountered, the man who had bolted from the scene of a murder.

To run away was a stupid thing to have done, I knew, but it was done and there was no going back. I considered calling the police, but something stopped me.

It was simply easier not to call them. How could I explain to the police that I had, to all intents and purposes, broken in to the apartment of a complete stranger to challenge his use of words in a letter to the press? It all sounded so ridiculous, and was certainly far from important.

Besides, I had no information which could help their enquiries. I was merely an innocent bystander. I certainly did not want to be seen to be wasting police time. I decided that the important thing the police should be focusing on should be the murder of the poor young man in the bath-tub, not a red herring in a well-tailored suit.

Irving's words over the dinner table at La Maison Sebastien re-played in my mind, and I told myself that I was in the public eye now, a figure of respect. To that end, surely this meant that I must do whatever I could to avoid being caught up in scandal or intrigue, whatever the circumstance? I had the good name of the London Clarion to uphold.

Indeed, not only that, I had my own reputation to think of.

I left my house in the late-afternoon in search of the evening edition, quickly returning to my lair after purchasing a copy from the vendor on the corner of St George's Drive. I do not know what I thought I would find, but was shocked as I caught the front page - yes, the front page - and read the headlines of the evening edition.

'MURDER IN HYDE PARK FLAT: man caught fleeing from scene!'

For the second time in as many days Payton Edgar had made the papers, although thankfully this time unnamed. But the subheading was incorrect, surely? *Man caught?* There was a poorly lit photograph of the post office beneath the headline and a rather badly written report. As I read on I realised that they must surely be talking about a different murder, on a different Hyde Park Corner, for it seems they had indeed caught their man.

"The gentleman, thought to be a vagrant, was seen running into Hyde Park and soon caught. He is as yet unnamed and is being held for questioning".

No, this was certainly the Pouche murder, but it seemed that I was out of the picture. I had indeed been followed into the park after my flight, only for some poor tramp to take the brunt of it!

Perhaps I should have felt some regret for what had happened to this unfortunate, and most probably innocent, man, but frankly I didn't. I felt just a curious kind of relief that the spotlight had passed over me.

Then suddenly it occurred to me; *a vagrant? A tramp?* Had the fool landlady not seen me standing there in my fine tailored attire? Did she not know the difference between toeless loafers and a brand new pair of bespoke brogues? And I had been wearing my homburg for God's sake! And now, because of that stupid woman's dire observational skills, some poor vagabond was for it.

However, I reasoned to myself, it was either that or hand myself in for no discernible reason whatsoever. Besides, the poor tramp was perhaps glad of the comfort of a warm cell.

I glanced back at the paper momentarily and then folded it over and dropped it onto the kitchen table. Yes, inaction was my only option. I must remain firm and have nothing to do with it. The only important thing at that moment was my meal that evening.

I made for the bathroom and began my toilette in preparation for the dinner with Irving and the Raqs Sharqi Club, where I intended to drink, to sparkle and, most importantly, to forget.

Before getting to know Irving I had barely given a second of thought about art on the canvas, and most certainly had never wasted my time pondering over any kind of contemporary art. And still, I cannot say I am any more inspired by colourful daubings after witnessing my friend in action - in the midst of his creative flow, so to speak. It seems like a rather silly pastime to me, especially if one's pictures barely resemble the person or item that they are supposed to depict. Irving's paintings were colourful affairs, but messy and haphazard all the same. Indeed, it was difficult to make out so much as an eye or a nose in some of his so-called portraits.

And I have never been one for historical documentation in oils. I prefer to enjoy life in the here and the now. A flower, for example, is meant to blossom and die. I believe that things should be enjoyed for the moment, just like a succulent meal.

On one occasion, over a dining table no doubt, Irving had suggested to me that, to some ears, this may sound like a somewhat ignorant opinion. Perhaps, I had stated firmly, but it is my opinion nevertheless.

At a push I would confess that I prefer photography over paintings, which is at least a true depiction of the subject. That said, quite why it appears to have become a celebrated mode of art is beyond me. Surely almost anyone can hold a box, point and click?

In the past few years I have been unlucky enough to meet a number of artists who, excluding Irving, turned out to be self-obsessed, unwashed and rather rude beasts with little understanding of the reality of the outside world. I would take a musician, or perhaps an author, over an artist any day of the week. Artists are the very bottom of the creative chain.

No, not true - I am forgetting the crowning idiots in the world of creativity; the actor.

I would take an artist over an actor any day of the year.

I actively avoid socialising with thespians as I have found them, without exception, to be egotistical, scene-stealing idiots with nothing original to say for themselves. I once spent a dreadful weekend in Whitby with the most irritating theatrical couple. His was a name so illustrious that even I had come across it, but I shall spare him from a naming and shaming, however deserved that may be. Suffice to say that he insisted on turning the entire gathering into something out of a poorly paced domestic matinee, with impromptu arguments here and sudden confessions there, the couple playing out their marital distress in front of the entire company with dialogue seemingly lifted from some second rate romantic novel.

It was the singular most boring weekend of my life to date.

I digress.

As promised, Irving called for me at eight o'clock, wearing neither the mustard or the pistachio suit, but instead sporting a rather conservative brown affair with a cream shirt beneath. At least he had worn the wing-tips that I adored, the ones that I had stumbled across one rainy Sunday afternoon, scandalously discarded at the bottom of his wardrobe. They looked good, and I was glad that I had coerced him to persevere with them. After appraising the man for a moment I concluded that his presentation was satisfactory. He was a handsome man, Irving, who alway managed to impress when he scrubbed up for dining out.

He looked distinguished. *A gentleman.*

I was careful to tell him as much, making sure to deliver my judgement with my very warmest smile.

'Thank you, Payton,' he replied distractedly.

I made no mention of the events of the previous evening and, thankfully, Irving did not probe much when he finally thought to ask. I had thought hard about what to say - or what not say - to Irving about my adventure in the Hyde Park flat, and had decided that the details were best kept to myself. I merely told him that Mr Pouche had not been available to speak with me, and that I had directly returned home.

This was more-or-less the truth.

There was no need to mention the bloody corpse I had discovered and the ensuing manhunt that I had caused. It felt just a smidgeon wrong to keep things from my friend, but it would do no good to fluster him over what was essentially nothing to do with me. I found myself telling him that I had calmed down, and had decided to forget all about the letter in the newspaper.

'Well I am glad,' said Irving in his light, genial manner. 'I had worried that you would carry on getting all hot and bothered, taking what is really a minor quibble and creating a drama out of it, which would do you no good at all. I'm pleased you are dropping the matter, I really am. Well done, Payton.'

I found this last comment more than a little patronising and struggled somewhat to let it pass without further discussion. I bit my tongue.

We walked along to the Belgrave Road where he hailed a taxi (Irving is very good at hailing taxis) and soon we were on our way. I kept my conversation to a minimum in the cab. Too often I have seen my friend blush at the glances of the driver as I wax lyrical about some antique trinket or other. Our scruffy driver did seem a little more inquisitive than most cabbies, to the point of even looking around and reviewing us both with a grunt as we sat and gave our destination.

The poor man most probably envied my style.

I sat back and allowed the thrill of anticipation to wash over me. I had never met Lord Charles Follett, but had certainly heard all about the man from the numerous headlines about his charitable donations. Meeting the proprietor of the illustrious Follett Gallery would indeed be a thrill.

'Why are they called the Raqs Sharqi Club? What's that about?' Irving had asked when first fingering the invitation.

'That, my dear friend, is one of the many things that I intend to find out,' I had replied.

And here we were, finally, headed for dinner. Knowing that Irving had been sniffing around the gallery a fair amount of late, I probed a little further as to his understanding of the club itself. His reply was infuriatingly vague.

'I really don't know very much,' he said lazily, and yet again I was astounded at his care-free attitude towards people of eminence. The man had a baffling lack of regard for the prestigious. He went on.

'I spend most of my time with Jessica Hatch, the curator. I know that she is one of them - one of the Raqs Sharqi, I mean. She makes up the seven. She has great respect for Lord Follett, but is a little nonplussed about the wife, I seem to recall.'

'Seven members? I see...'

The group was even more elite than I had anticipated.

'And who else makes up the Club?' I enquired gently.

'I really don't know. Nobody really knows. But I do know one thing - that one of their members died a few weeks ago.'

'Really?'

'Yep. Some Russian doctor. Jessica was quite cut up about it at the time. Died suddenly, by all accounts.'

My mind swam, and I confess that I felt a little dizzy with anticipation. The reasons for my invite was suddenly all too clear.

'So there is an opening?' I muttered.

'I beg your pardon?'

'An empty place at the table, so to speak. This can't be a coincidence,' I declared decisively, breathing in deeply with anticipation. Irving was gazing out of the car window and for a moment I thought I would have to repeat myself, but eventually he caught up on my comment.

'What can't be a coincidence?'

'Well,' I said, 'I can understand why they might invite you for dinner, featured artist at the gallery and all that, but why specify *me* in the invitation?'

His answer, when it came, was not appreciated.

'I don't know. To make up the numbers?'

'Rubbish! They want Payton Edgar! It's obvious! They want celebrated restaurateur and food critic Payton Edgar to join the Raqs Sharqi Club! To join their exclusive ranks!'

Irving laughed, not harshly, but enough to gall as the taxi swerved to the kerb and came to a stop all too harshly.

We had arrived.

After paying the man I circled the car to hear my friend speaking as he crossed the road. Not wishing to miss out on any important detail on our hosts, I found myself cantering a little to keep up with him as he talked,. He was muttering something about taxi fares. I did not need to hear this, nor did I need to respond. His next comment, however, invited response.

'And please, please don't mention your Mesopotamian pottery tonight, Payton.'

'I beg your pardon?'

He paused as if gathering his words before he went on.

'Whenever you are out to impress, you bring up your damn collection.

'I am extremely proud of it! Some pieces could be considered priceless!'

'I know, Payton. I know.'

I walked on in a hurt silence for a while, but soon forgot my irritation for a daydream. I pictured myself at my place at the table of Lord and Lady Follett. Sitting at the table of the Raqs Sharqi Club, entertaining my peers with witty observations. At my side, Irving was most probably thinking of nothing more than getting the evening out of the way and heading back to another late-night painting session.

We turned a corner and found ourselves facing the grand entrance of the Follett Gallery. It was well lit, the elaborate stone pillars at the fore casting shadows over the rising building behind. A huge central door up front was visibly bolted.

'We go around the side to the East Wing,' said Irving as he crossed the forecourt, walking a bit too quickly for my liking.

'Do slow down, Irving, please!' The last thing I wanted to break into a sweat before taking my place at dinner.

The East Wing was no less grand than the main building, but we entered through what can only have been a staff entrance that was situated around the side and hidden within a jungle of rhododendrons. It was cooler in the shade, cold even. Just a few steps down the corridor Irving stopped and rapped on a sizeable oak door, which was swiftly opened.

The door-opener was an oddly familiar face, a man of mature years, white haired and impeccably neat in his servant's garb. I couldn't place exactly where we had met before, but I had seen many of his type in the past, the grey-faced maitre-d who resents being nothing more than a welcome-mat to the wealthy. He nodded briefly and stepped back to allow us in, and as he did I was convinced that I caught a flicker of recognition in the man's eyes. He was, however, far too professional to say anything.

I concluded that he must be familiar with my face from one of my many and varied dining experiences, and I handed him my hat, stick and coat without comment.

We moved through into an extremely remarkable space. The main room of the East Wing had been converted into a dining room for the evening. The walls were formed of cold stone brickwork with a few choice portraits dotted about. In the centre of the far wall sat a substantial dark fireplace, unlit. The floor beneath us was an immaculate polished marble. A lengthy oak dining table stretched out in the centre of the room, giving the whole area the air of the great hall in a medieval castle. One half expected the place to be full of busty serving wenches and mead-swigging knights.

There were a number of people already seated around the table.

The room fell silent as we entered, and a short, wiry man stood up from his seat at the head of the table and made his way towards us with a funny, jumping sort of gait. He wore a curious velvet green suit with golden buttons which gave him a kind of pantomime appeal. His face crinkled into a smile, revealing his years. The teeth were preserved and pristine, disclosing the wealth of their owner. Above his brow rested a bushy fumble of hair, not unlike a sleeping red squirrel, that swept down into a fine red and grey specked beard below. This magnificent red squirrel was clearly a magnificent ginger toupee, I observed silently and not without malice.

'Mr Spence! Mr Spence! Do come in!' the man said, his voice a surprising boom in contrast with his slight frame. He extended a hand in my direction which I took a little uneasily. It was a somewhat hot and moist appendage, not to mention holding the strength of five men in his grasp.

'And you must be Mr Edgar. Charles Follett! So glad you could come.' He ceased crushing my digits and moved over to Irving to repeat the gesture. During all of this a female had risen from the table and was coming up behind him.

My heart skipped a beat as I saw her face.

A very familiar face. It was only a second or two before I made the connection.

Horse-face.

The last time I had seen the woman she had branded me a pervert and I had said a number of unflattering things in response. Before me was the woman I had the misfortune to meet in the park only the day before. The woman with the little yapping dog. Oh, my goodness me! Charles Follett made the introduction.

'My wife, Lady Follett.'

Oh, no.

Chapter VI

In which Payton Edgar holds court

Dear Margaret,
My mother won't let me play my beat records. I adore pop music and own every record in the top ten. I keep the volume down low, especially in the evenings, but when she is in Mother still makes me turn it off. What can I do?
Kate, Sidcup

Margaret replies; I am with your mother on this one. Beat music is nothing but a nuisance, and if I were your mother I'd do more than turn off the record player – I'd throw it out the window! I hear that Bridge is popular these days. A far quieter pursuit than noisily walking the Hit Parade.

For a moment I didn't know where to look.

I glanced over to the familiar servant, realising that he had been the mute companion with the yapping dog on that unfortunate morning. The valet had a wry smile on his face, the corner of his mouth was up-turned just enough for me to catch it. Lady Follett was greeting Irving in high, almost hysterical tones.

'Mr Spence, welcome! So good of you to come! What a thrill!' she trilled before producing a burning stick from nowhere and taking a deep drag. Two plumes of smoke streamed from her flaring nostrils.

'Good evening, Lady Follett.' said Irving, kindly.

'Oh! Please, call me Bunny! I have sat for you and your brush was so kind, so we are surely on first name terms, my sweet!' Horse-face's voice was as thunderous in volume as her husband's but scratched almost as though the woman were stricken with laryngitis. She turned to me. 'And this must be the notorious Peter Edgar! So nice to put a face to the words!'

Over the years I have had to become accustomed to the mishearing of my name, but something about the way this ridiculous woman said "Peter Edgar" rather got my goat. However, it was another word she had spoken that had really stuck in my craw. *Notorious*? Never before had I been described as *notorious!* I pondered on this for just a few seconds before discarding the label as a compliment. I should perhaps be merely content that she was greeting me rather enthusiastically, clearly ignorant of our previous acquaintance in St. James's Park.

'Payton,' I muttered automatically. '*Payton* Edgar.'

'My wife is a great admirer of your work, Mr Edgar,' Lord Follett droned, ignoring her gaffe. Such a fan as to not even know my name, it seemed. He went on. 'That and the society pages, of course.'

'Oh, my heavens!' the ridiculous woman exclaimed while waving her claws in the air. 'What that Beryl Baxter doesn't know!'

Lord Follett was talking over his wife's rapturous ejaculations. 'Now, come along and sit down, sit down, meet the Club.'

I could not take my eyes off of Bunny Follett as we moved to take our places. She was short and squat and positively glistening with jewels. Her hair had been pulled up into a bunch and clipped rather haphazardly, forming an auburn haystack that wobbled as she moved. Perched halfway down her bulbous nose were a tiny pair of spectacles with a delicate chain that looped around her neck from ear to ear. I prayed that the woman would refrain from pushing them up the bridge of her nose and taking a good long look at me.

As it happens, aside from a shaky exchange during dessert, she did no such thing and remained in blissful ignorance at our connection throughout the evening. Much to the sly servant's chagrin, I am sure. In fact, Lady Follett hardly appeared to observe very much at all, for she was far too busy either smoking herbal cigarettes or downing glass after glass of what I observed to be neat gin with ice. She was never without a cigarette in her outlandish holder for the entire duration of the evening.

The Folletts took their places and Lord Follett proceeded to introduce me to the company.

Irving sat to my right, and placed beside him was a striking young lady in dark horn-rimmed spectacles. Her neat features were heavily made up with blood-red lipstick and deep blue eye shadow, the eyebrows penciled to a fine line. Her hair had been lacquered back to form a smooth black cap on her scalp. There was something rather feline about the young woman, and had she issued a purr as a greeting I should not have been surprised.

41

'Mr Edgar, this is Jessica Hatch, our curator and a valued friend,' said Lord Follett, at which she did not purr, but instead thinned her lips and gave a furtive nod over a glass of white wine.

'And across the table from you we have The Right Honourable Mr and Mrs Ercot Mason.'

The name was familiar, but the man opposite was unremarkable. He was around my age, or perhaps a few years older, with a shock of white hair swept back from his brow. There was something of the scientist in his appearance, yet I was sure that this was not his game. It took a second before I placed the name and the person.

Ercot Mason, a Member of Parliament - not to mention a notorious political bully. I had seen this name grace the newspapers many, many times, and rarely in a favourable light. The man was tarnished with the label of being an angry, warmongering oppressor in the field of politics. Parliament may be littered with short-sighted diehards and idiot autocrats, but Mason was surely the worst of the bunch. His ridiculous rants against the ills of society were more suited to be shouted from atop a box at Speaker's Corner than from the benches of the House of Commons. Mason, I recalled, had enjoyed many well publicised spats with the home secretary, St. John Townsend.

Despite all this, however, I forced a smile, which was barely returned. The man's pale lips were as thin as pressed linen.

Beside him sat his wife, a hideous goat of a woman, skinny and brown with dark, smutty eyes sunken deep into her skull. Her lips were also as thin and tight as to be none existent. Mrs Mason wore a plain lime green summer dress and a flimsy grey cardigan which hung from her bony shoulders like washing from a clothes line. She did not move, smile or greet us in any way. Her eyes remained fixed ahead on the glass of water that sat in front of her, untouched. There was a conspicuous, unusual tension about the woman. I had seen this type before. She was the wife of a political name - a silent bookend, dressed conservatively and ever present at her husband's side.

There was an empty seat to my left.

'Wine, gentlemen?' bellowed Lord Follett, and before we could answer the stiff butler was topping our glasses with what turned out to be a rather delectable Pino Noir of the Romanee-Conti vineyards. And then more generous splashes of gin for our hostess, naturally.

The evening turned out to be split into halves, the first of which consisted of the type of polite conversation that one makes in unfamiliar company, from our side of the table at least. The second half, once the wine was freely flowing and we had all warmed up a little, was far more satisfactory, for Payton Edgar sparkled with quick wit and erudite charm, even if I do say so myself.

However, it was in the first half of the evening, just as young Jessica Hatch was giving us a rather saucy account of her experiences on the art scene in New York, that the final member of the Raqs Sharqi Club arrived, and he did so in a most disruptive manner, considering that we were just being served with our long-awaited starter.

There was the absence of a knock before the door burst open and a fussy, disheveled gentleman stomped in, huffing and puffing as he went.

'Ah!' breathed Lord Follett form his place at the table, 'Sir Maurice Williams at long last!'

The newcomer wore a long overcoat despite the warmth of the evening, which he removed to reveal a pair of loose cords and a tired and ugly patterned jumper. I did not recognise the face, but most certainly did recognise the name. Again, it took me some time to identify exactly where. He took his seat beside me and as he did so I caught a strong waft of two distinct, unwelcome scents; methylated spirits and mothballs.

'Wonderful!' sang Bunny Follett through swirls of smoke. 'The club is complete!'

My eyes scanned over the members of this elusive club. There were the opulent benefactors Lord and Lady Follett, the crusty politician and his wife, the feline curator and this unappealing newcomer. As the man took his chair Jessica Hatch mewed sadly.

'It seems a shame to say we are complete, without Victor.' Her clear tones cut through the moments silence and all eyes turned to her. Oh-ho, I thought to myself with some excitement, the seventh member, now departed.

'Irving mentioned that particular piece of bad news. I'm sorry to hear it. What happened to him?' I enquired discreetly. Irving's sharp sideways glance told me that I had not perhaps been as discreet as I had intended.

Bunny Follett sniffed and whined as if in sorrow, although there were no tears in her eyes. 'The poor man, I miss him too. He was struck down - on his golf course.'

'Lightening?' I said with some surprise.

The woman looked at me as if I were insane. 'No. A heart attack.'

Charles Follett gave a sharp shake of the head, the red squirrel wobbling.

'A great pity. The man was a wonder with a mashie.'

Clearly this exchange rankled the tatty newcomer, for, starved of the lime light, he cleared his throat loudly and then spoke out with cut-glass diction, as if young Miss Hatch had not spoken.

'So sorry that I am so very late, my darlings. It has been a rather pestiferous day from start to finish. 'Tis hard grind to educate the proletariat.' His glass had been filled and he took a great gulp from it as Lord Follett resumed his hostly duties.

'Mr Spence, Mr Edgar, may I introduce Sir Maurice Williams.

Although he needs no introduction!'

'Pleased to meet you, gentlemen,' the newcomer coughed through his beard, issuing no eye contact whatsoever. He chose instead to address his host. 'Have I missed anything?'

Bunny Follett smiled, exposing what can only have been a brand spanking new set of dentures, so white and regular were her teeth. 'We have only just started, my dear,' she said, slurring her words just a little.

I sat back and contemplated the brown onion, ale and cheddar cheese soup that had been placed before me. Maurice Williams. *Sir* Maurice Williams. I had seen the name many times, but where? My questions were soon to be answered, as the new arrival was determined to hold court at the table for some time, with the others fawning over his suspiciously perfect diction.

'Can you believe it? I practically had to hitchhike here, darlings! Most unsettling I must say, when the greats of our time are reduced to being turned down by so-called public transport.' He gulped down some more wine as we quietly tucked into our soups. I noticed that his was to remain barely touched, the man was talking so much.

'The early evening performance finished a little late as it was, to be followed by the usual swathes of ravenous autograph hunters. My fingers are worn and cramped from signing, and before I knew it Father Time struck at the nine. And, would you credit it? In my rush I left my damn wallet back in the dressing room.' The man rolled his 'r's in a peculiar manner. 'I simply cannot fathom just what has happened to the taxi service in this city of late. It took me a ridiculous amount of time to hail a carriage, well over five minutes, during which time I almost threw myself under the wheels of a few that drove on by, empty. Finally I received a carriage and explained my financial predicament, but the fool cabby was a philistine. A damn philistine! *"Do you recognise the profession, my man?"* said I, as is my tradition. He claimed not to know what I was talking about, refused to grant me a free subscription and drove on!'

'Never!' exclaimed Bunny Follett.

'It's happening all over! Just the other day I chose to take in the latest thriller at the picture show. One craves escapism, sometimes, from the hard grind of true theatre. I had just survived a very tiring matinee, and I had to pay to get in! To pay! Just like the drones around me! I was aghast. *"Do you recognise the profession?"* said I, to which the toothless harpy in the ticket booth replied *"cash only, mate!"* Can you believe it? What was once a noble and respected profession has been reduced to that of a street singer, thanks to-' he gulped and whispered the word through gritted teeth, '-television!'

'So you are an actor?' said Irving, delightfully innocent as always. There was a hissing sound as a few of our fellow diners sucked air through their teeth in surprise at the naivety of my friend's question. It was a great moment.

Lord Follett chuckled somewhat nervously. 'Mr Spence, Sir Maurice is one of the greatest stage actors of our time. He is the West End! A highly talented, and most respected, gentleman.'

'Bless you for that, Charles,' grumbled the actor before turning to look past me with a demented light in his eyes. He addressed Irving directly.

'I am a traditional actor, Sir. Shakespearian and knighted for my grind, not one of these two-a-penny film stars coming over here touting for business, barely able to string a sober sentence together!' He bellowed all this out over the table as if he were still on stage. I edged my seat a few inches away, as if to reduce his volume. 'What was once our great towering tradition of theatre is dying, poisoned at its roots by screens of the large and of the small variety. Armchair Theatre! What rubbish! True theatre requires toil, sweat and tears! There is simply nothing on heaven and Earth than can top the feeling of standing out front with the boards at your feet. The smell and dust and the feel of greasepaint, pigments and powders! I tell you, convention shall always win through. As long as there is breath in my body and a sell out in the stalls, we shall win through.'

I suddenly recalled reading these words before, as Sir Maurice was renowned for his contempt of the rise of television as well as being an unrelenting self-promoter. The man was always complaining vociferously in the comments section of The Clarion. A small silence followed his ridiculous outburst, during which I'm sure he expected applause. Instead he held the silence by taking a long, noisy drink of his wine and then, to my great despair, began to speak again. He proceeded to hold court throughout the rest of our soup, returning repeatedly in his prose to attack what he called *"televisual make believe"* and bemoan society for its lack of consideration for those stricken with what he referred to as *"the acting bug"*.

The man was a fool.

Tired of his grandstanding, I turned and whispered discreetly to Irving. 'I would rather go to a nudist's funeral than go to see one of his plays,' I quipped, and we sniggered a little. Sir Maurice was immediately distracted.

'Excuse me, Gentlemen. I was speaking!'

Hardly any of the other club members got a word in as Sir Maurice droned on and on, and I could see that his dull oration was, for some unfathomable reason, accepted by all. However, Ercot Mason did pipe up at one point in a very telling exchange. Sir Maurice had made a comment regarding his dresser who had recently moved to Ireland leaving him with an apparently incompetent young Indian lady, and then he paused to take a few spoonfuls of soup, most of which was to drip from his moustache and beard in-between courses.

'Charles would sweep the country clean of Indians and gypsies if he could,' declared horse-faced Lady Follett without a flicker of care. 'Oh - but he doesn't mind the blacks, do you dear?'

Lord Charles had just filled his mouth, but spoke anyway.

'Damned hard workers, the blacks.'

'Immigrants,' grunted Mason sharply, 'are what will bring this country down, mark my words. That fat fool Townsend will insist upon opening up our doors wider and wider, and before you know it our country will be raped and pillaged beyond all recognition!'

'Now, now, Ercot! Save it for the golf course,' Lord Follett piped up in a head-masterly fashion. 'No politics at the table, we all agreed that.'

It was not hard to see that those gracing the table of the Raqs Shari Club were merely puppets of the Folletts. Mason seemed to take this order from Follett amiably, only frowning when his shrivelled wife attempted to speak. She needn't have bothered for her soft words were inaudible.

'Oh, do be quiet, Mildred, please!' Mason snapped a little too loudly, and his wife's lips tightened back into position. Unlike her dining companion, Lady Follett was not a woman to be silenced, and she spoke out with an air of rich disgust.

'Well I think the breakdown of our society is entirely down to the lack of traditional family values...'

'Here, here!' Mason grunted.

'Bunny, dear, hold it down!'

'Well! You may frown, Charles, but this is not just politics, it is a simple fact of life!' She continued, but not before another slug of gin. 'Underage intercourse and intercourse out of wedlock is all you see in the papers these days. And what follows, too. A taste of honey? We certainly wouldn't have had such wanton abandon in my day. Nobody respects the values of marriage any more. And then there's divorce!'

'Bunny!' Lord Charles growled, to no avail.

'Well you may scoff, Charles, but Ercot knows what I'm talking about, isn't that right?'

Ercot Mason raised an eyebrow lazily as she went on.

'I know they're talking about it at Westminster, don't tell me they're not! Making it even easier for all and sundry to divorce! So many young girls these days, flitting from man to man. And men are no better! Tarts on each arm! It is a plague, pure and simple!'

'Hardly a plague, my dear,' Lord Charles droned with a smile. 'A boil on the bottom, perhaps, but a plague?'

'Be quiet, Charles. Nobody sees things through these days. Marriage is not an option, say I. It is not something to be played at like some flibbertigibbet. It is a sacred institution!'

'Come now,' Jessica Hatch purred over her wine, her calm words like a cool breeze. 'One cannot stay in a loveless marriage.'

There was something telling about her words, so coldly delivered.

'For better or for worse!' Horse-face spat out with an admirable gusto. 'I will not associate with divorcees. Marriage is sacred, there're no two ways about it. You will see, Jessica, when it happens to you. Yes, before marriage one must consider the future and once it is done to damn well stick with it!'

Sir Maurice chuckled indulgently. 'What was that quote? Hollywood brides keep the bouquets and throw away the groom!'

'It is no laughing matter, Maurice!'

'Quite so,' Sir Maurice said, dryly. 'Divorce is indeed a plague on our humanity.'

'Well said!' Lady Follett went on. 'And not only that - divorce leads to illness, mark my words. And I'm not talking about the common cold! Cancers of all kinds are directly caused by divorce, not to mention heart defects and strokes. A plague indeed!'

Thankfully the food was to arrive and interrupt our hostess's nonsensical bluster and it was just as our main courses were set before us by the mute servant that the evening took a more enjoyable turn.

Lord Follett raised his glass.

'Ladies and Gentlemen, before we begin our delightful main course - a toast.' We lifted our glasses in unison. 'To our distinguished guests, Mr Irving Spence and Mr Payton Edgar!' A chorus of cheers followed, a gesture that was extremely welcome. The hum of gentle conversation filled the room as we tucked in. I waited for a lull in conversation before speaking up.

'Please, let me tell you an amusing anecdote regarding my ancient Mesopotamian pottery!'

I had said this warmly across the table to Bunny Follett, at which she held up a wrinkly palm.

'No, no, no, Mr Edgar. W-what I want you to tell me-' she was now certainly slurring her words, for the considerable amount of gin she had imbibed was surely kicking in. 'What I want you to tell me is this... what made you think of becoming a restaurant critic? You must enjoy it, I suppose?'

My moment had arrived.

I took a sip of my wine, and carefully smiled at my hostess. I felt all eyes rest on me.

'My dear, for me, it is a dream come true. I am a Gourmand. An Epicure. Enjoyable eating is, and always has been, my favourite pastime, and so to write about it was simply the most natural step to take. I had owned my special little restaurant for a small number of years, ever since the last slice of ham was rationed. The Gazebo, in Wimbledon. You may have heard of it?' I allowed a pause but after a few seconds silence did not wait any longer for confirmation. 'It was a most successful venture. I believe that the Times called the food *"a gastronomic delight"* and The Clarion said that I had *"raised the bar of quality for London restaurants"* - although do forgive me if I am misquoting a little there.'

I knew that I was not.

'But this success was still not enough, and so a number of years ago I sold the business and, after time spent travelling on the continent, I began to develop my dream and desire - a desire to change our country's eating habits. You may agree with me when I say that England's restaurants are often drab, the choices we are offered far too limited and therefore our appetites as a nation are practically moribund. It has been this way for so long that this has become accepted. But I will not accept it! Are we still rationed? No! And yet I think we are at war! At war with ourselves and with our palates!'

There came a gruff cough from the actor at my side, yet I persevered.

'Payton Edgar was, it seems, desperately needed by The Clarion as a culinary pioneer to launch their restaurant column, and so I embarked on my two-fold mission. My first, to improve our nation's food and my second, for myself, to find the perfect meal.'

I would, of course, never confess that I also posed as Margaret Blythe for the agony aunt column. Not in this company. Not in any company.

'Goodness! And have you found it yet, the perfect meal?' This from Lady Follett who was clearly entranced by my story.

'No.' I stated simply and poured myself some more gravy.

'We'll tell our chef that you said that!' said Jessica Hatch with a glint in her eye and a flick of her head. 'So what's it like to be a critic? Do you have to be terribly rude all of the time?'

I laughed, and then pondered on this for a moment during which time Irving answered for me.

'Yes, he does,' he said, sending a ripple of laughter around the table. I noted that neither of the Masons cracked a smile.

Indeed, Mason's grey stare across the table accompanied a cold question.

'What exactly would a restaurant critic do throughout the war?'

I took his query for what it was; a challenge to justify oneself once more.

'Work extremely hard as head chef in the airborne forces, Mr Mason. I was a provider of vital strength for our nation's fighters.'

Here, the actor gave a chuckle.

'Someone had to prepare the powered eggs and dehydrated pota-toes, one supposes!'

I ignored his jibe, for I was watching Mason. His expression was one of disapproval and I pondered on his role during the war. Clearly he thought mine insubstantial. Bunny Follett provided the answer.

'Ercot was a Grenadier guardsman!' she chirruped proudly. 'Served in - Africa, was it?'

'Tunisia,' the man replied. 'I kept my feet firmly on the ground.'

I was to get no chance to retort.

'And so what would you say,' said Sir Maurice challengingly, 'of the meal before us?'

I examined my plate. 'Honestly?'

'Honestly!' The Folletts said together, both smiling as they chewed.

'Please, be as rude as you like!' mused Lady Follett with a mouth-ful.

I cleared my throat, and throughout my little monologue I was thrilled to hear bursts of laughter come from those around me, with even Mr Mason eventually nodding approvingly.

'I was presented with a rather anaemic looking cut of lamb which was drowning in an unnecessarily lumpy mint sauce, akin to the mush Nanny would serve when I was yet in nappies. This meal had already broken one of the main rules in food presentation, that a diner should always be able to pour the accompanying sauce to one's own taste. In this case, I certainly would not have been as heavy handed with such a sub-par condiment. The meat itself was stringy and uninteresting, and we shall dwell on it no further. The supplementary vegetables were uninspiring choices despite being competently prepared, and yet I had a certain feeling throughout the meal that something was missing.

'A traditional English meal when prepared and presented well is like a symphony, with each component bringing its own melody to the orchestra. The closest this meal got to orchestration lay with the afore-mentioned strings in the meat. No, this meal was more like a Cub Scout band on a wet Sunday rehearsal. The simple fact was that with the pota-toes, carrots and meat and the unpardonable limp excuse for a floret of broccoli on my plate, within the meal there was just... not... enough... green! However, I will endeavour to finish on a positive note, and say that the ambiance was spot on, and the company - divine!'

A new feeling came over me as I sat back and surveyed the smil-ing faces around the table. *Bliss*. There can be no other word for it. The admiration and appreciation washed over me and, I have to confess, I savoured it. Better even than a fine wine or succulent steak, that sensa-tion of adoration was divine.

I had finished to a resounding applause, with only the malodorous actor beside me declining to join in. I shot him a sideways glance and a sly smirk - who was holding court now?

Chapter VII

In which Payton Edgar eyes a vacancy

Dear Margaret,
Every Friday I go to my friend's house for tea. She is a widow,
and terribly lonely. My problem is that she bakes the most unap-
pealing cakes and brews the worst cup of tea imaginable. I cannot
begin to describe the consistency of her rock buns. I do not wish to
offend her in any way, but have started to dread our Friday together.
Any advice?
Contented knitter, Islington

Margaret replies; Oh, dear contented knitter, you say that you do
not wish to offend her, and yet you allow her to offend you with vile food-
stuffs each and every week. I suggest, if you think you are so much bet-
ter, that you take a flask of tea and some of your own cakes in a tin when
the next Friday rolls around. Tell her exactly what you think of her bak-
ing and show her what a real cake should taste like. A good friend is an
honest friend.

More questions came thick and fast throughout the rest of the
meal.

My fellow diners were terribly interested in all aspects of my career, and all the attention was so flattering that I quite forgot that I was
dining with some of the most unsavoury, snooty people I had ever had
the misfortune to meet. Irving sat beside me in comfortable silence for
the majority of the time. He was quite happy to remain anonymous, having never being a fan of the limelight. As usual he was drinking quickly,

the top ups of wine being far more frequent in his quarter than any other. Irving didn't often drink, but when he did he could really take it on.

The dessert came, and I was very pleased to see that it was a badly produced syrup sponge pudding, and thrilled my audience with yet another review without being asked. By this point the pleasing combination of wine and attention had kicked in. I did not dare to think what the chef might have thought about all this, and was pleased that the kitchens were well out of earshot.

'There are,' I declared, 'many stodgy traditional English desserts that, in my opinion, would make far better doorstops than they do puddings. Spotted dick is one, bread-and-butter pudding another, but the syrup sponge is the worst of them. A true sandbag of a desert, the syrup sponge is often a heavy, over-sweet and gloopy affair with little to commend it. However, if one must attempt this hardy perennial, then one should aim for a delicate, light affair, involving gentle preparation with as much airing of flour and folding of eggs as possible without overly straining the wrist. I can only imagine that the poor soul who prepared this sponge pudding nodded off during the folding stage. The sponge we were presented with was as light as a dumb bell and only half as tasty. Even the insipid and overly-thin custard failed to lift this weighty, barely edible mistake.'

Certain members of the Raqs Sharqi Club were growling their appreciation at my appraisal. And then, suddenly and without warning, I was taken away, far from the dining hall where we sat, back to that damp little flat at Hyde Park.

The image of that dead body in the bathtub flashed back to my mind. It was not twenty four hours since I had made the grisly discovery in that grim little bathroom, and now here I was, hobnobbing with what was seen as the upper echelon of London society. The dead man's glassy eyes stared at me in fear and surprise.

And then, as my fellow diners' chatter died down, something else happened to shock me back to where I sat.

Bunny Follett sat upright and thinned her eyes suspiciously.

'Very clever, now-' she put a little finger to the corner of her rucked lips, '-have we met before, Mr Edgar? Now I think of it your face is very familiar!'

'No, Lady Follett, I should certainly remember if we had,' I replied swiftly, summoning up some pretty impressive bravado. Thankfully Sir Maurice caused a distraction by pushing back his chair and breaking his silence.

'Well, I may be a culinary novice, Lady Follett, but I thought this meal was, as always, nothing short of a triumph. Good hearty British fare, just what I like. Now, I will retire to the easy chair, if you don't mind.' He pulled out some papers that he had been sitting on. 'I have an audition piece to prepare for tomorrow, and shall take some quiet time now it seems the show is over. If I may have a little snifter of something-or-other or other to accompany my mediation?'

A bottle was presented to the man.

'Ugh! Port? I think not! Nothing but strangulated wine! Vile! No, no, no! Cognac!'

He gestured his order to the Follett's valet, nodded curtly at the rest of the table and made for the armchairs at the far end of the room. I was disgusted to see him pull out a pair of pince nez which he then squeezed onto the bridge of his nose as he began to read.

He really was the most pretentious fop.

'I shall go and get cook to rustle up coffees for the ladies, I think,' said Bunny Follett as she straightened up before addressing her husband. 'Be a dear and see how the gents want their whiskies.'

Charles Follett looked to me and I nodded eagerly. He listed an impressive range and I opted for the single malt from Glenlivet. Irving declined the offer and was led away to the easy chairs by Jessica Hatch, who clearly admired him and enjoyed his company. This left me alone at the table with Ercot Mason and his shrivelled prune of a wife. Her eyes remained focused on that barely touched glass of water on the table in front of her. We said nothing until after Charles Follett had reappeared with a whisky for me and a cognac for the politician. He then moved away to join the others.

'Do you like golf, Mr Edgar? Mason enquired.

Golf, like cricket and football, has always been a mystery to me. Now I wished I had spent more time in Thistle House with the men from the Clarion's sports pages, smoking cigars and totting up the league tables.

Yet I was not about to tell the truth. Not with so much at stake.

'I have been known to enjoy the odd hole or two.' I replied, hoping that my terminology was sufficient enough to deceive. I was relieved that Irving was out of earshot.

'Then you must come golfing with us. We could do with another caddy . Mildred gets terribly tired of holding the clubs, you see.'

He laughed. Beside him, Mildred Mason smirked, her eyes fixed downwards. I was left puzzling as to whether or not this was a serious offer. This could be bad, for if I were forced to accept the invitation it would be only a matter of minutes before the man realised that I had never so much as held a golf club in my life. Thankfully however, the topic was an easy link in to what I needed to discuss, and the ideal diversion.

'I was sad to hear about the Doctor.' I said, gently.

'The Doctor?'

'Your recently deceased? On the golf course?'

Mason raised an eyebrow. 'Victor? Bah! Silly fool! Too much money and no sense, I say. Rather spend his mountains of cash on expensive mowers and bunkers than in helping to run this country right.' From this I gathered that he had declined a donation of some sort to Mason's party, and quite right too. Mason emitted a long sigh.

'Still, he loved his golf so much it is only fitting that he should go out on a green.'

'So, this means there is a-' I searched for the word, '-a vacancy within the Club?'

'A what, sorry?'

'A vacancy, in the Raqs Sharqi Club?'

Mason leaned in closer, a shrewd expression on his face.

'Why, I suppose there is, yes.'

'Well, it stands to reason-' I began before stopping myself, quite unsure of how to continue.

Mason leaned back, sipped slowly on his brandy and smiled. 'Anyone in mind, old chap?'

This was getting interesting.

I mirrored his actions, sipping my drink mysteriously before speaking. 'I had wondered, well, being a great fan of good food and good company-'

'Oh, yes?' he said with polite interest.

'Well, I imagine a position in the Raqs Sharqi Club is swiftly filled, and I would hate to miss out on an opportunity-'

'Indeed?'

'I imagine that Lord Follett would be looking for someone with taste and style. Even with a smidgeon of notoriety, perhaps.'

There was a pause.

Suddenly Mason burst out laughing, and not a little snigger, but an uncontrollable guffaw. He was shrieking like a child at a circus. Even his skeletal wife beside him was showing her teeth. Suddenly, he let his smile drop.

'Do you really think that you could join *us*? Be a member of the Raqs Sharqi? Hah! I think not, old chap. No offence meant but, well, you were born to be a party piece, not a club member! A clown, not a ringmaster! Ha!'

I was puzzled, and this must have shown on my face.

'You have been very entertaining tonight, Mr Edgar, but that is all you are here for, for entertainment. What do you think this is, a free-for-all? This is an *exclusive* group, you fool! A prestigious group that needs entertaining. You were invited as an act, and what an act you have been!'

He emitted another great bellow of laughter. Beside him, Mildred Mason's bony chest puffed in and out as she guffawed in a sequence of short snorts.

'I don't understand-' I stumbled a little, perplexed. The man made no sense.

'Why do you think we are called the Raqs Sharqi Club, for God's sake?' Mason saw my questioning look and put down his glass, leaned in closer once more and spoke to me as if I were a simpleton.

'It's very straightforward - you are here to belly dance. That is all.'

'Belly dance?' I asked. He emphasised his boredom with a sigh before speaking.

'Do your homework, Mr Edgar! The Raqs Sharqi is the belly dance. The dance of the East. We invite people to dine with us for entertainment, to study them as they entertain us - to dance for us, if you like. And you danced wonderfully tonight. I think the Folletts thought you were most amusing.' He smacked his pale lips together sneeringly and then leaned over the table, his voice lowering to a most unwelcoming growl. 'But you won't be back. And, most certainly, you will never, ever be a member of the club.'

After holding his position for a moment with that ghastly sneer on his lips he sat back and drank in silence for a minute, letting his words sink in. His rancid wife was still snorting to herself. My heart had sunk at his scorn, and I felt like a fool. What sort of people invite somebody to dinner just to laugh and gloat over them?

'Yes,' Mason continued casually with a flick of the wrist, 'we've had all kinds here, some better than others. A magician, a fashion model - she was good, gave us a turn and all. We had a postman, lord knows why, that was Bunny's doing. We even had a bloody immigrant.'

At this, Mildred Mason cast a puckered scowl down at her cutlery.

'What else? A dog trainer, a barber, a ski instructor...'

Ercot Mason continued to list absurd occupations as I sat, red cheeked, in silence. After a minute or so he had finished speaking, but I had not heard a word. I pushed my unfinished drink aside, stood abruptly and, making no excuse to the Masons, began my walk to Irving through a cloud of putrid cigar smoke. Behind me I could not fail to hear Mason's nasal laugh as he issued one last rebuff.

'It has been so pleasant to meet you, Mr Edgar. Do come and visit Mildred and I in our darling country house, won't you?'

I could just see their faces in my mind as they sneered cruelly behind my back. By the time I reached Irving I was in a state of near apoplexy. And yet I contained myself, all too aware of the company that surrounded me. I stood beside Irving and quietly, meekly, asked him if we could leave.

I wanted to go home.

Chapter VIII

In which Payton Edgar chews over delicious revenge

Humiliation!

When I returned home I threw my coat aside and made straight for the drinks cabinet. I had barely spoken to Irving on our return journey from the Follett Gallery, and had been glad to close my front door on the world and gather my thoughts alone.

Without really thinking I fixed myself a stiff whisky without water and then barely touched it. Mason's words were floating around my mind again and again.

You were born to be a party piece, not a club member.

Anger welled up in my gut.

A clown, not a ringmaster!

For a moment I thought I might cry. I found myself wishing that Miss Kemp were up and about, to happily offer her no-nonsense opinion in that cool calm way of hers. Miss Kemp respected me. She didn't see me as a clown. Far from it.

But it was late and the house was still.

I paced the room, picturing Ercot Mason and that leering snarl of his. Heat welled up in my chest.

All this was doing no good for my ulcer.

In an attempt to sooth my rage I forced myself to sit, took in a long, deep breath and followed this with a gulp of my drink. But it was no use, for a moment later I was back on my feet and over to my bureau where, rested on top, I had proudly placed Irving's invitation for dinner with the Raqs Sharqi that night at the Follett Gallery. I switched my glass for the letter, and deftly tore it up into the tiniest pieces that I could, dropping the shreds to the carpet without a care.

Revenge!

I would get my revenge on each and every one of the repulsive Raqs Sharqi Club. I would show them that nobody treats Payton Edgar with such callous disregard. Yes, somehow, by any means- and as soon as I could - I would indeed enjoy some revenge.

Delicious revenge!

Chapter IX

In which Payton Edgar happens upon some answers

Dear Margaret,
I have a terrible problem with mice and cannot seem to get on top of it. They have nibbled a hole in my favourite sweet-pea linen curtain panel and leave droppings behind my love seat. I have tried poison, and even a cat, but they ignore the poison and the cat is so lazy it just lies there and watches them. Do you have any suggestions?
Yvonne, Hampstead Heath

Margaret replies; what on earth do you think I am, a rat catcher? I don't think for a minute that your biggest problem is mice - I think that it is your lack of taste in home furnishings. Your vile sweet-pea panel sounds like it is better off devoured, and anyone who refers to their two-seater as a "love seat" deserves an infestation if you ask me.

Once more I found myself going into hiding.

For the next couple of days after my dreadful experience with the so-called Raqs Sharqi Club I moved very little, saw very little, spoke very little and did very little at all. The fury I had felt on the night of that awful meal had been diluted somewhat and I was left with a new feeling, a muted feeling of frustrated irritation. As usual, Lucille was scant comfort in my time of need. As I reached out to pet the bothersome animal she would slink away from me as if to agree with everything the hateful Mason had said; that I were nothing but a court jester and a fool.

The days seemed interminably long and drawn out, and very little of note actually happened to me during my period of - for want of a better word - sulking. I had even pushed away Grace, and after she had made me a nice mug of Horlicks one evening, too.

'Is something wrong, Payton?' she had been forced to ask as I grumbled over my milky beverage. I was almost enjoying this particular sulk.

'Would you miss me if I went away, Grace?' I found myself asking.

'Away? Do you mean if you went on holiday, or if you died?'

'Either suits me,' I replied.

'Of course I would!' sang Grace, honestly. 'But I think a holiday would do you the world of good. You never go anywhere. You're thinking of taking a trip somewhere?'

'Perhaps,' I had replied, mysteriously, and she had the good sense to leave it at that.

I barely thought about the corpse I had discovered in the bath tub, so all-encompassing was my ire at the events of the Raqs Sharqi meal. Everything seemed flat and lifeless. One thing that did spark an interest, albeit only a flicker of interest, was the news that the poor vagrant arrested following the death of Fabien Pouche had been released, uncharged.

The unfortunate man had probably found himself sitting back in the cold darkness of a park and pining for a return to the warm cell and the basic services provided within.

In the run up to his exhibition opening, Irving had been deeply embroiled in all things creative, and I had kept out of his way. He seemed to be under the impression that the dinner with the Folletts had been nothing short of a triumph, entirely unaware of the set-up, with the members of their stinking club treating me as nothing other than a wind-up toy! Fury bubbled through my chest each time I thought of it.

A toy! A plaything! It was unforgivable!

We had enjoyed a fairly low key evening on the Monday night at a restaurant near Euston, armed with my pad and pencil for the next review. I was careful not to mention to Irving anything I had learned about the Raqs Sharqi Club, but it was constantly on my mind. For the first time since the start of my venture as a restaurant critic my notes were sparse and my heart was not really in it. I did write the review, but it was somewhat restrained and nowhere near as scathing as the meal and service itself warranted.

The letters for Margaret Blythe even failed to ignite a spark in me.

Dr Margaret was in a foul mood, and the public would suffer in her replies. I produced a rather savage attack on a grumbling housewife, driven to distraction by the barking emitting from the dogs home that she chose to live adjacent to. The woman had a poorer command of the English language than the dogs of which she complained, and Dr Margaret gave her a short shrift, but perhaps with rather too many personal attacks to be fair and I duly destroyed the piece and filed it in my waste paper basket. This was swiftly followed by the usual prurient and coarse correspondences received that I refused to include on Dr Margaret's page.

Yet again, some of the words within were inappropriate in the extreme.

I put my creative impotence entirely down to the emotional bruising I had suffered at the hands of the vile Raqs Sharqi Club, and on day four my simmering and seething came to a boil. I renewed my vow of vengeance. I would not act immediately, but I would bide my time and then strike at the heart of their pointless club when they least expected it.

Yes indeed. I would see their club crumble away to nothing.

An opportunity came out of the blue, most unexpectedly, as I was sauntering through Vauxhall. This was the first day that week that I had woken feeling any kind of strength inside, as if the bruises sustained to my character on attending that damned meal were finally fading. The morning air was a little cooler, refreshing almost, and town seemed pleasantly calm. I had taken in a pair of trousers to be - well - taken in, and was hoping to get to the butchers in time for a satisfactory cut of beef for Grace to prepare. It was as I headed for the butchers that I passed the steamy window of a tea shop.

A smooth face through the glass caused me to stop and do a double take. Dark eyes peered back at me through the condensation, and I found myself giving the natural response of a smile.

It was the French girl from Ferrier's restaurant. Therese.

My friendly gesture caused a startling reaction, as she jumped back from her stool and made hastily away through the darkness inside the café. Somewhat alarmed by this, I stepped up quickly to the door of the establishment, only to bump into the girl as we met face on. We both jerked back sharply in the doorway.

'Therese-' I began.

'Go away!' she gasped and made to shove past me. I would never allow such insolence to pass, and duly blocked her route.

'What is wrong, my dear?'

She was shaking a little, I could see, and it dawned on me that she was frightened.

'There are people in here!' she nodded inside the café, 'they see you now, and what you do. Now move away or I call police!' She was indeed scanning the street for a passing bobby.

'Therese, I don't understand. What have I done?'

She stopped and looked me straight in the eye, a cloud of disbelief moving across her dark features. There was something about the girl, she was arresting to look at.

'What have you done? You come see me, you ask about Fabien, and now he is dead!'

I tried to stifle a laugh.

'That had nothing to do with me, my dear! Nothing!' Looking down at her I could see just how frightened, and upset, she was. I knew that I should step away, to leave the poor girl alone, but Payton Edgar has never been one to shrink back from false accusation.

'Do I look like a murderer?' I asked. My choice of words upset her even more, but I persisted. 'Well? Do I look criminal?' I fingered my lapel pointedly. 'This is Saville Row's absolute finest, for goodness sake!' The girl did not falter, but it was clear that she was listening.

'I asked you about Fabien because I did want to see him, but about something entirely, well...*trivial*.'

It hurt me just a little to say that word, but there was nothing else for it but to come clean.

'My name is Payton Edgar and I am a journalist for the London Clarion. I live in Clarendon Street, Pimlico, with my cat, my elderly aunt and her nursemaid. I enjoy listening to Bach and reading classic literature with my feet up in leather slippers. I never have, and most certainly never would, hurt a fellow human being in my life!'

She blinked and continued to look deep into my eyes. I appealed to her one last time.

'Would I give you my name and address if I were a murderer? Would I?'

Her shoulders relaxed and for a second she looked helpless and fragile. I gestured back into the café and gently offered her a fresh cup of tea. Soon we were sitting opposite each almost comfortably, and I dare not imagine what onlookers took us for, as with her Gallic features and cosmopolitan air the girl was clearly not my offspring.

The first thing that I said opened the gates of her history and I did my upmost to offer her a quiet audience. She spooned far too much sugar into her cup and told me stories of her life without any further questioning. Once she had accepted my innocence it was surprising how the girl was able to talk, seemingly keen to share her experiences, which were many and varied given her few years of adulthood.

She was a sweet, lonely young thing, and I did my best to keep up with her sprawling story.

As I had suspected she was indeed from Southern France, born to a dying mother in a tiny village at the foot of some mountains not far from the Spanish border. Soon after her birth her father had taken her and an older brother across the border for work, where, eventually, they had been caught up in the war and pulled back to their homeland. Her account was simple, the second world war as seen through the eyes of a four year old. Simple and brutal.

She talked of losing her brother in a bombing, of bringing her father to England, and of climbing a catering hierarchy from kitchen hand to cook in the hotels of London. She made these places sound like majestic palaces of wealth and glamour, clearly having been able to ignore all the rats and filth a young worker must have come across in the Capital. She talked of cooking for her ailing father and then nursing him as he died. For Therese, England was a place of solace, a place of money, creativity, and most importantly a place of peace.

Her tale should have been devastating. It was certainly peppered with enough pathos and tragedy to form the sort of moving stage musical that I would definitely go to great lengths to avoid. However there was a sadness about the girl that was fresher, something about her life today in the kitchens of London was making her speak so openly.

She shook her head sharply, as if shaking off dark thoughts, and then addressed me abruptly.

'So why you look for Fabien? Please tell me truth.'

Slowly, reluctantly, I told her everything. I told her who I was, and about the restaurant review and about the demoralising letter in The Clarion.

'So you not like my restaurant, eh?' Therese grunted, looking up at me with what I hoped was a comical malice.

'I assure you, young lady, I did not mean to upset you in any way. Only that cretin Ferrier. It is not your restaurant, it is his. I'm sure that you are a very able cook, but to be a very able cook you must be prepared for challenge and dissatisfaction from those in the know. I know how it feels to be criticised myself. And so I had to see the writer, this Fabien Pouche, you understand? But I didn't want to hurt him - heavens no. I never could. I simply needed to get to the truth. You see, I have a, well, a difficult relationship with your employer, Monsieur Ferrier, and-'

'He write the letter,' Therese stated with the casual wave of a hand.

A long pause followed.

'I beg your pardon?'

Therese sipped her tea and swallowed. 'Ferrier. He write the letter,' she said again.

'Well, that's what I thought at first-' I began, only to be interrupted.

'I hear him talking about it, laughing about it in the kitchen. Sebastien read that review in the newspaper and he is very angry. You complain about his restaurant! He not like you at all! He will write a letter in reply, he say, and he will be just as rude. And then he say to us all in the kitchen *"give me a name, any false name"*. Fabien say "Fabien Pouche, you use my name but pay me for it!" And Monsieur Ferrier, he did. He owe him his wage anyway. Fabien not write English, he not write the letter.'

I watched the girl sipping her drink innocently for quite a while.

Unbelievable! I had been correct all along, and it was Sebastien Ferrier behind the whole stupid letter! It was indeed a personal attack. I should have felt something akin to gratification, satisfaction, even, at being proved right yet again, but I did not. All I felt was a mild anger that I had taken the bait so easily, and that Ferrier had got me into the sticky situation with the corpse in the bathtub.

This revelation, however, tied up the mystery of the letter and drew a line under the whole torrid affair. I was reluctantly grateful. Having had confirmed just what I had expected all along, I felt surprisingly little ire towards the French restaurateur. It was as if I had used all my anger up over past few days.

Therese had dipped her eyes down once again, her pretty face taking on a shadow of sadness. I sat and watched her for a while, and it was a good few minutes before I spoke with a simple observation.

'You are a sad little thing!'

Then tears came and I immediately regretted my words, for I had not wished to cause upset. She cried through three paper napkins as I sat patiently sipping on my lukewarm and over-milky coffee and thinking to myself *what would Dr Margaret Blythe do*?

Despite the tears I realised that I had done the girl a favour, that she had been given her only opportunity to think, to consider, and even to cry. In usual circumstances wild emotions frighten me, and I would run the proverbial mile from any emotional confrontation. Perhaps I was changing. I sank for a while into glorious self-inspection.

Were the experiences of recent years, since my divorce, shifting who I was? Had fronting the pointless problem page made me an even better person? Could it be possible? After a time I rose out of my reverie and realised that the sniffing girl at the table before me was still talking.

'You see, I loved him,' she croaked almost inaudibly.

Now I was speechless. What was the girl expecting me to say? I bit my lip, feeling more than a little hopeless. The things that Dr Blythe might say in response to this pitiful display seemed wholly inappropriate at that particular moment. Therese gathered herself a little before continuing.

'Fabien came to work in the winter time. At first, we did not speak even though he was French too and did not have any friends in the city. Then one Saturday our kitchen hand not turn up, and I help Fabien with the washing up. I am very angry. I am cook, not cleaner! And he laugh at me, and we fight, and then... it changes. We laugh a lot, and I love him. I love him! We laugh so much, he so kind and funny. And handsome too.' Her eyes were sparkling with remembrance now. 'I do the wrong thing - I tell him I love him, but he not mind. He was very… very tender to me. We grow so close. Oh, I know he is a rat, all men are. He never show up when he promises to. I lend him money, which he never pay back, but I not mind.'

She weaved her fingers together.

'And then, at the kitchen one day, a customer, a man, approaches Fabien, gives him money! I not know why. The man says they meet that Friday, and I know Fabien goes. From that moment, I lose him. I lose him to some bad gang, I think.' Her face had paled, the light smile had gone.

'I'm sorry,' I said, letting a moment of silence pass. I really was surprising myself with my sensitivity that morning. I felt I should ask something.

'When was this?'

'The start of the Summer,' she said with a resigned tone. 'He still work with us after, but is quieter, and not happy. And very, very tired. I think he is on bad drugs, but he says no, and we argue. And he never borrow money from me again, he not need to. But he no longer laugh any more. Fabien is gone. And now he is dead.' Her face crumpled to tears once more.

This time I did look around me to other tables in the café, realising for the first time the interest generated by a mature gentleman entertaining a young woman in tears. Two wrinkled elderly ladies in headscarves were certainly enjoying the show, but it didn't matter to me at that moment. I gave then an indignant glare before turning back to my confidante.

Let them look.

Therese gave a great sniff, as if pulling all her sorrow deep back inside, and adjusted her posture, sitting upright.

'I know you not hurt him, Sir. They did. They make him unhappy. They killed him.'

I could not hide my curiosity. 'What happened?'

'I not know.'

'You should go to the police, my dear. The boy is dead!'

'Never!' she replied sharply.

'But who are they?' I said, 'Who did this? Who was that man?'

She shrugged. 'I do not know! Fabien never tell me, he very quiet about it. I think he with some gang of bad people. That where he get the money. But I know one thing - the people, one day he call them something strange. Name of a big fish. Kind of shark. The racks shark…'

'*The Raqs Sharqi?*'

The words were out of my mouth without a second thought.

'That is it! I remember it well. He in with them. They kill him, I know.'

The world around us stopped as she said the words. The Raqs Sharqi? Had she misheard? This made no sense. The kitchen boy could never have been a member of the club himself. And then, as I sat back in my chair I heard Ercot Mason's sneering drawl float back into my consciousness.

'We've had all kinds to dinner... a postman, a dog trainer, even a bloody immigrant...'

An immigrant.

The late Fabien Pouche.

PART TWO

Chapter I

In which Payton Edgar begins an investigation

Dear Margaret,
My best friend is so much more beautiful and stylish than I
am. I am afraid that I look rather frumpy and old-hat compared to
her. I try my hardest with my hair and make-up and the latest fash-
ions, but I just cannot keep up. Any advice?
Betty, Bermondsey

Margaret replies; *Does the humble farmhouse chicken allow itself*
to be seen with the preening peacock? *The answer is "no", and with*
good reason. *Birds of a feather flock together, my dear.* *Don't waste*
your time trying to polish an already rusty doorknob. *I suggest that you*
aim your sights a little lower and find yourself some new feathery
friends.

I had avoided my Aunt Elizabeth for some time, and should have
known that it couldn't last forever. At the most inopportune moment I
was bound to find myself summoned.

I had been enjoying a pot of tea and a plate of custard creams with
Grace Kemp. Sharing my homestead with Aunt Elizabeth and her current help should have been a tiresome affair, for I enjoy my peaceful soli-
tude and my creature comforts, and sharing has never been something
that came naturally. Miss Kemp, however, was a like a cool breath of
fresh air. Around the house, she kept herself to herself, was happy to
help with all sorts of chores, and - most importantly - she was an excel-

lent listener. She had an air of honesty and frankness that elevated conversations beyond the banal.

She enjoyed home cooking, and we had been talking about the difficulties of making a good roux when she had posed an unexpected question.

'Still thinking of taking that holiday?' she had enquired. I had quite forgotten that I had alluded to such a thing during one of my sulks, replied with a shrug and quickly changed the subject back to Béchamel sauce.

As I contemplated a third custard cream she gave a squeak.

'I nearly forgot! Your aunt has asked to see you, Mr Edgar.' She said this with a simple, perhaps sympathetic smile and I soon found myself outside my Aunt's lair, tight fists at my side as I prepared myself. I knocked first and then entered the bedroom.

I had tried to get on with Aunt Elizabeth, I really had. I had welcomed her into the house at the end of the previous year and suffered her complaints and taunting ever since. And still, as I stepped into her room I hoped for something - anything - nice or even just pleasant. A pleasant word of thanks, rather than a barrage of insults.

I should have known better.

'Good morning, *Margaret*,' Aunt Elizabeth declared dryly as I entered her room, baring her yellow dentures with a wicked snarl. She was, as usual, sitting up in bed as if she were stricken by illness and not simply elderly and lazy. For the umpteenth time I cursed the fact that she had discovered my alter ego.

'Grace tells me that you wished to see me,' I replied, direct and straight to the point. Before Aunt Elizabeth could reply, her vile stray ginger moggy appeared through the open window. The cat was increasingly scrawny and unkempt each time I saw it, a true disgrace to her breed. She leapt onto the bed and cast a thin eyed glare in my direction before curling up in my aunt's lap. Aunt Elizabeth pushed a gnarled knuckle into its fur.

'I want to ask you for something,' Aunt Elizabeth began. She fixed me in a glare as if to dare me to refuse. When I made no response, she went on. 'It's not very often I ask you for things...'

I couldn't let this pass.

'Not very often? How about last week? That implement you so desperately needed-'

'The pill cutter? That cost pennies!'

'And what about that foot bath you were so keen on?'

'Pooh! That was before Christmas!'

'Grace tells me you never use it!'

'I don't like getting my feet wet.'

I took in a deep breath and steadied myself for what was to come.

67

I could tell by the look on Aunt Elizabeth's face that I was about to be hit with no run-of-the-mill request.

'I would like a television set,' she declared with incommodious simplicity.

Wrong-footed somewhat, I took a moment to reply.

'A television?'

'Yes, have you heard of it? Small box of talking people?'

'But-'

'Most houses have one these days, Payton. Television is the *in-thing*!'

I swallowed heavily. The *in-thing*? The *in-thing*? This coming from a woman who would not be out of place encased in glass at the British Museum!

'And how, pray, do you intend to get to the living room to view it?'

'Pah! I want a television in here, Payton, in my bedroom!'

The woman was unbelievable!

'You would like a television in your bedroom?' I stammered in disbelief. 'We don't even have one in the living room!'

'That is your choice, darling nephew. You really don't know what it's like for me. I lie here day after day, night after night, bored out of my brains. Have you any idea how it feels to be stuck here alone, listening to that clock, staring at the walls-'

'You have that moggy!' I pointed out.

'Poor dear Titty is bored too, aren't you dear?' She scratched at the cat's head.

'You have your books,' I replied swiftly.

'Read 'em all!' Aunt Elizabeth snapped sharply. 'I need a television set!'

I felt that familiar heat rising in my chest.

'Out of the question! You summon me here to ask the impossible-'

Aunt Elizabeth let out a sharp cackle.

'That isn't why I asked for you. I just thought I'd put in the order. And you can consider it an order. Look at you, standing there, mouth open, gormless. You really don't know why I asked for you, do you?' she asked coldly, to which I issued an exaggerated shrug. What on earth was wrong with her now?

'You have shamed yourself,' she went on, her dark eyes widening. And there I stood, at the foot of her bed, like some disobedient schoolboy before his headmistress. I could not let this be.

'If you are going to speak in riddles, Auntie, then I will leave. Is this about the problem page again?'

She cackled.

'That too brings shame on your head, I cannot deny it, *Margaret*! But there is something else.'

The cat raised its tail and rested it to cover it's eyes, as if it could not bear the sight of me. My aunt had paused, but I was not about to fill the silence.

'Today,' she announced eventually, 'is exactly one year to the day since my darling sister, your dear mother, passed on.'

Silence.

I wanted to shrug once more. I wanted to hold out my palms in question. I wanted to say *"so what?"* Mother and I had never been close. Of course I hadn't remembered. Of course I hadn't thought about it.

Why should I?

'Is that it?' I asked softly. 'May I leave now?'

And as I turned to go Aunt Elizabeth tore into a torrent of words, a wave of words that following me out of the room. I caught the words *selfish, ungrateful,* and then *television* and then – that word again – *shame.*

I stormed up the staircase to my attic study where my books and maps were kept, and where the chair was plump and comforting. Yet I did not sit. I paced wildly, casting out all thoughts of Aunt Elizabeth and her ridiculous anniversary and returning my mind to more pressing issues.

For a few days after Therese's revelation I had been brooding on exactly what my next steps would be. In my mind I had defined an enemy, with each member of the pretentious Raqs Sharqi Club in my sights. I had also given myself a time limit. Before the summer cooled into autumn I intended to bring down their useless, disrespectful venture and crown myself victor in the fight against the disrespectful insolence they had demonstrated so coldly.

The only question was - *how?*

I allowed the tips of my fingers to touch my globe, and then let it spin carefully, watching the countries and oceans roll on by. The answer, I was certain, lay in the mysterious death of Fabien Pouche and his connection with their Club. Therese had been close to the young man, and she was no fool. She knew that the association with them had brought his downfall, and I intended to prove it. I spun the globe once more and then returned to my pacing.

It took me some time to decide where to start. The catty curator, the vile actor, the politician and his wife or the Folletts themselves? None of my options seemed particularly inviting, and it was with a certain devil-may-care attitude that I hatched a plan.

The last words I had heard from Ercot Mason had stuck in my mind. His sarcastic invitation to tea at his house may have been a plummy jibe, but what if I were to take him up on it? What if Payton Edgar were to attend the Masons' place with a sincere naivety about the nastiness of the whole Raqs Sharqi project? Surely they could not turn away a pleasant visitor who had been genuinely invited to tea? And if that visitor were to bring up the subject of Fabien Pouche, what could they do?

I became thrilled at the thought. It would require something of a performance on my part, but I did not doubt for a moment that I could do it.

My pride was at stake.

To find the address I required, I had to call one of my contacts at the Clarion. It is wonderful to work for a newspaper such as the Clarion, for one has access to worlds such as politics or show business that your average lay person could only dream of. Grumpy old politico Thomas Lee gave me the address without question. After I had scribbled it down and given thanks, I began to prepare myself for a day in the country.

When I say country I really mean Potten Way, just north of Watford.

This is deep darkest countryside to us city-folk, and much as poets would have us believe that England is proud of its rolling hills and dense woodland, I have never understood the appeal. In my opinion the dreary, mud-splattered fields and miserable, decaying cottages with crumbling brickwork leave much to be desired.

And sheep are simply eerie creatures, standing about like balls of fluff all day long, doing nothing but eating grass.

In spite of this, one should always dress up for a day in the country, and it was after some deliberation in my mirror that I opted to wear the classic blue/grey tweed two piece and navy tie with my Standard Oxford shoes, the need to outsmart Mason in the wardrobe department being far more important than my comfort in the heat of the day.

To make matters worse, I was forced to journey by bus. After carefully studying the timetable, minimal as it was, I had noted the time of the last bus home, which came through just after teatime.

My journey was unremarkable, and thankfully the bus was quiet enough for me to sit alone. I was careful to sit on the shady side of the vehicle and kept my brow-mopping handkerchief to hand. I have never been the greatest traveller, and it was with equal amounts of relief and apprehension that I stepped from the bus. I had been dropped off opposite a sloping, weary-looking cottage with a fussy thatched roof. One became immediately aware of the difference in the air, the clear, sterile silence being so much at odds with the smoky bustle of the City.

Suddenly the still air was punctuated with a loud mechanical choking. To my far right a figure in a flat cap was leaning over a lawn mower, which eventually shuddered into action with a deep, repetitive phut-phut-phut. The man began to stride across what was evidently the village green.

On my left a small and somewhat dowdy elderly lady dressed in a faded flowery smock was playing bowls on an undersized green, seemingly by herself. Aside from this figure and the lawn mower, there was no other person in sight.

After following a pathway through the green I arrived at a rather sad looking village hall. For a moment I studied three posters which had been strung upon large noticeboard, one warning me that Potten Way Summer Fete was on its way, one calling me to prayer and one scruffily written advert for a *"dog walking woman"*, whatever that may be. I moved on and passed a shadowy graveyard to my right. I had soon come to the conclusion that, in such a neat little village it would be fairly simple to locate Number One, Briar Lane, residence of Sir Ercot Mason.

I was to be proved correct.

Many of the houses I passed proudly displayed their numbers alongside absurd names such as *"The Vines"* (there was no evidence of vines neither on nor around the building) and *"Honeysuckle Cottage"* (once again, the absence of honeysuckle was notable). I headed onwards, and had only walked for a minute or two before I found Briar Lane and caught sight of a narrow, perfectly manicured lawn, behind which stood a rather grand white turreted house with deep red paintwork at the frames. From the road I could see the fancy number one in ironworks mounted upon its nearest wall amongst a number of flowery hanging baskets.

As I approached the building a plaque came into view beside the house number. This had been hidden from view by the bulky black car that sat in the driveway baking slowly in the morning sun. Aside this car was a second, smaller car of the sporting variety.

The plaque on the wall read *"Ivy Cottage"* in swirls of vine on a beige background. To give the Mason family their dues, there was indeed a mass of sprawling ivy across the nearest portion of the house which justified its appellation. A little further along, besides the large oak front door, sat a stone dog with a stone collar and a chipped stone slipper in its mouth. I had nearly stumbled upon it, and I resisted the impulse to kick it aside as it sat looking up at me, hungrily. I would not have wished to scuff my toe-cap.

Without pause I rapped on the impressive lion-head knocker and waited.

I was to stand unattended for a few minutes before rapping once more. The cars were present in the drive, and therefore I expected the house to be occupied. Stepping back a little I looked to the upper windows which were dark and netted. I moved to the bay window at my left and peered through the well polished glass. Again, nets obscured my view, but I was sure that I caught sight of a shadow silhouetted by the back windows, a shadow which moved sharply aside as I pressed my nose up to the glass.

Somebody was at home.

I returned to the door and abused the knocker once again, a little louder this time, determined not to have had a wasted visit. I knocked again.

Eventually, the lock clicked, and the door opened.

I experienced a sudden unexpected flash of discomfort as Ercot Mason stood tall in the doorway. Despite the fact that there was a half-smile on his lips, his stance was somewhat confrontational. He wore a black shirt tucked into grey flannel trousers, the sleeves rolled up as if he had just finished the washing up. He extended a dry hand.

'Mr Edgar! What a surprise.'

There was not even a glimmer of surprise on his politician's face.

I shook the hand briefly. 'Good morning, Mr Mason,' I said, opting to begin with the necessary pleasantries. 'I do hope I am not calling at an inconvenient time? You said to come to tea, and I was just on a pleasant little ramble when I thought I'd pop by. I do hope I am not disturbing you?'

He slithered backwards a little. 'No, no, not at all. Come in, come in!'

I stepped up into the shade of the house and was led through a bright ornate flowery hallway into an even more floral lounge. Large irises patterned the walls amongst ugly green swirls. The carpet, though thick, had been covered in the centre of the room by a large oval rug of pink and red petals, aside which sat a plump cream leather sofa. A substantial arrangement of roses burst out of a garish patterned vase on the gilded mantelpiece above a redundant fireplace, sending a powerful floral scent around the room.

The place was the very picture of a comfortable country house.

'Mildred is upstairs changing, she will be down in a minute,' said Mason. 'Please do sit down.'

I sat and found myself sinking alarmingly deep into the plump cushioning. Mason weaved his fingers together and threw out a question.

'Too early for a tipple?'

I coughed before replying. It was not even eleven. 'I think so. Too early for me anyhow, thank you.' Mason strode over to the fireplace and leaned his elbow on the edge, smiling in my direction.

'Work going well for you?' He tossed out this casual pleasantry as though reading from a script.

'Yes, yes,' I said, 'Thank you very much.'

There was a pause.

'So then,' he began, raising an eyebrow and pursing his lips, turning his word into a question. The man must be baffled as to why I would care to visit.

Bide your time, Payton, I said to myself. Even though you are on Mason's territory, you are in control here.

'You have a very pleasant abode,' I stated with forced innocence.

'Yes, yes, we rather like it. It is our second home of course, a comfortable base away from the bustle of work, if you like. Mildred keeps it well, and we have no kiddie-winkles to mess up the place. Now, where the devil is she?'

This was the first hint of impatience I had witnessed, but he was saved by an urgent scuffling noise behind me. I turned to see the fragile Mildred Mason standing ghost-like in the doorway. She wore a dainty summer dress of pastel greens and pinks and around her shoulders was draped a light beige cardigan. On her feet were a garish pair of fluffy pink slippers that clashed with the wateriness of her dress.

Rather incongruously with her comfortable attire, she had on her face a look of wide-eyed fear and she stared over at her husband for a moment before shifting her eyes downwards to the floor. Her short greying hair was more ruffled and boyish than before.

Mason greeted his wife as if she were a princess at a ballroom.

'Mildred, darling, you look sensational. Come through, sit down.'
Strange that he should order the woman formally into her own living room. And yet, she did not move. Her eyes remained cast downwards.

'Mr Edgar has just popped by for tea,' Mason said darkly. 'He was on a ramble.'

Mildred Mason said nothing.

'In his best suit, it seems,' her husband added pointedly.

I ignored this crack and stood firm, issuing a wide smile.

'Good morning, Mrs Mason. Beautiful day, is it not?'

I received no response of any kind whatsoever. Instead, Mason spoke for his wife.

'I think a pot of tea would be in order, Mildred. Don't you?'

'Tea would be lovely, thank you,' I was quick to answer.

As the tea was made, Mason and I exchanged some more polite words about the weather and the village. I heard all about the miserable Parish and the troubles of the tiresome bowls club, and then some nonsense about a badger on the village green. I was keeping up my innocent visitor guise with considerable skill, and Mason had no cause to break through his strained veneer of acting as a genial host. I took my time to admire the ugly vase atop the mantelpiece, and was duly treated to a horribly boring story about its purchase.

He then went on to matters of fox hunting, and I was thankful when Mildred Mason clattered back into the room with a tea trolley.

'Goodness!' I exclaimed, genuinely surprised by the lavishness of the spread that had arrived. 'What a feast! And a most striking tea set.'

'Yes, the tea set was a welcome inheritance from Mildred's side. A rather rare Royal Worcester set, don't you know? Pour now, Mildred.'

She did as she was told. The cup clattered nervously in its saucer as she handed it over to me.

'Sugar?' the man enquired as his wife did the work.

'No, thank you.'

'Rock bun? Buttered scone?' Mason continued.

I produced my sickliest smile.

'Well I really shouldn't, but I will. It is time for elevenses, I believe?'

And so I munched on a rather grim rock bun as Mason prattled on about something one of his constituents had said to him at Church the previous weekend, a tale he clearly considered to be terribly amusing when, in actual fact, it was predictably wearisome. I was only half listening, studying the docile Mildred Mason as she sat cowed in the farthest armchair, an untouched milky tea on the table before her. I realised she had not said a word at all that morning, seemingly content for her idiot husband to do all the talking.

It was as if the woman were her husband's servant, the poor thing.

Mason had reached a climax in his story, and I proffered a polite chuckle at what he clearly deemed to be something of a punchline. I turned back to the man, for it was time.

I made my move.

'Actually, there was something I meant to ask you about, Mason. What was it?' I placed a finger to my chin and pretended to rake over my memory for a moment. 'Ah, yes. You mentioned having an immigrant to the Raqs Sharqi Club at one time or another. A Mr Fabien Pouche, I believe?'

Mason didn't miss a beat in his reply.

'Can't say as I recall the name, Edgar. They all look much alike to me. Young chap, he was. Entirely unremarkable.' He sipped his tea. 'Perfect brew, Mildred, my dear.'

I persisted.

'And yet it is not every day you have an immigrant sitting at the table of the Raqs Shari Club. There must be some detail you recall-'

'Well, we've had so many guests to dinner over the years, don't you know?' Mason cut in, pointedly drifting away from my question. 'We had a catwalk model, that grumpy old postmaster-'

And now it was my turn to interrupt.

'I was under the impression that Mr Pouche became rather more than a guest for the night. Am I right?'

'Mr Edgar, I really can't tell you anything for the simple fact that I know nothing about the lad. You may as well ask me for the lowdown on that damn dog trainer we had one night. Damned dull do that was. She didn't even bother to bring a mutt with her.' He finished his tea with a slurp. 'The man was an immigrant with an interesting tale, and that is all. We don't fraternise with the lower classes, Edgar. So no, sorry, old chap. Nothing doing.'

And so with this my investigation came to a halt.

The man was clearly immovable, and his mute wife about as insightful as a broom handle. I finished my tea and, after five more minutes of polite conversational clap-trap, made my excuses and left.

Mason had shown me out, leaving his wife to clear away the tea set. He behaved as if my visit had been an entirely pleasant and natural experience, even clapping a hand jovially to my shoulder as I stepped out of the doorway.

I returned, dejected, to the bus stop.

As I waited for my ride I pondered on my next move. I was unsure as to whether Mason had been making light of his encounter with Pouche. It was feasible that he had indeed had nothing to do with the young lad, and that another member of the group was involved. But who? And why?

More importantly, what was to be my next move?

By the time the bus arrived back at Victoria I had realised just what I had to do next, and had hurried back to Clarendon Street with renewed vigour.

"*We don't fraternise with the lower classes*", Mason had sneered. Then, perhaps, this was exactly what I should do next. My next move was obvious.

The lower classes; the eyes and ears that had been around the club but in the shadows. Those who are in the best position to observe the truth behind a group like the Raqs Sharqi bunch.

The staff.

Chapter II

In which Payton Edgar avoids some piddle on the parlour floor

Dear Margaret,
We have had the misfortune of having a family of blacks move
in to the house next door, and I feel that this has let down the tone of
our whole neighbourhood. A few days later they came knocking on
the door and I was so frightened that I hid in the back, and have
managed to avoid them ever since. I cannot let the children out to
play in the side garden as it leads on to theirs. My husband is a very
busy man and leaves me to deal with this kind of thing. Now I feel
trapped inside my own home. What can I do about this?
Mrs Pitts, Barnet

Margaret replies; I am glad that you wrote to me with this conun-
drum, Mrs Pitts, as it gives me the opportunity to say this; if any Clarion
reader ever writes such condemnatory and asinine claptrap as the letter
above to my postbag it will be treated with the only necessary reaction –
a direct line to my wastepaper basket. You are not trapped in your own
home, Mrs Pitts, you are trapped in your own stupidity. Please reassess
your attitude and return the delightfully considerate (not to mention very
British) gesture of calling in on your new neighbours before your chil-
dren grow up thinking that foolishly avoiding the varieties of life is a
normal and acceptable way of behaving.

It was not hard to locate the Mayfair residence of Lord and Lady
Follett.
Earlier in the year they had invited Irving to an undoubtedly dread-

ful Spring garden party in aid of malformed children. Despite some relentless badgering on my part Irving had refused to attend, but the floral-bordered card remained wedged between a jam jar and a hastily sculpted Buddha on his mantelpiece. Slipping the invite into my pocket unseen was easy, as my friend was in a paint-spattered, distracted creative flux. I could have stolen all the furniture in his house and the shoes from his feet and I dare say he'd have failed to notice.

Mayfair.

Once a place where each and every doorstep was scrubbed to within an inch of perfection, housing the richest of the rich, before the richest of the rich were bombed out of the area and replaced by industry. Now the area stood as a curious mix of grandiose town houses and meat packing firms. I sauntered along Curzon Street and sat for a while in Berkley Square before finding myself standing before Tower House, Grosvenor Street.

The steps leading up to the front door of the Follett's private residence were indeed well scrubbed, but worn and high, with shining iron-work running alongside of them. The door itself was the kind of over-sized town house door with an elaborate knocker that really suits a wreath at Christmastime.

I was left waiting for some time after pulling the bell.

The door eventually opened to reveal a harassed looking young lady in a surprisingly old fashioned maid's attire. She forced a smile and peered at me through crooked glasses.

'Good day, Sir. May I help you?' she asked in a superior tone.

Politely, and not without some authority, I introduced myself and requested to see Mortimer, valet to Lady Follett. The young lady's face fell as if I were not worth the strain on her facial muscles, her tone dropping to a cockney drawl.

'Servant's quarters in the back, mate. I can't let you through the 'ouse. You'll have to go through tradesman's entrance down that way.'

She indicated a stairway leading down to my left and the door was closed abruptly. Naturally, I was more than a little disgruntled at being treated like some common-or-garden bread deliveryman, but nevertheless did as I was told and stepped carefully down some moist steps and through a damp alleyway to find another, smaller, unkempt door at the rear of the building. After waiting a moment nobody appeared and I was forced to use the weatherbeaten knocker. Flakes of paint fell to the ground as I did.

The same maid appeared once more, but this time the door was not opened wide.

'Sorry, Sir, to waste y' time. Mr Mortimer, you see, sismorningofftoday.' Her eyes remained fixed at the ground and she spoke as if it were not worth the pause between words.

'But I must see him,' I said, 'it is of vital importance.'

'Sisdmorningoff. Not in, right?'

Peering through into the darkness behind her I could just make out a slippered foot poking out from an armchair. I took a chance.

'But I can see his foot!' I ventured. The foot disappeared, and the maid remained inexorable.

'Sismorningofftoday. Sorry.'

'It really is very important!' I persevered.

'I'm sorry but-'

'It's alright, Katie, I'll take it,' said a deep, tired voice from the darkness. The maid grimaced, stepped back and the door was opened to me.

I followed her through a small lobby and found myself in a wonderful Victorian parlour with a cold hardwood floor and pale yellow walls, opening into a similarly decorated kitchen to the right. It really was like stepping back in time. Grand black cabinets sprawled against the far wall, stopping only for the simple iron fireplace. Mortimer remained seated, cooly appraising me from a noticeably worn armchair. Beside him sat a half glass of milk and an open book. The maid busied herself between the parlour and the far kitchen and I took a moment to admire the air of the place. In its prime, these rooms would be filled with three or four times as many staff, and must have been quite a sight.

Ah, the steam and bustle of a Victorian kitchen!

'Mr Edgar! Quite a surprise visit.'

If Mortimer was indeed surprised at my presence he did not show it on his face, despite his words.

'What can I do for you?' he asked, promptly adding 'I won't make you a cup of tea.'

The man was a cold fish.

'I do apologise for interrupting your day off, but I am here to enquire after a friend of mine. I gather he has spent some time in the company of-'

'His name?'

A very cold fish indeed.

'A Mr Fabien Pouche.'

I would place my hand and swear on the Bible that I caught a rapid flicker of recognition from the valet, but that was all. The maid, on the other hand, dropped her tray atop a surface with quite a clang. I am certain that Mortimer would have denied all knowledge of the man had his colleague not gasped dramatically.

'You a friend of Fabien, then? Why didn't you say? Where the devil is he?' she said with a squeak.

Mortimer shot her a weary glance.

'Haven't you got the silver to do, Katie?'

I addressed the maid.

'I understand he attended a meal with the Raqs Sharqi Club.'

'Then you *understand* more than I, Mr Edgar,' Mortimer put in sharply. 'I am not a social secretary, you know. And anything I have seen or heard whilst in my employ-' here his eyes sparkled somewhat, for he had clearly seen and heard plenty, '-is not my business. And it is most certainly not yours.'

That told me.

Nevertheless, I persisted,

'But you will have seen-'

'No, Mr Edgar.'

'I'm just thinking that you may have heard someth-'

'I am afraid not, Mr Edgar,'

I paused to gather myself.

'But there is-'

'I think not, Mr Edgar.'

Realising I was to get nothing from this characterless bookmark of a man, I set my sights on the maid, who evidently had more to say on the matter. If I were to squeeze any information from her, however, I would need to do it out of Mortimer's earshot.

'Well then, I can see I have wasted my time. Good day to you, and thank you so very much for your time.'

Mortimer grunted and did not reply. I backed slowly into the lobby, where I loitered carefully. Within seconds I was thrilled to see Mortimer stand abruptly, leave the rest of his milk and vanish into the house. I waited for a minute and then crept back into the parlour.

'May I have a word, Katie?' I said gently.

'Oh, Lordy, Lordy! You still 'ere?' she clutched a hand to her chest. She had been setting up a tea tray, and the buns glistened invitingly.

'I have to ask about Fabien,' I began, lowering my voice with a faux concern. 'I haven't heard from my friend in a while. I am worried about him. When was he last here?'

The maid thinned her eyes at me.

'Youreally'isfriend?'

'A very good friend, yes.'

Behind her the vile little dog of Lady Follett's pushed its wet nose through a doorway, and for a moment I feared that old horse-face would follow. I was relieved to see that it came alone. It tottered across the floor, four tiny paws pattering skittishly on the cold hard floor.

''e y'ant been 'ere for some time,' said the maid.

'When did you see him last?'

The maid would have gone on, had the back door behind us not slammed shut and interrupted our little conflab. A short round woman entered from outside, clutching a sizeable box of filth-encrusted eggs. She stomped past me with barely a glance and made for the kitchen.

'What do we say about friends in the parlour, Katie?' she boomed.

'Oh, Dolly, this man's 'ere looking for Fabien.'

The cook came back into the kitchen doorway with a rolling pin and a grim look.

'Well you won't find him here, snooping around. He'll not come back. Gave him a good clip round the ear I did, for messing in my drawers. You a policeman?'

The maid spoke for me.

'Man's a friend, 'e says.'

The cook snorted.

'Well when you see him, you can tell him he's welcome back here for another clip at the other ear, but that's all.' She turned back but called over her shoulder. 'Did you give him the purse, Katie?'

The maids face dropped and she moved over to one of the sturdy cabinets and pulled open a drawer.

A ragged wallet was tossed over to me.

''e left that here last time. Give it to 'im when you see 'im,' said the maid. 'There was no money in it!' she swiftly added.

From this sharp addition and the pitch of her voice I guessed that there may have once been a few notes within, which had probably found their way into the maid's purse. I smiled and pocketed this potential clue. Suddenly the maid gave a scream.

'Oh, gawd! Prince's gone an' done a piddle on the floor again, Dolly!'

The tiny dog stood blinking innocently, a few feet from a puddle in the corner of the room.

'Get him out of here!' the cook bellowed. I am sure that she meant the dog, however I also took my leave with a genial farewell. This went unheard over the domestic chaos unfolding in the kitchen.

I was barely at the end of the road before, unable to contain my curiosity, I stopped to examine my find. Unfortunately, the wallet contained very little. There were a few faded, scribbled receipts of little interest, an old bus ticket, some second class stamps and a couple of tattered business cards; one for a taxi firm, one for '*La Maison Sebastien*' and one more that was decidedly more interesting.

This was a dog-eared business card that read;

Dame Terry House
Guest House to the stars!
66 Kilburn High Road

London.
(Please ring bell. Equity desirable)

I had heard somewhere or other about small hotels that label themselves show-business establishments, lodging travelling actors in need of a room and quiet understanding, no doubt. But what had this to do with Pouche?

There was only one member of the Raqs Sharqi rabble that fitted with this theatrical connection, I thought to myself with a creeping distaste.

Chapter III

In which Payton Edgar takes in a show

Dear Margaret,
I am crippled by superstition. My mother brought me up to believe in omens. If a black cat crosses my path I am in a stupor all day long. If it is the thirteenth day I can barely venture out of my flat. I never walk under ladders and woe betide me if I put my hat on the wrong way round! I find it difficult to get out and meet people, and struggle to keep down a job because of this. What can I do?
Myrtle, Hampstead Heath

Margaret replies; Don't blame your mother for your ridiculous beliefs. My own mother used to say that two women must never pour from the same teapot, and always ensured that she said "rabbit rabbit" on the first of the month. Did it bring her luck? No. She died a lonely and bitter old woman, and the same will happen to you, Myrtle, if you carry on with this rubbish.

I didn't even try and ask dear Irving to accompany me to the theatre, for a number of reasons. Perhaps the main reason was that, once again, it was simpler not to have to explain my actions. It was far easier to go alone than be forced to suffer questions and disagreements over my careful handling of the Fabien Pouche situation. When it came to it, I was quite happy to go unaccompanied, for it would be easier to put my plan into action without Irving shuffling in his seat and wishing he was back at home with his easel.

He knew how much I hated the theatre, and would surely probe

82

incessantly into my reasons for going. And besides all of this he was far too busy, spending much of his time at the gallery with young Miss Hatch, putting the final touches to his exhibition before the grand opening.

It was for these sound reasons that I kept Irving out of it.

The play was Hamlet at the Old Vic, and it was an entirely dreadful experience from start to finish. The seats in the place were worn and uncomfortable with barely enough leg room for a contortionist dwarf. Worse than that, a slender lady wearing something akin to a Victorian bonnet seated herself in the row in front and took some considerable persuasion to remove the offending article. The play itself was so dull that I was in half a mind to tap on her shoulder and ask her to replace the hat back on her head, as staring at its laces and ribbons would have been twice as interesting as anything occurring on stage.

I have avoided Shakespeare ever since being force-fed his baffling wordplay at school, and with good reason. Nobody seemed to mind that fact that three quarters of what was said was riddling rubbish. The actors all seemed to be enjoying themselves enough, with bellowing Sir Maurice Williams certainly putting the 'ham' into Hamlet. At times like this I wished I were a theatre critic, for there was plentiful material to work with. I saw much to criticise, despite the supposed caliber of the performers.

My mind wandered through my thoughts of the day as the actors prattled away on the stage. At one point, some woman called Gertrude was telling Sir Maurice that *"all lives must die"*. There was much talk of death on stage, and I found my thoughts returning to my mother, and the anniversary of her death.

I felt a flicker of anger towards Aunt Elizabeth. Of course I hadn't counted the days since her death, and why should I? The words *ungrateful* and *shame* danced across my mind, and then I recalled my aunt's ridiculous request. A television set in her bedroom indeed!

I spent the final act of the play entirely caught up in these thoughts, and then, mercifully, it was over, and following an overlong session of undeserved bows, the curtain finally fell.

I edged away from the throng of over-dressed miseries that were milling about outside the theatre and crept around the side of the building to where I had spotted the stage door. The absence of the swathes of autograph hunters Sir Maurice had alluded to was notable.

I knocked with some confidence, and the door was pulled open by a smooth faced young man in a striped cap. He said nothing but looked at me questioningly.

'Would it be possible to see Sir Maurice-'

'No autographs tonight,' the boy grunted.

I raised a finger along with my voice. 'I am no fan!' I said abruptly, an extremely true statement that I quickly followed with an equally extreme lie. 'I am a dear friend. He is expecting me.'

'Name?'

I forced a smile and gave my full title, following which the door was slammed in my face. I was making a habit of waiting outside closed doors, and I was to stand like an idiot outside the stage door for some time before the man returned. To my great relief, not to mention my surprise, I was invited in.

The backstage area was even grottier than I had imagined, with none of the flamboyance and pizzazz of the theatre we are always hearing about. The air was stuffy and there was an overpowering smell that reminded me of having the decorators in. Paint and glue, no doubt. The fishy, ripeness of the stench was unpleasant in the extreme. The young man at the door was leading me through dimly lit creaking wooden passages, and I had to skip a little to keep up with the lad.

Soon he stopped, turned and knocked on a large door with *"DR2"* boldly painted in black on its face. After the quick knock, the young man was gone, once again leaving me waiting alone by a closed door.

'Come!'

The command was issued by an unmistakably plummy voice from within the room. How a man can make one simple word sound so very irritatingly salient I shall never know. Grasping the handle, which was strangely sticky to the touch, I pushed open the door into the dressing room of Sir Maurice Williams.

The man was standing before a dressing table cluttered with jars of make up, brushes, three wigs on plastic heads and numerous vases of flowers in various states of decay. He wore a hideously patterned Noel Coward-style gown, and was drawing on a pipe. Sir Maurice really did look ridiculous, and I stifled a chuckle. He waved a hand to beckon me in and completed his inhalation, puffing smoke about him through an 'o' shaped mouth. White make-up had been thickly applied to his face, giving the impression of an alarming mask, with dark eye sockets and deathly white skin. Much of the makeup had infiltrated his outrageous beard, and some had melted away at the sweat from his brow. He issued a broad, somewhat disarming smile.

'Mr Edgar! A pleasant surprise indeed!'

I did not believe that for a second.

'Sir Maurice, good evening.'

'Sit! Sit! Sit!' The actor pointed to a worn wicker chair to my left and I sat obediently, the chair creaking under my weight. Suddenly I noticed that we were not alone, for in the shadows of the far corner sat a youth in a curious frilly cream blouse with a far-away look on his face. The lad can't have been far past voting age, and he too wore dark make up about the eyes, with what can only have been rouge at his cheeks. He was to sit, blinking slowly in a sedated silence for the duration of my visit. Something told me this was not a relation of Sir Maurice, but something else entirely.

'Drink?' Sir Maurice enquired, holding aloft a half-bottle of whisky, to which I nodded. The man was behaving as if he had expected my visit and it was more than a little unnerving.

'I have just seen the show-' I began, rather obviously.

'Yes, yes, of course.'

A pause.

'Well?' Sir Maurice gasped impatiently, clearly keen for my glowing review of his triumphant performance. He had made the assumption that I was primed with praise, and I was careful not to disappoint.

'Astounding!' I lied. 'Absolutely astounding.' There was another lengthy pause as, for a moment, words failed me. Insincere fawning such as this is really not Payton Edgar's style, for I am proud to be an honest man. Forthright, perhaps. Brutal even, if the situation demands it. But very rarely insincere. It was important, however, to get on the right side of the man, even if it required giving some undeserved praise.

'Yes, astounding. And, well, outstanding. Thrilling.'

'Oh, yes?' Sir Maurice ventured with a cocked bushy eyebrow.

Clearly the man expected more, and I was about to continue when I was saved by a loud rap at the door. This time the knocker did not wait politely for instruction as I had, and the door opened wildly.

A tall, thin brunette entered, adorned in a flowing red gown that would not have looked out of place on a Hollywood starlet. It took me a few minutes to realise that here was Ophelia, the rather dowdy woman on stage, transformed.

'Darling!'

She glided across the floor and sent a kiss flying past each of Sir Maurice's floury cheeks. She ignored the lad in the corner.

Sir Maurice bowed his head gently and raised the two glasses in his hand. 'Just in time for a tipple, as always.' His consort took one glass hungrily and turned, seeing me for the first time.

'Oh! Hello.' Her eyes thinned as if she couldn't place me. 'Are you in the company?'

Sir Maurice moved past her and handed me a noticeably smaller whisky. 'My dear, this is Mr Edgar, an acquaintance from the Evening Clarion. He saw the show tonight.'

'Critic?' she shrieked. Sir Maurice gave a sharp shake of his head.

The newcomer seemed disappointed at this and, without reply, turned to her fellow actor.

'It did go well, tonight, didn't it, darling Mo.'

This was not given as a question, but a statement, and Sir Maurice was quick to agree, lavishing the woman with flowery praise. Ophelia lapped up his adulation like a child after a dance and then threw down her whisky in a manner that would make a spirit-swilling navvy proud. In a split second she was holding out her glass for a refill. Sir Maurice obliged her and, to my horror, spun the spotlight back onto me.

'Mr Edgar was just about to tell me what he thought of my Hamlet.' He replaced the bottle and lifted his powdered chin up in my direction. 'Well, Mr Edgar? We have somewhat enhanced the existentialist bent of the piece, wouldn't you say? Did you have a particular moment of enlightenment?'

Thankfully, I had prepared for this moment by carefully studying the theatre programme from cover to cover during the all-too-brief interval.

'I thought,' I began carefully, wishing I could sound more confident, 'that highlighting the contrasting themes of revenge, uncertainty and death was a very bold move.'

They stood looking at me blankly, clearly wanting more. I focused on my prey, Sir Maurice.

'It has been said that the crown of Hamlet has been passed down from actor to actor over generations. In your hands, Sir Maurice, the crown shone brightest, having found its true home.'

I felt a little swell of repulsion in my belly at this insincere flattery, but the man seemed pleased enough at my words. However his co-star interrupted with a groan before he could respond.

'Is that it? What about me?'

I realised that Sir Maurice had failed to introduce me to the young lady, and for a fleeting moment was unsure as to how to address her.

'Madam, you were sensational. Truly…sensational,' I said, quite surpassing any fawning I have ever done before. For a moment I felt as if I was going to be sick.

Ophelia issued something of a snort.

'Oh. Well, that will just have to do, I suppose! I am used to something more, well, directive. One feeds on it, you understand.' She turned unsteadily and, after receiving a third top up, took the glass away with her without a parting word. Sir Maurice stood for a moment, with a sneer on his mouth until he was sure that she was gone.

'Good God! Talentless harlot!' he spat, topping up his own glass before addressing me with a toothy snarl. 'Since the advent of television this profession has been awash with lucky amateurs and dreadful charlatans! They think that just because they had a name on screen that they have *a name*! Girls like that think that theatre is all bright lights and lollipops! So very far, far from the truth. Theatre is blood and sweat, Mr Edgar! Blood and sweat! Well, I am sick of it. This production is a joke.'

I thought back to watching Sir Maurice studying his papers

through his ridiculous pince-nez, and gave my calmest smile. 'How did your audition go the other day, Sir Maurice?' I enquired innocently.

He bit on his lip for a moment before answering.

'I have another on the horizon,' he said sharply and somewhat dismissively, which I took to mean that it had not gone as he had hoped. The actor tellingly glanced down to a pile of papers on his desk, at least two of which I noted with interest were stamped with the letters "*B.B.C.*"

Sir Maurice caught me eyeing his papers and, as he continued to speak, rather obviously covered them with a grubby grey towel. He then padded over to his dressing table where he sat, with his back to me, rubbing at his face with various rags.

'The thing about the theatre, Mr Edgar, is that it relies upon a stern ship to tackle the soaring waves of public expectation. Any weak spot, any failing, becomes a hole in the ship's hull. Are you with me? Before you know it, you have a sinking ship.'

His nautical metaphor had failed to impress, but I took his references to a weakness within the crew to mean the young actress who had just left the room. As he continued it seemed that he moved on to bemoan other members of the company, and fleetingly returned to his nauseating boat concept, words that I am certain have been repeated many a time over to anyone foolish enough to listen.

'Even our director is an oaf. The captain of the vessel needs to be a strong, confident leader, not a weak-kneed nancy! The man has simply no vision. And the set! I trust that you saw our problems with the set? This production relies far too heavily on properties! Surely you must have thought so? Even the most ignorant playgoer cannot fail to notice that the stage is heavily cluttered with un-necessaries. The only vital part of any play, Mr Edgar, is the actor, and our director simply cannot understand this. Strip it down, I say, to bare boards and bare feet! Bare boards, bare feet and *bare souls*. Give a novice actor too many properties and they will hide behind them like birds in a bush.'

At this point he jumped up and clasped a stained velvet cushion to his chest.

'Their performance will be muted, and they will fiddle mindlessly. They will hide and they will fiddle. This production is full of mindless fiddlers! Now! Take away the pointless properties-' here he flung the cushion aside to land clumsily in the lap of the daydreaming boy in the corner, '-and an actor has room to breathe, to express himself. To be naked. To be in his natural form, stripped to the very essence. Stripped to the very soul within. Laid bare.'

My mind was racing with ways to return back to the subjects I wished to discuss. I did not require nor desire an acting master class. Sir Maurice was preaching very much to the wrong person, and I worked hard to keep up my pretence.

'Sir Maurice that is extremely astute of you-'

'Indeed!'

'-but if we could turn to other matters, I have to confess that I came here with a purpose. A matter of great importance.' This declaration came out firmly, for I had tired of Sir Maurice's flimsy talk and badly needed to get to the point. I did not give him a chance to speak, much as he would have liked to.

'I wish to talk about Dame Terry House.'

There was a moment of silence before he spoke, after mouthing the words slowly.

'And who is she?'

This was not a good start.

'Sir Maurice, it is not a person but a hotel. Surely you know it it? A guest house, for actors.'

'Pah!' he spat. 'Never heard of it! Can't abide the places. Full of sissy nobodies moaning about the fact that nobody understands them, convinced that they have a talent worth sixpence! Pantomime nobodies! I haven't time to talk, Mr Edgar, about people and places that mean so very little to me.'

His words were so unyielding that I have to say I rather believed him.

He returned to face the mirror and proceeded to dab at his crusty face harshly with some gauze which he soaked in a medicinal-smelling tonic. Taking a deep breath, I laid my cards on the table.

'You will have heard, however, of *Fabien Pouche*.'

With this name I had caught him by surprise, and he faltered noticeably. The soiled gauze was abruptly dropped, and he turned slowly to face me. His gaze was dark with suspicion. He pursed his painted red lips and studied me as if seeing me for the first time.

'What do you know of Fabien?' he eventually growled, his voice lower and noticeably devoid of bravado.

My heart leapt a little, for I had clearly put my finger on something. His reaction had been strong, almost violent, and perhaps I should have been more wary.

'You are aware,' I continued, 'that Mr Pouche was found dead several days ago?'

Had I known the effect my words would have, I would have laced the news with a more gentle tone and an altogether kinder approach.

Sir Maurice blinked, gulped and glared at me. Even despite the smears of greasepaint I was sure that I saw the colour drain from his face. Suddenly and with an unsteady lurch, he stumbled over to one of the creaking wicker chairs and sat heavily, his mouth hanging open. It was a while before he spoke again, and this time with a whisper.

'Fabien is...*dead*?'

I nodded.

'Murdered.'

"Murdered?' Sir Maurice echoed emptily. 'Why…why would you say that?'

'Because it is true,' I replied. I allowed a heavy silence to settle.

The silence was interrupted by a young man in black who opened the dressing room door while knocking loudly, and was sent hurtling back out again by a firm shout from Sir Maurice.

'Get out! Get out!'

The door slammed shut. Once he knew that we were alone again, with only the unresponsive rag doll of a lad in the corner, the actor asked his question quietly, meekly, and with palpable grief.

'What happened?'

Fingering my drink with some discomfort, I was careful to speak slower, and softer, somewhat muted by the man's evident shock.

'He was murdered, at his flat. That is all I know.' At these words I realised that they were true; that was indeed all that I knew.

Then, much to my horror, Sir Maurice broke down in tears.

'No!' he breathed through his sobs. 'No! No!'

It is a very rare sight, to see a man cry, and for a few minutes I sat stiffly and rather awkwardly in silence. Unlike Therese's gentle tears over the lad, Sir Maurice's distress was uncomfortable in the extreme, his loud theatrical sobs and whimpers coming in waves. I tentatively threw him a clean piece of gauze from his dresser and waited as he dried his eyes. If the man had been involved in the young Spaniard's death he was certainly a better actor than I had given him credit for.

I discreetly topped up his glass, and it was not long before he was giving me some rather juicy details and my patience was rewarded.

He began by asking me to ensure that the door was closed firmly, and that we were alone. He made no reference to the lad in the corner who now appeared to be sleeping, despite all the commotion. Then Sir Maurice issued forth a rather incongruous query.

'You are not married, Mr Edgar? Is that correct?'

I replied in the negative.

'No,' the actor mused with an odd glint in his eye. 'I thought not.'

I could not think what the devil my marital status had to do with matters currently on the table, but kept quiet.

'You know Ferrier, of course? Sebastien Ferrier?'

'How could I not?' I mused with distaste.

'I was at Ferrier's new place, when I met him. I was dining with an exceedingly dull young actress. Pretty, and talented enough, but dull as ditchwater. But one has to keep up appearances, you understand?'

Here I was shot an unexpectedly animated look, and yet he did not allow me time to interpret it fully.

'And then I saw him. I looked up into the kitchens, and there he was. A very handsome young man, washing dishes. It enraged me that such a-' he fought for the words, '-fine-looking young man should be shut away, washing dishes for a living. It pulled at my...paternal instincts.'

I found myself frowning, trying to decipher his meaning. He continued.

'But what could I, a famous and successful public figure do to help the poor young, penniless man? I wanted to take him to dinner, to talk, but I could never be seen in such circumstances, you understand? And then I realised, the only way I could possibly get-' here Sir Maurice was faltering again, '-closer to the man, to help him you see, was to invite him as a guest for the Raqs Sharqi.'

At these words an indignant fury erupted within me. I swallowed, but could not hold my words.

'Yes, the Raqs Sharqi Club! What a ridiculous concept! I feel I must protest about this dreadful practice of parading people for entertainment, a most unreasonable and disrespectful-'

'Oh, what are you blethering on about now, Edgar?' Sir Maurice growled, unhappy at my interruption.

'The rotten Raqs Sharqi practice of farming talent merely for their entertainment!'

'Good grief, man, it's just a bit of fun!' snapped the thespian, sharply waving my fury aside. 'Just a bit of fun amongst people of a higher social and intellectual understanding. Leave it be! Just a bit of bloody fun, Mr Edgar!'

Sir Maurice filled yet another glass, pointedly neglecting to offer me a top-up this time. He went on.

'I think it's fair to say that Fabien wowed every member of that dinner party. He was something different, something more than previous guests, not some run down menial worker living in poverty that we could grill, or some dreadful performer we could chuckle at. He was gentle, and sweet, rather like a puppy. Obliging. And he had some wonderful stories of France to tell, and with surprising humour. Fair charmed the ladies out of their shoes. And I felt proud - proud to have introduced him into a higher society. Of course, the lad needed money, and we paid him well for it. The Folletts had him mowing the lawn of their town house, as did the Masons, I believe. And the sluttish Miss Hatch was most taken with the gentleman.'

Here his tone lowered.

'Perhaps a little *too much*.'

He sat and drifted away a little in remembrance of Fabien Pouche. In my minds eye I saw his tanned skin and fine teeth. After a brief moment, I gave a light cough before speaking.

'And you?'

'What?' spat Sir Maurice, as if coming out of a dream.

'Did he-' now I was the one struggling for words. I searched for an appropriate term. 'Did he...did he mow your lawn?'

Sir Maurice issued no reply. Instead he threw the contents of his glass down his hairy throat and then made a sudden leap for the whisky bottle. As he poured another generous measure, his face stiffened, the white of his eyes bulging in dark sockets. Suddenly, he turned on me with a powerful air of fury.

'Why are you here, Mr Edgar? To cause upset? Then consider this a job well done. But if you intend to harm my good name then, well! You have picked the wrong person!'

'I am here to find out what happened to Mr Pouche, nothing more.'

'Why?'

Not a bad question. I hesitated, finding no reply.

'Why are you getting involved in all this?' Sir Maurice spat, slurring his words somewhat.

I swallowed and thought of Therese in the kitchen.

'To help a friend.'

Sir Maurice rolled his eyes. Globules of spittle had rested in his beard, and he was now scowling. His welcoming façade was well and truly dropped.

'Pity the poor friend who looks to you for help.'

'I beg your pardon?'

'You are nothing but a bumbling fool, Mr Edgar! Get out, and take your stupid questions with you! It was embarrassing at dinner last week, you do realise that? You really did make a prized turkey of yourself. We all laughed at you, you know! Talking in that ridiculous way, acting like only you know what is best, when we all know that you are nothing but a trumped up fraud. You don't know half as much as you think you do. Food critic? Pah! A lame squirrel knows as much about fine cuisine! What a twit! Now clear out of my dressing room!'

I was leaving, and not because he had asked me to. And yet in the doorway I was halted by a yell.

'Stop!'

Sir Maurice lurched in my direction. He produced two small cards and folded them into my top pocket with a gentle pat, a furious sneer on his painted face. His whisky soaked breath got right up my nose.

'A present for you, Mr Edgar. After what you have said tonight about our play, I think you warrant a return visit. You are clearly lacking a certain literary acumen. Here, a couple of tickets for the matinee on Saturday. I think that you should watch the play again - perhaps when viewing it for a second time you will understand it.'

I stormed out of the room.

Chapter IV

In which Payton Edgar bears witness to some wanton behaviour amongst the rhododendrons

Dear Margaret,
I miss my husband terribly. He died just after New Year, and after forty-three years of marriage I cannot bear life without him. I have no reason to get out of bed in the morning, nor any reason to shop, sleep, eat or drink. I have no children to share my grief. I feel I shall never get over this.
Freda, Bromley

Margaret replies; "To be or not to be, that is the question". This quote from Hamlet is possibly the only thing that Shakespeare wrote that warrants any consideration. It may help you to know that mankind has mused on the pain of loss since the dawn of creation. I suspect a diversion is on order, to get out of the house more and attempt to enjoy life. However I most certainly would not suggest attending the current run of the aforementioned play at the West End. This poor excuse for entertainment lasts a bottom-numbing three hours and it's lead actors are consistently weak.

The launch of Irving's exhibition had rolled around all too quickly, and, wishing to avoid all things artistic or theatrical following my dire experience at the Old Vic, I was in mixed spirits about the evening's event.

The relentless sun continued to cook the capital and I had spent yet another day behaving akin to some creepy-crawly, hiding in the shade of my rock until the sun had burnt down and I could crawl out into the mildly cooler afternoon air at around four-thirty.

The afternoon in question turned out to be considerably cooler and breezier than in recent days, and I considered this a welcome sign of Autumn waiting patiently for its moment.

I had taken time to reflect on my evening spent in the presence of Sir Maurice Williams and had arrived at some mixed conclusions. Yes, the man was a fop, a peacock, and the very worst type of preening thespian, but something told me that he was no murderer. I could see that young Pouche had had a profound impact on the man, perhaps even enough to give him motive for murder for some reason or other, but still I could not see Sir Maurice himself getting his hands dirty.

I had also come to the conclusion that the business card containing the guest house address was nothing more than a red herring that had only led me into further trouble.

And so to Irving's exhibition.

I was to get an unexpected and exceedingly unpleasant surprise as I arrived at the Follett Gallery. I had arranged to meet Irving at the gallery at five o'clock, and it was exactly that as I came up behind the building and, instead of retracing the steps of my previous visit, took what I hoped was a short cut around the far side. I had in my mind the little door in amongst the rhododendrons that we had entered for dinner, however it turned out that my diversion was less of a short cut than I had anticipated. I pictured Irving waiting alone in the main foyer and quickened my steps.

As I carried on through the greenery in the direction of the road a rasping voice stopped me abruptly in my tracks.

'Stop!'

Had somebody called me?

'Stop! Stop!' the voice breathed with the urgency of a hushed tone. I stood planted firm, but could see nobody. Was I being watched?

It turned out to be quite the opposite.

After a few more tentative steps I caught sight of two shady figures through the foliage before me. It was clear that the figures were embroiled in a passionate embrace. I stepped out of view and positioned myself behind the trunk of a large oak, clenching my teeth in discomfort.

I could not cut away without the risk of being spotted.

'I must go, darling!' said a sharp voice that I instantly recognised as the severe tones of Miss Jessica Hatch, the feline curator. She emitted a low growl as she was kissed. A hairy hand was fixed to her lower back, the fingers splayed. Despite some attempts to peer around each side of the thick tree it was impossible to identify her companion. I strained my neck somewhat.

'Please, let me go now! We will be missed!' she laughed gaily, a gaiety which seemed at odds with the prim young woman I had met at dinner.

'One more kiss!' said a voice, and there was a chilling minute of silence as that one more kiss happened. I stood stiff and straight, not daring myself to breathe. Following the embrace Miss Hatch pushed gently back from her accomplice and danced away through the rhododendrons. I steeled myself and stepped aside, cautious of being seen as the male figure turned and made in the opposite direction. As he moved away I caught the clearer view I had been hoping for. There were no other words to describe my reaction - I was stunned into disbelief.

It was Lord Charles Follett!

The man was decades older than the professional young woman, not to mention being rather wizened and ugly, even more so when compared against Jessica Hatch's smooth features.

An odd mix; the sultry cat and the wizened old fox. Not for the first time in my life I mused on the alluring nature of money, as this was surely Charles Follett's only asset. The man was stumpy in build with an unfortunate taste in clothes and surely the worst toupee one had ever clapped eyes on - and yet his wallet was bulging.

The power of the pound.

I had to wait on the spot for some time before I was sure he was gone. Filing this experience away in my mind under *"interesting and useful information"* I clasped my hands together and then continued on my way. As I circled the corner of the building to approach the front steps I did not think for a minute that Charles Follett would change his course and move back in my direction, but this was exactly what he had chosen to do. To my horror, he caught me with a wave, a smile shining through the speckled beard.

The red squirrel was still sitting firmly atop his head, its coat looking perhaps a little wilder following his shenanigans in the rhododendrons.

'Mr Edgar, so good to see you again!'

Relief washed over me - he was clearly oblivious to my spying session just a matter of minutes before. 'Bit cooler this evening, what?'

I tried to appear relaxed and carefree.

'True, Lord Follett, true.'

'The Summer's not gone yet, though, I think.'

'Undoubtedly.'

'Here for the opening, eh?'

'That's right - wouldn't miss it,' I said, smiling.

'Jolly good, jolly good.!' Follett said cheerily. 'Just one thing, old chap, before you go...' Suddenly he moved in close, until his nose was practically inches from mine.

'You'd better watch it!'

'Sorry? I-'

'You, Mr Edgar, have made me angrier than a bag of tigers!'

The man's breath smelt of Polo mints.

'I beg your pardon?'

'You're a pest, Edgar. You have been buzzing about asking too many questions. Silly questions about things that are, quite frankly, no business of yours.'

Follett's face had darkened and he spoke through gritted teeth. The change in his approach was dizzying. The man suddenly looked menacing, dangerous even - a far cry from the simpering, genial host I had seen before at dinner.

'So I am telling you, gentleman to gentleman, to stop making a pest of yourself and stay out of my affairs. Or else! You have had your moment in the lime light, Mr Edgar. The doors of the Raqs Sharqi Club are closed to you now. After today, I don't want to see you anywhere near me, my home in Mayfair, my wife or my gallery.'

What could possibly have set this off? I was sure he had not seen me spying in the bushes. Of course, I reasoned, it can only have been one person - the cold grey valet must have grumbled in Follett's ear. I stood straight, stiff and silent, despite the man's dark threats. His eyes studied my face for a moment with some vehemence I was issued with one last threat.

'You know what happens to pests that buzz about at this time of year? They get swatted. Stay out of it, Edgar! I mean it! After the launch today I don't want to see you round here again!' Follett growled out these words before turning pointedly and heading out towards the road. Had he known that I had just gathered some ripe information on his personal exploits then I imagine his approach would have been altogether more genial.

I had the ammunition needed to ruin his name and standing in an instant!

Unimpressed, I decided to overlook his asinine intimidation. The man was about as threatening as that fluffy toupee. I carefully considered my options.

Of course, I was attending the launch for Irving's sake, to support him and endorse his body of work. But then, there were other benefits to be had. Besides observing the founders of the Raqs Sharqi Club in their natural habitat, my other objective that afternoon was to speak with the frosty Miss Hatch about her relations with young Fabien Pouche. Her motivations seemed, at best, indistinct.

Rancid Sir Maurice had told me how taken with Pouche the curator had been, but if she were having an affair with filthy rich Follett, what would she want with penniless Pouche? Could Pouche have found out about their tryst as I had, and threatened her? In many ways I could see the girl as the spiky, ferocious type, who might just go to any lengths to get exactly what suited her. For a good few minutes I was lost in thought.

My imagination was in full flight.

I snapped out of my reverie and was soon climbing the grand steps of the Follett gallery, where I rapped on the ostentatious door with as much confidence as I could muster. The door swung open and I was admitted, unchallenged, by a handsome young waiter. I was one of the first to arrive by the looks of things, as there were only a few bodies dotted around the airy foyer.

I was instantly annoyed; Irving wasn't anywhere in sight.

My eyes scanned the impressive lobby. There were none of Irving's paintings here either, only aged landscapes in ostentatious frames.

As is customary on such occasions the organisers had accommodated for many more visitors than would surely appear. The vast cloak room stood deserted, with numerous empty coat-hangers piled up like old bones, awaiting an influx of the stinking old furs that London's elite tend to sport in spite of the weather. Along one side of the foyer a long table was laid out with endless empty glasses which sparkled in the light. I barely had time to draw breath before the young waiter who had opened to door to me moved over and offered me a drink.

I asked politely for an orange juice. One would have thought that I had requested the fresh nectar from a hummingbird's beak. The young man looked puzzled momentarily, and then replied that unfortunately they did not have orange juice, and would I care for a glass of champagne instead? I asked politely for a glass of water, only to confuse the poor chap once more. It appeared, rather extraordinarily, that plain water was also off of the beverages menu. He issued a winning smile.

Would I like a glass of champagne instead?

I requested a small red wine, wearily. The young man gave a polite smile and darted away, only to return seconds later with a glass of champagne, which he presented to me with shameless pleasure, as if it was just what I had been waiting for. Tiring of this game, I reluctantly took the glass in hand and gave my thanks.

The drink was to accompany me for the majority of the evening, the champagne slowly warming in my grip until it came to rest back on the drinks table at the end of my visit, warm, barely touched and with all its fizz faded.

I began to search for Irving, and within seconds I was stopped in my tracks by a light touch on the shoulder and a familiar bovine snort.

97

'Payton Edgar! Sweetheart!'

Behind me stood a woman dressed in a purple symphony of wool and chiffon. A purple shawl over a tight fitting purple trouser suit and veiled hat, she stood clutching a matching purple handbag.

Beryl Baxter.

I greeted my friend with some genuine pleasure. Mrs Baxter was a fellow employee of the London Clarion and one of my few colleagues which, when pressed, I would perhaps call a friend rather than a passing acquaintance. Beryl had been the voice of the society pages for many years now. She had a natural flair for collecting scraps of gossip where nobody else could, and it had not been long before the column was titled *"Beryl Baxter's Society"* rather than the original, simpler, *"Society"*.

One would imagine such a person to be sharp-witted, cutting and even perhaps cruel or dismissive, and Beryl could certainly be any of these things should she choose to be, however she also had a good head on her shoulders and was never one for unwarranted disrespect. Her column, often candid and forthright, had gained a reputation for fairness and clarity, much like the woman herself. However, while she effortlessly maintained all this within the workplace, such scrupulous control did not appear to stretch into her private life as she was currently on her third divorce, seemingly collecting husbands as one in her position might collect fine silk scarves. On the numerous occasions that we have been thrown together Beryl has proved to be peculiarly enjoyable company, not to mention a fountain of information.

And now, following my uncomfortable experience with Charles Follett in the rhododendrons, I was genuinely pleased to see her. Beryl was also just arriving, and was removing her scarf and shawl as she spoke.

'Darling Payton! So good to see you here. Not your scene, though, surely? Or are you taking over every single column of the Clarion now, darling?' Beryl always spoke to me with a tinge of playful sarcasm in her tone. 'Are you to be the new art correspondent as well, Mr Edgar? Should I fear for the society pages?'

'No, no, no,' I replied brightly, 'I am a friend of the artist!'

'Ah, yes, of course, of course.' Beryl had pulled off her gloves and was depositing them into her handbag.

'And how do I look, Payton?'

She twirled a little with her tongue firmly in her cheek. I am ashamed to say that she caught me off guard and I struggled a little in my reply.

'You look very, well, very presentable this afternoon, Beryl. Very - well - *different*.' The word had come out before I could stop it, for there was something different about the woman and it was a minute before I saw just what it was. Beryl had always been a wig wearer, however her usual mousey, towering wig appeared much lighter and livelier, almost yellow.

'Oh, yes!' she laughed, 'my new look! Do you like it? I'm up to speed - nobody's wearing their own hair these days, and wigs are the latest thing, so I am finally in vogue! Bright colours are in, darling, and I have always wanted to be lighter, blondes having more fun and all that. Seen the latest *Tatler and Bystander*? Not one of the girls in its pages are sporting their own curls, believe you me.'

I nodded politely.

'Of course,' Beryl continued in her sing-song voice, 'damn hot and scratchy these synthetic hairpieces, you know. Still, fashion has never been about comfort, quite the opposite of course. Anyway, Payton, enough about me. Have you got any news for me?'

By "news" she meant column fodder, though why she always insisted on asking me I could never fathom. The woman should know by now that when it comes to scandal or gossip I am hardly a big player in café society. And yet there *was* something I knew. At that very moment in time I was in possession of some genuine headline-grabbing, first-class gossip - the sordid affair of Charles Follett and the gallery curator. I also had learned one or two things about Sir Maurice, who had already made a number of appearances in Beryls column, usually shamelessly promoting his latest piece.

Yes, I did indeed have some "news", as Beryl had put it. My problem was that I was unsure just what to do with it. It seemed cruel to gossip blindly, and I felt unprepared. I needed time to formulate the best use of the information I had so far gathered on the Raqs Sharqi mob and their stupid club.

I had, unfortunately, mentioned the prestigious invitation to Beryl, and she had the memory of the proverbial elephant.

'Of course! You'll have had that meal with the Raqs Sharqi gang by now? How did it go? Come on, I've got five minutes.' Beryl pulled out a notepad and pencil. 'Go on!'

I shrugged. 'Beryl, I don't know what I can possibly tell you-'

'Who was there, what were they wearing and what did they say? That kind of thing. I know that Lady Follett's something of a heffalump, but her husband's no fool. Did he mention any savvy investments? I hear he's leaning towards politics - anything there?'

I replied in the negative, as firmly as I could.

'Fashion? Evening attire? What were the ladies wearing?'

'I couldn't possibly comment on that.'

'Rumours? I assume there was alcohol involved. Someone must have let something slip!'

I shook my head, my chin high.

'Nothing? Not even a titbit?' Beryl sighed with disappointment and then licked the lipstick from her front teeth. 'Well, never mind! You know my number if anything comes to mind, darling. There should be enough swingers around here this evening to give me something tasty. Do you know, I had luncheon with a very promising Welsh young thing the other day, a guaranteed singing sensation. And do you know what I have done? I am so certain of her success that I have popped her name down on a piece of paper, dated, which I have in my handbag so that once her star is risen I have proof of my prediction. She's one to watch, believe me.'

Suddenly she pointed to my glass. 'Where did you get that?'

'The-'

'Well I shan't stand around waiting. If my memory of these caterers is correct one could starve before I am handed a canapé. I had better drop my wrap in first, though. Lovely to see you again, Payton. Keep in touch!' And with that she swept away to the cloak room. As she moved away I stood for a moment in quiet contemplation.

At the right time, the woman could be useful to me.

Chapter V

In which Payton Edgar is immortalised in art

Dear Margaret,
My husband can't stay out of trouble. He is always up to no
good, buying or selling stolen goods and the like. I am well provided
for, but would much prefer him to have a proper job. He says he
doesn't want to be caged in a nine-to-five job and prefers to do
things his own way, but I am worried he will only get into more
trouble. What can I do?
Caroline, Purley

Margaret replies; It sounds to me like you have made a rum
choice when it comes to husbands. Some men cannot help getting into a
fix with the law, and I suspect that it will only be a matter of time before
he is well and truly caged, as you put it, and this time as a jailbird. In-
deed, had you provided your full address I would have passed it on to the
authorities immediately.

I found myself alone in the gallery foyer, clutching the unwanted
champagne and searching for Irving. My poor friend had struggled so
much with the last exhibition of his work, and I was anxious that, this
time, he should be relaxed and content with sharing the fruits of his
labour.

I needn't have worried.

I found him over by the bar, and he was not alone. It soon became
apparent that offering my support for that evening had been an entirely
unnecessary move. Jessica Hatch stood close up to his shoulder, purring

something into his ear. I watched as Irving responded with a polite, re-laxed chuckle. The woman certainly moved quickly from man to man, it was only a matter of minutes since she had been draping herself over Charles Follett's shoulder. The young curator cut quite a formidable fig-ure at Irving's side, and I was surprised to see how she almost matched his height as she gently laid a hand onto his forearm

As I approached, Irving had been smiling absent-mindedly at the ceiling, but the beam of pleasure he gave me as he noticed my arrival quite restored my confidence in the man. His broad smile made it worth attending, despite all of the nonsense that had happened in the rhododen-drons. Miss Hatch sensed a change in her companion and cast a lazy look over a bony shoulder in my direction.

I noted that she cooled off somewhat as I approached.

Irving wore the divine cream suit that I had suggested, with a chocolate brown tie and a red carnation at his lapel. Miss Hatch coun-tered this cheeriness somewhat by sporting an outfit that would not have been unwelcome at a funeral; a narrow black dress covered by a stiff black jacket. She hadn't bothered to use the sleeves, instead draping the jacket over her shoulders. Only the occasional glistening of tiny sequins in the cut of her hem gave any indication that this was anything other than a solemn affair. Her face revealed no suggestion whatsoever that only moments before she had been in a passionate embrace within the gardens outside.

After greeting Irving with a friendly handshake and returning the curators ridiculous cheek kisses with some discomfort, I enquired polite-ly on the progress of their exhibition.

'We are primed and ready for action!' said Miss Hatch a little omi-nously, thinning her eyes and nudging up once more to poor Irving. 'This show will knock them out.'

I appreciated the fact that she was saying this as much in support of Irving as anything else, and warmed to the girl just a little more. And yet I could not help but feel wary of the markedly intimate relationship she appeared to have with most men. I watched her for a moment as she drew a cigarette from an impressive silver case and allowed Irving to light it.

As Irving knows I care not for London's reaction to his latest cre-ations, much as I have always wished him success. Over the years I had learned that whether people actually admire a piece of art is often neither here nor there. On the contrary, a poorly received or controversial piece of work is usually found to be more successful due to this very notoriety. As an artist, Irving had never strived for success, but after turning to por-traiture he had produced a huge body of work within a very short period.

I think it's worth pointing out once more that I had been instru-mental in events leading to this success.

And yet, although my friend had required a fair amount of gentle persuasion to agree to exhibit, to look at him now you would see an artist with a relaxed, confident air about him, and I wasn't sure I liked it. Irving was much more suited to working alone in his studio with an air of flighty distraction than to the expeditious business of the art world.

'Mr Edgar,' said Jessica Hatch, waving her cigarette in my direction, 'I'm sure you are bursting to see Irving's most glorious collection, hung in all it's beauty.'

I offered nothing in return but a dry smile which, I knew, Irving would understand. My indifference to his work was something that I dare say he rather valued in me. The man clearly had enough fawning admirers.

He stood grinning at my nonchalance.

'Shall I give you a quick tour, Payton? Before the rush hour starts,' he said gently, and was about to lead me away when an operatic bellow stopped him in his tracks.

'Mr Spence! I say! Mr Spence!'

Horse-faced Bunny Follett had entered her gallery. She tossed aside a growling mink as she made her way over to us on loud wooden heels. Mortimer, the stiff valet, was suitably prepared for this action, catching the creature before it hit the ground. He clutched it tightly as if it might have run away. I was careful not to meet his eye.

Thankfully, there was no sign of the objectionable, incontinent pooch.

'Lady Follett!' said Irving smoothly. His courteous address could have melted the heart of any woman present, and indeed Bunny Follett did for a moment reveal her chalk-white dentures. She turned to the curator.

'Jessica.'

'Bunny.'

There were no kisses exchanged between the two of them, I noted with interest.

'Quick puff I think, Mortimer!' Lady Follett turned and allowed her aide to light her cigarette. She took in a noisy lungful and then pulled the holder from her lips. Her words were circled in smoke.

'Mr Spence, I am simply thrilled to be able to spend this evening with you. My bridge was cancelled at the last minute, I'm sure that you are delighted to hear.' She took a few more noisy drags on the cigarette and then swivelled from side to side as gracefully as her bulk would allow in attempt to show off the foul swamp-green dress that had been squeezed over her lumpy trunk.

'What do you think, darlings? It's a De Groot creation, of course. A saucy number, I know, but one has to shock at times, doesn't one? Even if one is, ahem, touching middle age.'

Touching middle age? The woman was delusional and ridiculous in entirely equal measures.

She smiled forcedly at Jessica Hatch as she pawed at Irving. 'I'm sure you don't mind, my dear, if I take him off of you? I shall need the tour from the artist himself, and nobody else!'

'Be my guest,' said Miss Hatch, stepping back a little from Irving's side. Lady Follett handed her smoking stick to her aide who silently withdrew. She then immediately drew in her cheeks and widened her eyes.

'Cigarette out now, I think, Jessica!'

The young woman scowled before dutifully dropping the remains of her smoke to the marble floor. She squashed it with the ball of her foot, her face a picture of displeasure. This mild rebellion went unnoticed by her employer.

'Is Lord Follett not around?' asked his wife, referring to her husband as formally as any other person would be expected to.

'Charles has not appeared as yet,' said Miss Hatch. It was at that moment that Bunny Follett noticed that there was one more person present in this little group, and she gave me a look of surprise as if I had just popped out of thin air.

'Oh, hello!' she gushed, 'I didn't see you there. Bunny Follett.' She offered me a limp gloved hand and continued in a high squeak.

'And you are-?'

To be forgotten once was excusable, even fortunate given the nature of our first rendezvous in St James's Park. However, to be forgotten twice, and after spending an intimate evening together only a matter of days before in which you had been introduced as a "*great admirer*" was inexcusable in the extreme. The woman was steadily climbing higher on my list of vengeance. In reply, I kept my voice low and stern.

'Payton Edgar.'

I might as well have said "*Liberace*" for all the attention she paid my words.

'Delighted to meet you, and all that!' She chimed in the most irritatingly off-hand manner. And then she caught herself.

'Edgar, you say? Mr Peter Edgar? Perhaps I am acquainted with your wife? I had a Mrs Edgar to bridge at one time…'

'I doubt it, Lady Follett,' I said through gritted teeth. 'We are happily divorced, and she moves in quite, quite different circles.'

A hand was waved in the air. dismissively.

'Pah! Don't talk to me about separation!'

'I wasn't about to!' I replied. I certainly did not wish to hear a repeat of her nonsense about the sanctity of marriage. Suddenly, Beryl Baxter swept up to our little group and greeted Irving and Miss Hatch before fixing her attentions on our hostess like a homing pigeon.

'Lady Follett! Good evening!'

'And you are?' came the unsurprising reply.

'Beryl Baxter. We have met before, Lady Follett. The De Groot Fashionista at the Mayvere? You wore a divine De Groot number, I recall, and the cutest emerald tiara!'

Beryl was talking Horse-face's language.

'Beryl Baxter, of course! Of the society pages? Never miss it, my dear!'

I saw an opportunity to cause a little stir, and took it.

'Beryl, Lady Follett and I were just discussing divorce!'

Beryl chuckled cheekily. 'A subject so very close to my heart!'

Lady Follett pulled the corners of her puckered mouth up into a smile with some effort. 'You are married, I take it? Would I know your husband?'

'Happily divorced, Lady Follett. Three times over!'

I could have clapped as Horse Face's expression darkened with distaste. Beryl went on, oblivious to Follett's reaction.

'Number one was a cheat and liar and a thief, marriage number two barely got past the honeymoon as the man only had eyes for the pageboys, if you take my meaning. And then number three turned out to be married already - to his damn business!'

She continued, entirely oblivious to Bunny Follett's displeasure.

'I am currently working on husband number four, a man with prospects. But we all know where that will end. I simply can't help myself!'

I cannot deny it, I delighted in watching Lady Follett as she digested this particularly unsavoury piece of information. She shook herself, and turned away from Beryl.

'Where the devil is Sir Maurice, Mortimer?' she hissed at her miserable aide. He studied his wristwatch.

'It is only a quarter past,' he said dryly. 'He will no doubt be late, as is his bent.'

Bunny Follett sighed dreamily.

'Sir Maurice Williams, such a delightful man!' She turned to me. 'Have you met him?'

Anger stirred within my belly. We had had dinner together! The woman seemed hell-bent on forgetting my entire existence! I would have said something clever and cutting had she not gone on in her ridiculous high tones.

'Such a delightful man, and so very, very talented! And what a way with words! I could listen to his smooth delivery all day long. He is the kind of gentleman who, when describing a particularly smelly tramp, would refer to the man as *fragrant*. Most amusing, and clever too! You know the type of gentleman.'

105

I most certainly did.

'Well, no use in hanging around here for him,' continued Horse Face with a sneer. 'Mr Spence and I must leave you now. I demand an exclusive tour of the exhibits with our dear artist here. I trust my portrait has pride of place? I expect no less! Take your hands off him, Jessica. You can't be hogging the dear man all night can you? Now, where are my spectacles, Mortimer? Mortimer!'

With that she pulled poor Irving away with an unladylike tug at his arm, her manservant rushing after her with thick glasses in hand. Beryl hadn't stopped grinning.

'Did I say something wrong?' she chuckled before draining her glass and moving away for a refill. Jessica Hatch and I stood together and watched Lady Follett as she pulled Irving around a corner. She must have caught the look on my face.

'The woman is an ass,' uttered Miss Hatch, just loud enough to be audible. Glancing at her I pretended that I could not contain my surprise.

'I understood that you were very loyal to the Folletts?' I asked.

Miss Hatch cocked a penciled eyebrow. 'I am - in my way.'

She drained her champagne glass, giving me the opportunity to reach out to her and proffer a second helping. She did not decline, and within a minute I had returned with a fresh bubbling flute. The foyer was a little busier by this time, with a few more fur-clad ladies and bow-tied gentlemen arriving as Miss Hatch and I watched on.

'You have been indispensable to dear Irving these past few weeks, Miss Hatch,' I said, more for the relief of something to say rather than to flatter her. 'He speaks very highly of you indeed.'

'The same could be said of you, Mr Edgar,' she mewed.

'We are indeed great friends.'

'Mmm. Yes.'

We stood in silence for a moment as I struggled with what to say next. In comparison to squaring up to the icy Miss Hatch, challenging Sir Maurice the previous evening had been a doddle. In the end, it was the curator that eventually broke the silence.

'Would you like to see some of Irving's work on display? I could show you?'

'Yes, perhaps, that would be…nice.'

She must have caught my reluctance, despite my chosen words.

'Not all of it, if you don't fancy. You don't strike me as an art lover, Mr Edgar. But there's just one particular room I think you should see. Did you know that there is a portrait with a dedication - to you?'

'Really?'

To say that I was surprised would have been an understatement in the extreme. Irving had mentioned no such thing. A portrait of me? When had he done this? I certainly hadn't sat for one, and probably would have refused had he asked. And there were surely no photographs of me I did not know about. I have always hated having my picture taken.

Why hadn't he told me that I had been captured on canvas?

The young woman moved away with short, rapid steps that I was set to follow. Her heavy heels sent a crack echoing around the room with each step. I was pleased to note that we moved in the opposite direction to Irving and Bunny Follett. I swallowed, realising that once again I needed to take the bull by the horns if I were to get any more information regarding Fabien Pouche.

'Miss Hatch-'

'Jessica, please!' she replied, sounding almost warm as she continued to clack along the floor.

'There is something that I need to discuss with you. About a young man-'

'Oh, yes? A young man? That sounds intriguing!' she exclaimed dryly without even slowing pace.

Clack clack clack.

'-a Mr Fabien Pouche.'

She may have paused on a foot for just a split second, but only just enough for me to notice the break in the rhythm of her steps. She continued forwards.

Clack clack clack.

'Yes, I know the name,' came the curt reply. We turned a corner into a larger bay.

'Are we there?' I asked as Miss Hatch continued to stride forth.

'Next room, come along.' she instructed sharply.

Clack clack clack.

Soon, my eyes rested on a familiar painting to our left, a painting in greys and greens of an elderly lady with an interesting face and large, sad eyes. The image of old Mrs Clay was the painting that had started Irving off with portraiture, and to my eye was certainly one of his better works. I feigned interest, for I was a little out of puff and wished to slow Miss Hatch down so I could get the information I needed. With an air of protest, I sat upon one of the wooden slats that formed a bench in the centre of the room.

'Please, can we sit? Just for a minute?' I requested gently. Miss Hatch stopped and turned sharply and somewhat impatiently. I gestured towards the portrait of the old lady and issued a fib.

'I wish to admire this piece for a moment.'

'If we must,' she replied. Miss Hatch, I noted, spoke as if she resented the time spent in between words. She did not sit straight away.

'Fabien Pouche-' I persisted, ever direct and straight to the point, '-came to dinner.'

'I know that, Mr Edgar. I was there.'

'And did you know-'

'-that he is dead?' she put in quickly. 'Yes, I read it in the paper.'

She bit her lip, glancing casually around the room. However the superior observations skills of Payton Edgar saw through this pretence of calm, for her bosom was rising and falling with the rapid short breaths of a young woman making an effort to suppress herself. I pushed forth with a clarification.

'*Murdered*, Miss Hatch.'

If she were shocked by this, she did well to hide it.

'Now you've had time to peruse it, what do you think of the piece?' she nodded to the painting by way of a distraction. Taking control, I disregarded the question.

'I gather the two of you had grown quite close.'

'Hah!' she laughed sharply, 'whoever told you that? And is it any of your business, anyway?'

Time for more lies.

'I was acquainted with Fabien too, Miss Hatch, and shocked to the core by what happened. I simply want to find out what happened to the poor boy.'

'And you think that I don't?' Her voice cracked and at last she sat, but did not settle. Instead, she glared at me for a while, and then issued a tired sigh.

'So, if you really did know Fabien, you wouldn't be that surprised at what happened to him. He lived a shady life. There was something dangerously attractive about the man, didn't you find? He never said anything to me. Well, we didn't talk much, if you get my meaning. All I can imagine is that he must have got in with a bad lot, as was his inclination. Lowlifes, criminals. What do you think happened? What do you know?' When I didn't reply she spoke again, wistfully. 'With men like him it is inevitable, I suppose.'

'He got in with the Raqs Sharqi Club' I said pointedly.

'Yes, but for one night only, as always. And that's quite the opposite of mingling with lowlifes and criminals, isn't it? Nobody else in the group really cared for him, anyway. He was just one of their little jokes, someone to boss around a bit, to get to do their lawn and trim their borders. But for me, he was different.' Her eyes sparkled for a moment.

'A real man.'

'Indeed,' I said, and surprised myself by venturing further. 'You were in love with him?'

She gave another of her sarcastic laughs.

'Love? Good Lord, no! What the devil gave you that idea? He was just a bit of fun, darling. Fabien was a little boy, really. He was like a lost child, looking to others to pay for things, to buy him treats. He was an idiot, and would trust anybody. Like a puppy dog, I suppose.'

She paused, and I allowed it to pass.

'But he was a naughty puppy! He was ever curious, nosing himself into the affairs of others whenever he could. And what he wasn't given he would try and steal, let me tell you. I know he went through some of my things on our second...meeting. I caught him. He gave me some ridiculous justification of course, said he was just inquisitive and interested in other people. What kind of excuse is that, to be rummaging in your clutch bag? It's not even as if I have much to steal. God knows what he was like at Follett's bloody mansion. Sticky fingers in every nook and cranny, no doubt.'

Another pause came, a longer one, and I feared that she was about to move on.

'Then why bother with him?' I asked.

Miss Hatch replied in high tones as addressing an imbecile.

'Fun darling! That's all he was to me, a bit of fun. If you knew him I'm sure that you understand. That particular puppy dog had no prospects, no money, no future - just a pretty face. What kind of life would we have together? Of course, he declared his love for me, but I told him what I thought of him. I need a man with potential, with money, who can promise me a future, and I've got that. What could he offer me but trouble? I would not let him ruin everything.'

'You have got a man with potential?' I smiled, the image of Lord Follett's hairy hand at her back flittering to mind.

For a moment we were sharing secrets.

'Maybe,' said Miss Hatch, slyly. However, it was clear from her demeanour that she would give me no more details on this front, little knowing that I already knew her secret.

'So,' I said, unable to keep the surprise out of my voice, 'Fabien was in love with you?'

For the first time I detected a glimpse of emotion. Just a glimmer in her eyes and a faint pinking of the cheeks.

'Pah! Yes, I suppose he was. I told him it would never happen. I have a future assured, and that, darling, is that.' She paused, looking for a minute at her long slender fingers on her lap.

'He was lovely, though,' she whispered.

I was about to speak when she interrupted with a flick of her wrist.

'Anyway! Fabien said he cared, but he had other things on his mind. He had other women, I know. I'm sure that one of these simply got bored of his good looks and did him in.' Her attempts to make light of the situation were unconvincing to say the least.

'You're sure that he had somebody else?' I ventured. Suddenly I heard myself - I sounded just like my ex wife, or one of her gossiping bloodhound friends.

109

Miss Hatch was nodding. 'Oh, yes. And I know where he met with her - they had a secret rendezvous, on a number of occasions, no doubt.'

'Really?'

'Oh, yes.'

'But how do you know?'

She stopped, and frowned.

'Just what is it to you?'

My reply, a sidestep, took just a moment's thought.

'A secret rendezvous. It just sounds so, I don't know illicit, and exciting.'

'Quite. Well I followed him there-' she said, hastily adding '-out of curiosity, you see.'

'Of course. Where?'

'Oh, my goodness! Nowhere special,' she cackled. 'Just some grotty guest house in Kilburn.'

'I see.'

Could it be? Could it possibly be the guest house to the stars? It was too much of a coincidence not to be true, however I managed to contain my excitement. Here I was, being directed to the guest house once more.

'Why was he there? Did you go in after him? Did you challenge him?'

She laughed. 'Oh my, no! I would be wasting my time. I just wanted to see what he was up to. I never found out the identity of the woman he was meeting, though. Some thespian floozy, of course. I didn't care. I really didn't.'

'Mmm, of course,' I replied carefully. Her expression betrayed her words and I could see that Miss Hatch had actually cared very much. It was obvious that one couldn't believe a word the young woman said. Her actions seemed jumbled, her story complicated by deceit and fibs.

And then, she opened up a little.

'Fabien was up to something, I know, but exactly what escapes me. And I decided to give up looking, and give up caring. Standing outside that guest house, I dropped him there and then and haven't seen him since. None of it matters now, of course.'

Her words trailed off, and we each sat with our thoughts for a moment.

'Well! Come on,' she snapped, standing abruptly. 'Just the next room and we're there.'

I followed dutifully after Miss Hatch, summing her up. I couldn't see her murdering Pouche, as she had spoken of him with a guarded affection and little else. Besides, she clearly had got her claws into Follett, not to mention Follett's money. Perhaps that was all she cared about. It was hard not to admire the girl, really.

Until we went into the next room, that was.

'So there is a picture in here of me?' I asked, moving straight over to a messy image of a young man's muscular torso, moving out of what looked like mud and greenery. It most certainly did not look like me.

'Is this it?'

'No.' said Miss Hatch, a note of amusement in her tone.

A canvas on the far wall caught my eye, a beautiful medley in blues and blacks which was quite unlike many of dear Irving's pictures. If it were indeed a portrait it was devoid of facial features. I was drawn closer to it, and as I did I sensed the colours moving to form shapes, shapes of no clear definition.

'I quite like that one!' I exclaimed.

'Well, good,' said Miss Hatch, 'for that is the one. *'Dedicated to dear Payton'* it is inscribed.'

'Really?' I moved in closer and saw that she was right, as there on a plaque besides the art were those very words. *Dedicated to dear Payton*. How so very wonderful! Irving had clearly meant this as a surprise for me, and the way it was presented in the centre of the large white wall certainly hinted that it was a jewel in the crown of his collection.

I was almost moved to tears.

And then I stepped aside of the painting to read the printed title. *The title.*

The title of this painting was to give me a shock, and to change my opinion of dear Irving rather rapidly. I read the plaque, sensing Miss Hatch smiling coolly over my shoulder. The title was one simple word.

One simple, horrible word.

"Pomposity".

Chapter VI
In which Payton Edgar drops a name

Dear Margaret,
I am terrified of running out of money. I am a full-time short-hand typist. I work hard and try hard to spend as little as possible, but still I am heading towards bankruptcy. My fiancée earns very little and spends very little, especially on me. All my friends at my hockey club seem to manage. Everything is so expensive these days. Any advice?
Penniless of Lambeth

Margaret replies; Dear me, penniless! If I were to receive a letter from all poor unfortunates who worry about money my postbag would be bursting at the seams. Financial concern is ubiquitous in modern life; of course your friends worry about money too. And as for your boyfriend, he sounds like a sensible young chap who knows how to save what little he does get, and you should be proud of that. As President Thomas Jefferson once said, "never spend your money before you have it". If you really require some parsimonious advice, I would advise you to spend less on lavish frills, starting with stationery. Standard post office stationery cannot be beaten. The fancy paper you used to write to me was unnecessary in the extreme.

Dame Terry House, home to the stars, was just as shabby and unfavourable an establishment as I had expected.

Situated on a busy road in Kilburn and sandwiched in between rows of typically bland Victorian terraced houses, the place had about it all the show business glamour of a pair of moth-eaten old socks.

I had left the Follett Gallery quickly and quietly. Standing before that vile piece of so-called art, my heart had broken a little. *Pomposity, by Irving Spence.* With that one ill-chosen word I had seen just what my friend thought of me. I had made a quick getaway, certain that, had I stayed, I would ruin his opening by loudly venting my disapproval. Besides, I had a perfect reason to leave - I had business to attend to, a lead to follow.

The building before me was crudely pebble-dashed with turquoise trimmings at the windows and a bold, peeling dark blue door. Unsurprisingly, the dog-eared sign in the window to my right read *"vacancies".* I considered knocking but instead was compelled to try the door without any fanfare. It was locked.

Then I noticed a button to my left, heralding a rusty plaque which read *"press for attention"* and so I pressed for attention. This promised attention was noticeably slow in coming, and it was a good minute before I could hear some noisy fumbling from within. I waited as patiently as I could.

The door was opened by a wide-faced elderly lady who positively glowed with a nervous energy. She wore a tawdry flowery pinafore over a drab grey dress and had her hands clasped together at her front, rather like a perched mouse. Although certainly over seventy years of age, her face was smooth and unwrinkled with only the hair cursed by a faded blue rinse and teeth like a piano keyboard giving away her years. The thick glasses magnified the crinkled, sagging bags under her eyes.

She was, for some unknown reason, grinning wildly, and she spoke with the unmistakable clang of a cockney. It was clear in an instant that this woman was pleasantly unhinged.

'Sorry, love, I was busy with me veg out back. May I help you?'

'May I please speak with the proprietor?' I asked.

'I'm so sorry, dearie - may you *what* with the *who*?'

'May I speak with the proprietor? The, erm, the owner of the hotel.'

'Ah!' she chimed, 'the owner! That'll be me, love. Here I am. Proprietor, yes, proprietor. Reenie Thomas. Welcome to Dame Terry House, guest house to the stars! Do come in.'

I allowed myself to be ushered through into a thickly carpeted hallway where I found myself politely asking if I should remove my shoes.

'Why? Trod in poop, have you?'

'Well, no, but I thought - the carpet...'

'Oh that's all right, keep 'em on, love, we don't stand on ceremony here! Come on, come on!'

As I shut the door behind me the unmistakable heady scent of soft, over-cooked cabbage hit me. Mrs Thomas scuttled to the foot of the

113

stairs where a makeshift desk had been erected, which, upon closer inspection, was clearly a sturdy old ironing press half-covered by a tablecloth. She shuffled some papers next to an empty guest book that lay open.

'Is it a single you're after, Sir? Usually is.'

'No,' I said quickly, 'I just need to talk with you for a minute, to ask some questions.'

Reenie Thomas, proprietor of the Guesthouse To The Stars, stiffened and stood frozen with alarm for a moment, rather like a dormouse before a combine harvester. She bore a befuddled expression. The man wanted to ask questions. This was clearly something new. Something was wrong.

'I don't...do...questions, dearie. You want to ask questions? What questions?' she stammered with uncertainty. I tried to relax the woman.

'Please, it's nothing to worry about, I promise. But it is very important - to me.' I issued my sincerest smile.

'Oh, well, if it's important,' she said, adding with a peculiar harshness, 'but I can't tell you anything about my guests, no, no, not at all. See I have very special tenants!' Her eyes twinkled. 'And we are very, very discreet. It wouldn't do to be telling you all about my guests would it, dearie? No.'

'I'm sure that you are extremely discreet, Mrs Thomas, and quite right too.'

I took a moment to look around at the gloomy wallpaper and hideous trinkets littered about the place. Heading up the stairs a number of framed photographs climbed the wall, each one a portrait of another star of stage or screen whom I was sure had never graced the steps of Dame Terry House, and never would.

'So!' I began, feigning appreciation. 'This is Dame Terry House.'

In saying this I had obviously pressed the woman's "introduction" button, and as she spoke richly and proudly without a hint of the cockney clang to her tone, I wondered which idiot actor had prepped the poor woman so harshly.

'Welcome, Sir, to Dame Terry House! Founded in 1947 and named after Dame Ellen Terry herself, acclaimed Shakespearian actress, a particular favourite of my dear departed mother. Mother was an actress too, you see, and I was born under the lights of the music halls. Ah! The Old Mo at Drury Lane! And here I am now! Yes, Dame Terry House, Guest House to the stars! We have nine comfortable rooms, mostly ensuite and with piping hot running water. Breakfast is included in our breakfast room - and no, before you ask we don't do breakfast in bed. No, no breakfast in bed. I won't have marmalade stains on my eiderdowns. Evening meal is optional, but requires at least six hours notice, that is to say requests must be issued before eleven in the morning. We cater especially for hard working members of Equity and guarantee complete discretion and the anonymity of our guests.'

She moved a little closer and spoke softly. 'We have had some very, *very* special guests.'

'I'm sure that you have,' I said quickly.

Mrs Thomas wrinkled her nose and dropped the bravado.

'Of course, we have started getting televisual types too, but I have to say they are far less fun than the theatricals. I think the theatre is so much more involving than television or the pictures, don't you?' She gave me no time to reply. 'I always think that you can sit and shout at the television as much as you like, but nothing would happen. There's the magic of theatre, you see? Theatre is live, right there and then. I don't go, though, not any more. Can't trust myself, see? I tend to applaud at the exciting moments. And I often think to myself what would happen - what if, in the theatre, sitting in the dark, right in the middle of an act, what if you shouted "Boo!" or something? I have to stop myself. I sit there, thinking what if I screamed right now? What would they do? It's so exciting to think of, sitting there in silence, and then-' and she screamed, '-aaaaeeeeiiigh! Just like that! Right there, in the theatre. I can't stop myself. A thrilling feeling!'

I was forced to stand and listen to this nonsense politely, and was glad when she moved on with a question.

'You are in the profession yourself? You look the sort.'

'Oh, no," I replied, rather too quickly, for the woman looked suddenly put out at my lack of theatricality. I realised then that to get the information I needed then I had to play ball, so to speak.

'However, I was speaking just yesterday about your establishment with my dear friend and confidant *Sir Maurice Williams*. You may have heard of him?'

Her eyes widened like puddles in a flood and I do believe that the woman was speechless, if only just for a moment.

'Sir Maurice has never stayed here!' she began with an air of suspicion.

'Oh, I know that. But you have your reputation you see, my dear Mrs Thomas. And favourable reputation spreads like a forest fire, especially among thespians. Dame Terry House was spoken of just last night by Sir Maurice in his dressing room.'

That, at least, was true in some respects.

'Oh, my!' Mrs Thomas exclaimed, clasping her dry hands together. 'Caesar! Prospero! Hamlet!' she cooed, and like a young child she was almost skipping on the spot. I had her right where I needed her.

'Now a friend of ours has been here recently, a Mr Pouche. I have to know when that was.' *And, most importantly, who he was with.* However, I told myself that I must be careful and take things one step at a time. I was relieved that she did not question why I needed this information but simply stood still, screwing up her face for a while.

'Pouche. Pouche? I can't say that I recognise the name. What's 'e been in?' She flicked her claw like hand through some loose papers on the makeshift desk. 'Pouche - no. We have had a Pollack a little while back, Swedish actress, she was. Or was it Norway? Somewhere wet it was. Spoke good English, whatever she was, but left the room in a terrible state. No, no Pouche here!' And then she caught herself. 'Not that I would be able to tell you if I had. Discretion, you see, dearie!'

'Of course, of course. I think you would remember him if he had been here, anyway. Very handsome young gentleman, he is. French. I suppose like many actors he changes his name for the stage. Yes, that must be why Sir Maurice is having so much difficulty locating the man.'

'Oh, it's Sir Maurice looking for this man, is it?'

I nodded eagerly.

'Well,' she shrugged, 'it can be a problem sometimes, stage names and all that. I had a man here last year registered as Jessop, said he was in pantomime in Croydon, stayed for two months and left without paying a penny! Turns out his name wasn't Jessop at all. Not even an actor - oh, no he wasn't! Shame on him, using the good name of pantomime like that. No shame, some people. And a while back we had a Mr Briar, said he was in that Hamlet at the Old Vic. Only he wasn't see? Turned out to be a one-nighter. There was no Briar. I only found that out after he'd gone. Paid up for a week, mind. Stage names, you see-'

I was determined to stay on course. 'But there can't be that many French actors in London, I suppose.'

'No, that's true,' she said thoughtfully. 'French, you say?'

'And handsome. Very handsome,' I added, for she struck me as the sort of woman to remember a handsome young man. I was pleased to see her blush just a little beneath the rouge. She remained motionless for a minute with a blank expression on her puffy face. And then, with a clap of her hands, she spoke.

'I remember him!'

It was like watching steam suddenly released from a trouser press. 'French and handsome. A lovely young man - here only last month. François?'

'Fabien?'

'That's it! Fabien! Such a lovely, cosmopolitan name! We chatted a little, he was standing right where you are now. So you know him, then?'

'Oh yes, he is a dear friend of Sir Maurice.'

'Well then, that's alright, dearie. Yes, he was here. We had a lovely chat. Nice boy, so charming. But he was only here briefly, and not as a guest. No, he wasn't a guest.'

'Oh?'

'Came in to meet with one of my guests, I recall. Stood right where you are now and asked for the man. Yes. I remember him, fine young man. And he asked for the man-' She stopped abruptly. The whole episode was clearly coming back to her in flashes. 'Funny you should bring this up, actually! He asked for that guest, Mr Briar, that man who left a false name. He was a grim sort of creature, but at least he paid up. Can you believe it? He registered as Briar, but that wasn't his name.'

'How did you know that? That Briar wasn't his name?'

'I saw-' She stopped herself mid-sentence.

'You saw...what?'

'Well - I, I wasn't prying!'

I gave a casual laugh. 'Of course not! But it seems you have been caught out by frauds in the past - there is no question that you would be curious as to his real name.'

'Yes, that's it exactly. And I was right, he wasn't Briar at all.'

'No?'

'No.'

I waited, but the woman had come to a halt, triumphantly.

Briar? Where had I heard that name?

Once again I had to lay my cards out on the table, in a risky guess.

'His name was Follett?' I ventured.

She blinked.

'Oh, no.'

'No?'

'No! Now, what was it?' She fixed me in a vacant glare. 'Who are those blokes? My old Uncle was one, called it *going to the lodge*. All secret handshakes and nonsense like that. Went a bit wild on it all in the end, poor Uncle Victor. Oh, what're they called? And why am I thinking about jam jars?'

The word she was searching for suddenly became clear, and I knew where I had heard the name.

Briar Lane, Potten Way.

'Mason,' I said firmly.

'Yes! That was it! Masons! Yes! Jam jars! It was Masons, just like the jam jars!' She smiled her keyboard smile and nodded with certainty.

'Yes, most definitely Mason. That's the man your young french friend met with.'

Chapter VII

In which Payton Edgar and Irving Spence exchange words

Dear Margaret,
I so want to start a family. My husband avoids talking about the issue, and fails to make any preparations for conception. I would like two children, a boy and a girl, in that order, and it has to happen soon as I am not getting any younger. However my husband refuses to comply. What can I do?
Broody, Lewisham

Margaret replies; In your letter you come across as impatient and demanding, and so it comes as no surprise to me that your poor husband should want to run a mile. Children can be nasty, noisy little things that only get underfoot and cost each and every pair of pitiful parents the earth, with little or no thanks in return. I suggest you take up a nice quiet hobby such as needlework or bridge to fill your time instead. Leave the poor man alone!

I returned home that evening with mixed emotions. It had been a busy day.

I had certainly observed enough about certain members of the Raqs Sharqi club to cause some significant rumblings within their clique, as was my plan. The torrid affair between the curator and the gallery owner was one piece of news that would cause immense rumblings. And then there was the insufferably bombastic Sir Maurice Williams with his crusade against television, and yet still with the words *B.B.C.* upon his audition scripts.

However, these observations were mere trivialities, for there was something else - something I was missing. There was more than a hint of darkness, even nastiness, about what had happened with Fabien Pouche around the table of the Raqs Shari Club. Exactly what this was had eluded me thus far, however one thing I could now be certain about was that it involved Ercot Mason.

I had only encountered Mason briefly twice, and yet all the unfavourable connotations associated with the man had been proven correct. Mason was rude, arrogant and bullish. One might say a perfect politician. And it had been obvious that he was a man used to getting his own way.

But what was his connection to Pouche? He had said in no uncertain terms at dinner that he loathed immigrants, and yet it appears that he had invited young Pouche, an immigrant himself, to mow his lawn! And then, according to the proprietor of Dame Terry House, he had met with the man in Kilburn in an undeniably illicit fashion.

Something here did not add up.

I grew certain that a visit to Mason should clear everything up. He was surely the key to the whole mystery of Mr Pouche's murder.

For what I think was the first time ever, I returned home to find Irving in my house waiting for me. Some time before we had exchanged keys for the sake of convenience, but never to that day had they been used. Irving was sitting in the dim light of my lounge, on the sofa, his arms folded, and I did not see him at first. I hung my hat and jacket and moved over to place my keys in the china bowl on the sideboard as usual. I looked around for Lucille, and it was only then that I caught sight of his pale face through the darkness, frowning like a sullen ghost.

'My goodness!' I almost swore out loud and felt as if I had jumped an inch or so in the air. 'Irving! You-'

'Welcome home, Payton,' he said gravely and with noticeable sarcasm. 'Where did you get to?'

I stood for a moment, forced to silence by the realisation that we were about to have an exchange of words, and perhaps even a petty disagreement. I did not think for a minute that we were about to have anything so strong as an argument. For all our differences, we had never argued before, so there is no reason to think that I should have seen it coming. Ours was an easy, harmonious relationship.

Until that evening.

It is not worth repeating all that was said. An onlooker would probably have admired my restraint as I stood and allowed Irving to vent his annoyance, telling me how he had searched in vain for me at the gallery, how he had stood alone for some time, and how he was stranded among gangs of what he called "over-privileged idiots". He did not

119

shout, but spoke loudly enough, and with a force I had rarely seen in him before. In another situation I would have most probably admired his fortitude.

He finished his ranting and looked to me for a response. I stood mute for a while. When I did speak, I did so with a deliberate coolness.

'It's very dark and quiet in here. Is Grace not in?'

Irving shook his head. 'And your Aunt Elizabeth is out for the count. But that doesn't matter. What about all I have just said? I needed you at the gallery. Well?'

I studied his face, knowing I only had to say one word and he would understand.

'Well?' he repeated impatiently.

'Irving Spence,' I said slowly, 'I have one word to say to you.' Here I paused for effect.

'Pomp-osity!'

There was a delightful moment of silence in the room while I enjoyed the clout of my rebuff. Irving was looking at me quizzically at first, failing to make my connection. The silence was so thick that I could even hear the grandfather clock in Aunt Elizabeth's room ticking rhythmically. After a while a look of comprehension spread over his fine features.

'Is that why you left so suddenly?' he asked, 'You weren't happy with the painting?'

I moved in a little closer. 'Oh, I did like the painting, very much so actually. It was the *title* that I have a problem with.'

Irving repositioned himself on the seat and then beckoned me nearer.

'Payton, sit down, please.'

I did as he asked, but slowly, careful to maintain my air of victory. Once I was seated, Irving spoke in a manner that I had never heard him adopt before. He chose his words carefully, and fixed his eyes on mine.

'Payton, I care for you, you are a dear, dear friend. And good friends need to be frank with each other.' He swallowed before continuing quickly. 'I can tell that there's something not quite right. All I ask is that you tell me what is going on in that muddled head of yours. You are a very special person; clever, thoughtful, amusing, charming even... '

Don't stop there, I thought, and would have blushed if I were of a sensitive nature.

'But you must talk to me. Half of the time I don't know what you're thinking-'

'Hah! I speak my mind all of the time!' I insisted, 'As you know, brutal honesty is my-'

'Payton! I am not talking about being brutally honest. I know that you are good and true, but that is not my point. My point is that you don't tell me what is going on in your head. If you had come to me after seeing the piece, and talked about it, you would see where I was going with it. You would see what that painting meant to me. It is the single most important painting in that whole collection, and for a number of reasons. So I need you to talk to me more, do you understand? To talk - and perhaps more importantly, to listen.'

This was all getting a little too *American* for my liking. I did not reply. My mind was fixed on the word *pomposity* and all its connotations. Pomposity! Airs, graces and arrogance! Egotism and narcissism! Pompousness! An ugly, ugly word.

Suddenly I felt a warmth on my right hand. Irving had leant forward and was touching me, his dry, workmanlike skin on mine.

'I did paint the picture with you in mind, but I had no title at first. In comparison to some of my works it took very little time to do, so strong was my subject. I wanted to catch the very drama of a dear friend.'

He removed his hand.

'I started it on the morning after our meal somewhere out near Bethnal Green, do you remember, back in the spring? That place with those gold ropes everywhere? You disliked the restaurant, you said it was over-themed. You hated the food even more. I can't remember the name now. It had pictures of boats on the wall, and flags everywhere.'

I grimaced, recalling a meal that I had easily forgotten.

'The Coxswain's Cabin,' I said wearily. Irving clicked his fingers.

'That was it, yes. Well, I came home and thought of you, of your essence. Your spirit is so strong when you are at work around creative food, testing something. The drive you have when you set out, the hope within you, the judgements, comparisons. Your appetite is insatiable, and I love it. All of that is so precious.'

He was losing me a little now, but I tried not to show it on my face. He continued.

'You are in your element at those times, and that's why your columns are so readable. You believe every last word of what you write. And I started the portrait, thinking of you. You must have seen yourself in it?'

I shrugged. 'I liked the... the blueness of it, I suppose.'

'Yes!' Irving was finding something to get excited about that eluded me. 'And within that blue, that formal presentation of you, what we see on the outside, within that is the art of you, the dashes of colour, of anger, damnation and control. And then there is the Payton Edgar I see, the considerate, thoughtful, gentle man. The warmth.' He returned his hand to mine and squeezed momentarily. His touch was warm and dry. Then he released it. 'That all came out in the painting. It is a tribute to the man I admire more than any other. To my very best friend.'

He broke off. We sat in silence.

His words had been welcome, akin to biting into hot buttered toast. This was the first time he had ever said that he admired me as a man, and as a friend, and I could not help but smile. Irving's eyes were glistening in my direction. Were those tears in his eyes?

'And then your review came out, just after I had finished the painting. And in it you referred to yourself as *"this pompous reviewer"* - remember? You'd had that spat with the head waiter, who knew who you were. You must remember? You were upset that he called you bombastic, and said your reviews were pompous nonsense. And in your review of the place, you said *"this pompous shipmate shall never dine with this coxswain again"*. Remember?'

I did indeed.

'You said it, with reference to yourself. This is how you think you are seen, for right or wrong. And your words said it all. In the picture I wanted to say that may be your label, the label that you give yourself, but here is the man that I know. And so I titled it *"pomposity"*. Do you understand, Payton?'

Surprisingly, I did.

I nodded gently, and we sat for a few minutes in a beautiful silence. Lucille padding softly into the room broke our moment. The cat was licking her lips.

'I fed the cat, by the way, with a bit of fish from that tin in the top cupboard,' said Irving, 'I hope that's alright?'

'Of course.' I said quickly, although it hurt me to smile, for this was my very best fish. I did not mention that I had been saving it for myself. No wonder Lucille looked so content. I glared down at her jealously.

Irving sat back with a sigh. 'So, where did you go then?'

'I beg your pardon?'

'After you left the gallery. You didn't come back here. Where did you go?'

To a guest house for actors in Kilburn on the trail of a murderer. Somehow, this all seemed like far too much effort to explain. I would have to tell Irving about the corpse in the bathtub, when I had already told him I had dropped the whole affair. And so I replied with a simple wave of dismissal.

'Oh, nowhere in particular.'

For some reason, Irving persisted.

'Where *"nowhere in particular"*?' he asked.

'Oh, it really doesn't matter.'

'It does, Payton. Tell me.'

'Well,' I lied, 'Just to the park, to think.'

'Which park?'

'Just…a park-'

'Which park, Payton?'

And now I was annoyed. Is not my free time my own to do with as I like? The man was sat in *my* house, uninvited, demanding to know where I had been like some miserable tyrant housewife! I fixed his gaze with mine.

'It doesn't matter which park, Irving. Do I demand to know where you are every hour of the day?'

Irving laughed. 'I am in my studio, usually, as you know.' He sat forwards. 'Payton, what are you up to? There's something you're not telling me. I have called on you a few times recently, with no luck. You have been out a lot. Mrs Montgomery said she saw you in a tea shop with somebody in Vauxhall, a young lady. What-'

'Spying on me, was she?'

'She just mentioned it, and I thought-'

'Irving, it is no business of yours-'

'This is just what I was trying to say to you!' Irving cried unexpectedly before leaping up onto his feet. 'And what about this?' I saw he was holding up the programme for Hamlet that I had left on the mantelpiece. I could not help but roll my eyes.

'Dreadful!' I uttered. 'Absolutely dreadful!'

'I'm not surprised. You hate the theatre, Payton, you hate it! When did you go? Who did you go with? What is going on in your head?' Irving was shouting now, and I sat for a moment, mute, before he spoke again.

'Secrets and lies! This is just what I mean by not talking to me!'

'You want me to tell you the truth? Always?'

'That's what I've been saying!'

'Well then! That was my best fish!'

'I beg your pardon?'

'My very best fish - that you fed to the cat!'

Irving breathed out forcedly through gritted teeth.

'Your best fish. Is that all you've got to say? It's not good enough, Payton. Simply not good enough. I'm going home.'

'Well - well you were not invited here tonight in the first place!' I shouted after the man as he stomped past me and out of the room. At the slamming of the front door, Lucille gave a piercing mew and darted away into the kitchen, where I heard the swing of the cat flap.

I was left in the dark, entirely alone.

PART THREE

Chapter I
In which Payton Edgar tries his luck on the tombola

Dear Margaret,
My fiancé is a mummy's boy. We met through my brother
who is captain of our football club, and we are due to marry next
month. My fiancé is jobless and 28 years old, and yet he acts like a
child. His mother does all of his chores, and often makes unfair and
snide remarks about my own domestic abilities, such as my darning
of socks. I'm sure that despite her rudeness she is a nice person deep
down. Should I try and get to know her better?
Sally, Bexley

Margaret replies; What on earth are you wasting time with this
young man for? If you marry him, you will surely marry his mother. And
why should you try and talk to the woman? She is clearly a loathsome
type that you can do better without. I suggest you look again at your
brother's football club and pick your star player a little more wisely this
time.

My sleep that night had been disjointed and unsettled thanks to the
horrible argument with Irving.

It was most unlike my friend to be the one to stir up unnecessary
drama, and my nose had been well and truly put out of joint. I lay in the
darkness of my bedroom with balled fists, contemplating his actions for
what seemed like most of the night. I was to catch only spatters of sleep
here and there. I simply couldn't see just what had upset him so much.

His juvenile behaviour had been vexing in the extreme.

There was, however, a little twinge of guilt inside of me, although why I should have been the one to feel it I couldn't fathom. Perhaps I should have shown more interest in his work and made a point of asking how his exhibition went, but Irving had never needed buttering up like this before.

Perhaps my lack of enquiry was the whole reason for his curious, not to mention ridiculous, outburst.

Sitting at my breakfast table the following morning, with the remains of my egg and soldiers on the table before me and Lucille purring on my lap, I decided not to go and see him straight away. Once I had tied up the loose ends on the curious death of Mr Pouche I would tell him all about it, and he would see just what I had been through and why I had kept it all to myself. I would be sure to stress to him that by keeping him out of the situation I had been acting out of concern only for him, wanting him to focus on his exhibition and not to worry about me, chasing high-society murderers about London.

Sitting there that late Summer morning I was entirely unaware of the danger that I would be getting myself in to. Perhaps I should have had just the vaguest sense of it, but there was none.

It is all too easy to see the banana skin only *after* one has slipped on it.

As it was, once I had snapped out of my early-riser's fog I was quite content in mood despite the silly upset with Irving. I tossed Lucille aside with a growl (hers, not mine) and prepared myself for a return visit to the countryside. If my seemingly fruitless investigations had taught me anything it was that Ercot Mason had lied to me from the very beginning. After claiming at first to hardly know young Pouche, now I knew so much more. I had evidence of illicit meetings in crumbling guest houses. And yet, what would Mason want with the lad? What did it all mean?

I was determined to find some answers.

After braving the unbearable bus ride once more, I gathered my bearings at the bus stop in Potten Way. I had prepared myself for the unsettling stillness of the countryside once again, however I was about to receive a shock.

I first noticed something askew at the bowling green. The same rake-like old lady was there playing bowls as before, however this time there was a small crowd of onlookers gathered at a flapping pavilion. On the green she had been joined by a plump friend with an unsuitably ostentatious floppy hat. The breeze that had picked up pushed with some force at its brim and threatened to blow the thing away, yet the hat-wearer seemed unconcerned. I, on the other hand, inspected the clouds with a grumble and cursed myself for not bringing my rain mac, for the weather did appear to be turning somewhat.

I moved on just a few strides before halting in horror. There were people everywhere.

The village Fete!

Faded bunting hung from post to post and from tree to tree, the tiny triangles of colour flapping wildly in the wind. From somewhere, a cheery ditty was playing over a tannoy. Busty housewives with head scarves and grey scrubber's elbows stood behind stalls or poured tea. A number of children darted about clutching balloons, and there was a noticeable deficiency of men in the small crowd. I had to pass through the periphery of the fair to get to where I needed to be, and did so with my head down.

I successfully passed the steaming tea tent, a number of white elephant stalls and a rather battered hoop-la stall before being stopped in my tracks by a fat farmer with his ham-fists clasped to a rope. At the end of the rope danced a petrified pig.

'Guess the weight of the pig, Sir?' the man grunted.

'No thank you!' I replied swiftly and ducked past him. The pig squealed as if appealing for freedom. And then, as I was nearing the clear roads at the end of my dash, an item on a stall to my left caught my eye.

While I am by no means a specialist, I consider myself to be something of a connoisseur of fine antiques, with a particular leaning towards the oriental market. Indeed, upon my mantlepiece sits a beautiful Tibetan singing bowl, in pride of place. It has, unbeknown to the casual observer, a slight chip upon the underside.

But here, sitting innocently on a tombola stall amid boxes of handkerchiefs and knitted Spanish señorita lavatory-paper covers, sat the most beautiful chocolate brown ceramic singing bowl I had ever seen. To see it plonked amongst a clutter of unwanted tat almost broke my heart. The idiot who had donated it to a rag-tag tombola simply had no idea what they had done. I examined it slowly and casually; there were no chips or faults in sight. It was a fine prize, and I simply had to have it!

I enquired as to its price, and was instructed sharply that I'd need to buy raffle tickets.

The lady manning the stall put me in mind of Olive Oyl from the Popeye cartoons. True to such cartoon stylings, her eyes almost popped out on stalks as I handed her a crisp note and demanded a number of tickets. Winning tickets had a nought or a five on the end of a two or three digit number, and I was searching for one-five-five. I began to open each folded ticket impatiently, screwing up each losing ticket and dropping it to my feet with a groan.

As I did this a small crowd of locals gathered behind me, eager to watch this well-heeled stranger try his luck. I had surely cleared away a good quarter of the tickets in the bowl. My first six tickets were duds, however I persevered with quiet confidence. A small pale hand reached through the crowd towards my stash of unopened tickets, and was pulled sharply back after I went to give it a sharp tap. Looking down I found the wide blue eyes of a village urchin blinking up at me.

'Very well, you may help me,' I said softly, and moved a couple of tickets toward her. 'We are looking for one-five-five.'

Ticket one-five-five proved to be frustratingly elusive.

I won a battered box of mens handkerchieves with the letter 'L' embroidered at the corner, a dented tin of scented ladies talcum power, a tin of peas and a small teddy that may have been a koala bear. My little companion won nothing. I set aside the other unwanted prizes and passed the child the bear before digging in my pockets and handing over a coin for ten more tickets. This was the last of my funds. I had to steady my hands, but each folded ticket proved to be fruitless. My heart sank as I dropped the final losing ticket onto the tabletop.

My extravagance had whipped up quite a stir at the tombola stall, and, swept along by my winning streak, a number of locals had purchased tickets eagerly. Suddenly a high voice called out and my heart sank.

'One-five-five!'

Olive Oyl handed a plump lady with tight curls the singing bowl as if it were a cracked cereal bowl. Blinded by grief and fury, I turned from the stall and stamped across the grass. Behind me the pig squealed as if mocking my loss. I had, however, only gone a little way when the little girl with the big eyes skipped into my path. She had the bowl, and held it out to me with a smile.

Instinctively, I reached into my pocket and pulled out my lemon sherbets. The girl took one, smiling, and I grabbed the treasure quickly before sticky fingers could do any damage. The girl skipped back to where her mother, fat and curly, stood with a smile. She handed the girl her koala and gave me a bright wide grin, with I returned appreciatively. It was only right that I should have the bowl, but it was a sweet gesture nevertheless.

In my excitement at the tombola I had been entirely distracted from my mission, but was soon approaching the home of Ercot and Mildred Mason.

I clutched the singing bowl to my chest and approached Ivy Cottage, Briar Lane, once more. The cars were still in place in the driveway and I was hopeful that Mason was home. I had not prepared myself with any kind of cover story this time, but it was too late to think of a plan. I

127

stepped around the vile stone dog, pushed my bowl carefully under my right arm and hammered on the door.

It was a good three minutes before my call was answered. I had persisted in my knocking, and the effort was paid off when Ercot Mason pulled open his front door with a surprising gusto.

'Yes, Mr Edgar?'

He had clearly seen me from out of a window and had prepared himself for a some sort of confrontation. The polite mask of my previous visit had been well and truly cast aside. His trumped up manner caused me to stiffen - the man looked as if he were priming for battle.

It was a battle I was going to lose.

'I must talk with you, Mason,' I announced before pushing rudely past the man and taking myself into his lounge. I wasn't about to be left hanging on the doorstep like an unwelcome pedlar. The place remained immaculately tidy and still carried the heady scent of flowers in bloom. There was no sign of the willowing wife.

Mason followed on after me, scowling.

'Look here, Edgar, I am terribly busy. We have to get to the village green. I am to judge the prize vegetables at a half past-'

'This will only take a minute, Mr Mason,' I began, filling myself with all the self-confidence I could muster. 'I came to discuss the Raqs Sharqi Club-'

'Good grief!' Mason groaned, 'And I thought, just for a moment there, that it would be something interesting. Some business deal on offer or a political favour perhaps.' The man went on, loving the sound of his own voice. 'But no, here you are, on and on about the bloody R.S. club yet again. Let it go, Mr Edgar! Let it go!'

'I will get to the point,' I said sharply, as much to myself as to Mason. 'I wish to talk about Fabien Pouche.'

At the name he did not as much as raise an eyebrow, but continued to look down upon me with a stony glare.

'That's a nice bowl,' he said coldly.

I had been running my fingers over the rim which protruded from my underarm, but was not about to be distracted.

'Fabian Pouche, Mr Mason!'

'We covered that ground on your previous visit, Mr Edgar.'

'Exactly! I believe you lied to me on my last visit, and that you have had relations of some sort with this young man, and I would like to know why. You registered at Dame Terry Guest House under an assumed name, and I insist you tell me all about it, Mason. I am on a mission to find out the truth!'

I stood my ground, blowing my chest out, my eyes wide. We glared at each other in silence.

Stalemate!

Turning from Mason's glare, I practically leapt out of my skin. Mildred Mason had slinked silently into the room and was standing at my shoulder, a serene look glazed on her grey wrinkled face. She wore exactly the same attire as she had on my previous visit, the dowdy dress, cardigan and fluffy slippers. It was her husband who spoke.

'No time for tea today my dear.' Mason leered in my direction. 'Mr Edgar won't be here long enough for drinks this time, I think. He has rather overplayed his hand.' His words were surely a veiled threat. Or was I wrong? Was I reading too much into his politician's sneer? It was hard to tell.

Mildred Mason stepped uneasily over to a wooden rocking chair that was located aside the bay window, and sat gingerly, clasping her hands together in her lap. Despite her weight the rocking chair barely moved an inch. The atmosphere in the room was strangely taut, a tension that had not been apparent on my previous call. It felt as if they had never had a visitor before and did not know quite how to deal with it.

It was all most peculiar.

'Mr Edgar was just asking after young Mr Pouche,' said Mason with a sneer. Although he had not reacted to the name his wife certainly did, her eyes widening with what could have been some degree of internal panic. And still she remained mute, her jaw fixed with tight lips.

Mason took his wife's silence as a question.

'You remember, dear? That young gentleman who came to the Raqs Sharqi dinner a few months back?' Mildred remained still and wordless and Mason gave a light chuckle.

'Mildred here took quite a liking to the young lad. Felt sorry for him, you see, scum though he was. No prospects, no education. Follett liked the boy too, for some unknown reason, and offered the lad a job gardening. Mildred here-' his wife appeared to shrink in her seat, '-piped up that we needed our lawn tending to, didn't you, dear? I can't abide gardening and she is always complaining that the lawn needs trimming, a menial task a leading statesman should never wish to do. Let nature take its course, I say. Still, Mildred, for one reason or another, requested his services and the lad came to do the weeding and to mow, just for the one day, I think, wasn't it, Mildred? Just the one day, a fair while back now?'

She nodded briskly.

Mason shrugged. 'That was a long time ago, however, and although he had his work cut out for him, he did a very poor job, to be frank. Quite without skill, he was. I paid him off and gave him his marching orders and that was that. Now we're in need of a gardner, but it's so hard to find quality staff, only jack-of-all-trades like young Pouche. Haven't seen him since, have we Mildred?'

She shook her head briskly.

And with that, Mason had finished his story. He did not ask why I should be concerned with the man, and so I told him.

'Young Pouche is dead.' I said, in a matter-of-fact manner. Neither of them reacted for a moment, until Mason spoke.

'Oh, that is a pity. Such a young and healthy lad. A pity indeed.' He gave no weight to his words. It was as if he were talking about a broken teacup. Nor did he care to ask how the young man had died.

'Was there anything else you wanted, Mr Edgar? Surely you don't wish to have a crack at joining the Raqs Sharqi again?'

His words had their desired effect, taunting me like a rag to a bull, his smirk even more so, and yet I kept my cool.

'There are indeed a few other things, Mason. Not least, I was wondering why you lied to me on my last visit. You said you had only seen Mr Pouche at his meal with the club. You said nothing about lawn mowing, or-'

'Mr Edgar, your last visit was a farce. I still do not know what you thought you were doing here. I merely humoured you and hoped you would leave sooner rather than later. I didn't think it necessary to tell you anything. I didn't then, and I really don't now. Who are you? A nobody in a Saville Row tailored suit is still a nobody.'

Keep calm, Payton. Keep calm.

'I wanted to talk to you about Dame Terry House.'

'Never heard of the place.'

'Guest house to the stars?'

'Nope.' said Mason swiftly, with the bluntness of innocence. Again, he did not ask why I should think that these words would be familiar to him. I bit my lip as he stood with the air of dismissal, staring calmly at me with the merest hint of a wry smile. This was not going so well, and a feeling of foreboding abruptly came over me. What evidence did I really have? Only the word of a batty guest house proprietor, and that evidence was shaky at best. Ercot Mason was so firm, so cold, so certain.

Suddenly disarmed, I felt the urge to flee. Mason appeared to sense this urge and called my bluff.

'Do you know, I think we will have that cup of tea after all, Mildred. My wife makes a delicious fruit scone, Mr Edgar. The envy of the village, you must try one.'

Mildred Mason floated to her feet, and I followed suit, although not without a struggle to release myself from the soft cushions. I clutched my bowl with care.

'No, no, thank you. I really had better be going.' As I said these words I was instantly annoyed at myself.

I had failed.

As I stepped out of the front door Mason was spouting good-natured remarks, as if we had shared a pleasant morning together like old friends. The man was an imbecile. He rounded off his spiel with a curt "*Good day*" and a closed door, the heavy knocker rattling briefly in response.

I stood motionless for a minute on the doorstep.

The sun had made a reappearance, the dark clouds seemingly dispersed. The twittering of birdsong appeared to mock me as I stood alone, cast out like an animal. Again I almost fell over the foul stone dog as I turned, and then I crunched through the gravel which outlined the front lawn with a feeling of substantial disappointment and the crushing need to leave the stinking village. All this time, with all my work, and still I seemed far from the truth behind the Pouche murder, far from exacting a sweet revenge on the intolerable Raqs Sharqi rabble.

Just as the Mason house had vanished from view I stopped in my tracks. Something of note had caught my eye, and I retraced my steps very slowly.

The grass.

The short, cut grass on the lawn. Mason's carefully manicured lawn.

At the corner of Mason's property I stopped and stared over its borders carefully. I stood motionless in thought for some time.

Mason had said quite clearly that neither he nor his wizened wife attempt gardening of any kind. He had claimed that young Pouche had come once, and some time ago. But if that was the case, why was the lawn at the front of the house so short, and the borders so well clipped? This lawn had been seen to recently, that much was clear.

A lie? Why would the man lie about the lawn?

My eyes wandered all over the green up to the domes of a summerhouse in the left corner, the roof almost covered by the branches of an overhanging willow. I hadn't taken much notice before, but now I had seen this hidden hut I was overcome with curiosity.

If Pouche had indeed mowed this lawn, this is where he would have gone.

The door had a number of heavy bolts and a large bracket with a padlock hanging from it, unlocked. I was somewhat blinded by my renewed interest, and before I knew it I was edging across the grass, pulling back two rusty bolts and fumbling with the flaky handle, which clicked as I turned it. As quietly as I could I opened the door of Mason's glorified shed.

The first thing that hit me inside was an unexpected smell - a vile stench of decay, an odour of farmyard proportions of foulness. I clutched my hand to my nose instinctively. A substantial number of flies circled the room.

Before me sat the mower, like some dormant sleeping beast. I touched its handle gingerly with my free hand, as if it would reveal secrets as I moved my fingertips over the grips. Pouche had been here, and recently, I was sure. What had happened? What would Pouche have done?

Some words that I had heard in recent days came to mind. It was the clear cut words of Jessica Hatch that floated into my consciousness.

'He was ever curious, nosing himself into the affairs of others whenever he could.'

Nosy. The man was nosy.

I looked around the dark wooden hut, nosily. Beyond the usual spades, forks and buckets, against the far wall, a tarpaulin was covering something rather bulky. To its side was a dusty work surface, a number of wires and screws dotted about it. On the surface was a couple of sheets of paper upon which were scrawled odd pictures, diagrams revealing some unrecognisable sort of mechanism. I moved from these penciled blueprints and stepped forwards into the shack towards the tarpaulin. I touched the cool sheet, my touch sending more flies scattering into the air.

I paused for a minute, and then lifted the sheet.

The loathsome nature, not to mention the bizarreness of my find, did not register for a minute and I stood looking down at it for some time in revulsion and incredulity. Dead eyes stared up at me in amongst blood and flesh. I was so transfixed by the horror before me that I failed to hear the footsteps behind me.

What I did not hear I certainly felt, as a cold hard weight cracked across the back of my skull. My vision blurred, and then the pain came. The last thing I heard was my singing bowl crashing to the floor and then I followed it.

All went black.

Chapter II
In which Payton Edgar longs for goose feather pillows

Monday Dec 17th

Dear milkman,

Regrettably, Tits have been at my bottle tops. Please use this tea towel to cover bottles following delivery.

Many thanks,

Mr Edgar, number 8

Tuesday Dec 18th

Dear milkman,

What have you done with my *Cheeses of Northern France* tea towel?

Mr Edgar, number 8

Wednesday Dec 19th

Dear number 8,

I gave the tea towel to my Mum. She loves cheese. I have re-placed it and will cover your milk in future as requested.

Milkman

Thursday Dec 20th

Dear Milkman,

Your cheap tartan tea towel is most offensive to the eye. Please replace with my original, *Cheeses of Northern France* immediately.

Mr Edgar, number 8

Friday Dec 21st
Dear number 8,
I have already sent the cheese tea towel to Scotland. I think the tartan tea towel is very festive. It brightens up your doorstep.
Milkman

Saturday Dec 22nd
Dear Milkman,
I have removed your vile tartan towel and replaced it. Please use my *china cups* tea towel and do not replace. If your mother likes china cups you will have to purchase your own. They are 10 shillings from Fortnum and Mason.
Please end correspondence.
Mr Edgar, number 8

Monday Dec 24th
Dear Number 8,
Merry Christmas,
Milkman

I awoke suddenly, calling out something about tea towels.
My head was throbbing. I was lying supine, my crown rested on something resembling a pillow. Yet it was far too hard to be my own fine goose feather affairs.
Even though I had opened my eyes, for a while I thought I was still in the Mason's summerhouse, such were the proportions of the room. However, the floor was cold and hard stone and not wood. Thankfully, the smell of decay had cleared from my nostrils. The light was dim, and I wasn't sure if it was my vision, which was blurred and shaken, or the room itself. Some time passed, and I stared upwards as shadows slid across the walls. The place I was in was definitely larger than the summerhouse.
I strained to recall just what had happened.
I had experienced a moment of clarity - how long ago now? - and opened an eye, awoken by motion as I was pulled backwards by strong hands along the cut grass of the Mason's lawn. My arms ached, but not as much as my head. I had seen a shoe, my left shoe, flip up and fall off of my foot, being abandoned on the lawn as I was dragged away. I had tried to focus on the shoe, and even in my dazed stupor I was aware of my loss. They had been a pricey purchase. I had fixed my gaze on the shoe in dizzy horror as I was pulled along. And then the dull thudding of my head had returned and once more all went black.
This time, gingerly opening my sore eyes, all I saw was a low

brick ceiling dotted with the odd flash of light. I blinked as the dots moved, realising that they were inside my eyes, moving as my vision did. Closing my eyes tight, I rested for a while. Wherever I was, there was no sound. Silence sat heavily all around me. My head spun. The dryness of my mouth was remarkable and my lips felt heavy against each other.

My brand new singing bowl! The heartbreaking smash as it had fallen rang in my ears.

And then those damn letters to the Milkman all those years ago came to mind. Why on earth had I been thinking about those? I tried to put the image of tartan tea towels firmly out of my head, and then accepted sleep once more.

The next time I awoke it was a little easier to open my eyes, and no flashes of light greeted me. I stared up at the dark ceiling for quite some time.

A noise to my right broke the silence, causing me to snap my head aside. At this a bolt of pain shot through my neck and I cried out involuntarily, wincing in agony. After a minute the pain abated and I opened one eye. The room was silent again, and dark.

Very dark.

Black shapes formed, a box high up on the far wall that was lighter and could have been a window. Beneath it, a shadow. I watched the hazy darkness for a while, my whole being exhausted.

And then the shadow moved. Just a little, but enough to catch my eye. I drew in a deep breath.

I was not alone!

The figure against the far wall sat motionless for some time, so long that I began to think I had been mistaken, and that it was simply furniture. I couldn't take my eyes from it, and I felt my heart racing with a fear the likes of which I had never felt before. The shape jerked again, emitting a clinking sound, the sound of heavy chains against stone. I tried to focus. The figure was like a wizened shadow of a person, almost that of a child, with a small amount of what I guessed was moonlight bouncing off of its round and shiny crown.

Beneath the hazy glare of its bonce I made out two large eyes, far whiter than the face, staring in my direction. I heard a whimper, but it was not my own. The creature watched me from the darkness with those horrid moist, glistening eyes. I struggled to catch my breath as fear rose up into my throat. It was all very exhausting.

The shadow moved into a crouched position and slowly, very slowly, moved across the stone floor towards me. Chains dragged ominously against stone as the white eyes sparkled through the dark, wide and unblinking.

I told myself that I must move, that I must go somewhere, but could not fight the wave of lethargy that arose in me. My head pounded, my arms heavy at my sides.

Resting back on the hard pillow, I felt myself drifting away helplessly, back to sleep, to dream of tea towels once more.

When I next awoke my headache had dwindled and now my head felt just a little bruised.

My vision was certainly better, and I stared up at the dusty cobwebs above me for some time. The moonlight had faded into a nebulous daylight and outside there was a familiar noise I had not heard for some time - heavy rainfall. With it drifted in the distinctive smell of cool wet drops on warm dry ground, a tarry, earthy odour. I lay staring upwards and listened to the beautiful, orchestral sound of heavy rain. A fat spider hung in the corner, motionless. After a while I felt strong enough, not to mention brave enough, to turn my head.

This time, I could see.

The pale box shape I had identified on the far wall was indeed a small window, now casting two hazy beams of sunlight through filthy glass. I could see long blades of grass creeping up around the frame outside. Wherever I was, I was certainly below ground level.

Beneath the window, hunched in a shadow, sat the figure.

Many things are more frightening in the dark, as our imaginations fill in the unnecessary details of what we most fear. As a child, the looming shapes in the darkness of my bedroom had proven themselves to be a hanging shirt or an open wardrobe door when reexamined in the cold light of day. But there was no such comfort this time. Setting eyes on the creature in what little daylight there was only made me wish for the darkness again.

My heart beat wildly in my chest.

The figure was cowering in the shadows of the far corner. It was a small crouching human shape, but a shape with glistening wet black skin, a round black head and those large white blinking eyes. The mouth appeared to be a straight row of glistening metal teeth, fixed in a wide grin. It was crouched on all fours, and I could see the boney prominences of its spine rising and falling gently as it breathed.

The head was twisted and it was staring directly at me.

There was a sudden flash of light in which the creature, poised in its twisted crouch, was illuminated, and those metal teeth flashed in my direction. This was swiftly followed by the crack of thunder which shook the earth beneath us and rumbled away across the sky above. Rain clattered heavily against the small windows above.

I willed myself to remain calm, trying desperately not to cry out. My limbs felt heavy, almost numb, as I clutched my hands to my chest. The low bed on which I had been resting was tough and had been unforgiving on my poor bones. I lay there, for how long I do not know, staring at the creature, this shiny beast.

It glared back in my direction.

It was a while before I convinced myself that the creature was not crouched to attack and, tired of the silent sparring, I tentatively turned my eyes back to the ceiling. The hot pangs of sheer panic that had cast themselves across my chest. slowly abated. *Where was I? What had happened?* I longed for Lucille to pad over to me, to nuzzle her furry little head into my palm and lick my fingers with her horribly coarse tongue, following which I would awake in my lovely antique oak sleigh bed and shake off this nightmare.

Unfortunately, nothing so welcome would happen.

The clinking sound I had heard before, like grinding metal, brought me out of my thoughts, and I glanced back over to the creature. It had moved ever so slightly, and was resting against the wall with knees drawn up to it's breast. For the first time I saw the chains leading from a large iron ring on the floor to the beast's ankle.

It was restrained.

This should perhaps have given me reassurance, but it did not. It merely added to my confusion. My legs lay heavy and I wondered if I too were chained to my post. I raised my head, my neck throbbing, but could see no chains on my ankles, thankfully. Just one shoe on, one shoe off. My poor shoe!

When I was strong enough, I could run. And I would indeed run.

Hours passed, although how many I could not have said. The cobwebs wafted a little above me, dancing to the heavy rain that pummelled the ground relentlessly outside.

And then came the footsteps.

These were followed by an incongruously jaunty jangle of keys and the click of a lock before the door creaked open. A man stood, silhouetted in the doorway, the keys dangling from his hand, looking for all the world like a Sheriff in the wild west. Ercot Mason stepped forwards into the light. He was, as usual, smirking that vile smirk.

The old door banged shut behind him, sending the creature opposite into a tight ball against the far wall with the clanking of its chains. It feared him.

'Good morning, Mr Edgar!' His arch tone was almost warm.

What had he expected? A cheery reply? My mouth was dry and sticky, and I struggled to push out a single word.

'M-morning?' I heaved myself up with a sore elbow and managed to sit, my head seemingly taking a little longer to rise up. I blinked the pain away.

Mason laughed. 'You don't even know what day it is, do you? This is probably your tomorrow, I think. Or perhaps the day after.'

Casting my sore eyes around I took in the room, a cell to all intents and purposes. Cold brickwork formed the walls, with rusting metal implements fixed within the cracks. There was a rusty gin trap mounted on one wall, with many chains anchored all around. Had there been an iron maiden standing proud in the corner I would not have been surprised. Straining to look over my right shoulder I saw that the room continued a little to the left of the doorway, a small corridor leading nowhere that was decorated with numerous posters and pictures on the walls. There may have been a desk or some such thing in the far corner. What looked like cloth flags were hanging from the ceiling of this uninviting corner. The cold brick floor of the place was dusty and uneven, and spattered in a number of places with strange dark stains.

The bed beneath me was a small number of folded blankets on the hard floor and my pillow consisted of cuttings of cardboard tied together by bands. To the right of my bed sat a dog's bowl, half filled with water.

This was not good. Not good at all.

'You just couldn't leave it be, could you, Mr Edgar?' said Mason disapprovingly. 'Well, this is what you get for your dogged perseverance. It's all your own fault, quite frankly. You're going to have a fun few days, I think. Mildred and I have never had a guest quite like this before. It will be a privilege.'

I spoke, although my throat was dry, so very dry.

'Mason, let me go. Please!' This feeble plea was all I could muster, but already he was shaking his head.

'You will remain our guest, no questions. Anyhow, I did not come down to chat with you, Mr Edgar. I came for Mildred.'

He turned pointedly and approached the creature, which shuddered and whimpered. I watched in horror as Mason held and caressed the beast until it lay silent and spent. For a few minutes he ran his dry fingers across its skin, emitting a curious, deep scratching noise. The beast's skin was thick rubber.

Eventually Mason fumbled with the chains and released them from the creature's ankles.

After grabbing a tight hold of its wrist he pulled the fragile being to its feet and dragged it to the door. As they passed through the shadows of the room I saw the bones of the creature's shoulders and spine clearly defined through its rubber skin. It was only after they had left, the door had been locked and I had sat for a minute or two in silence, that I accepted what I had just seen; Ercot Mason leaving with his wife, Mildred

Mason, in his grasp.

Suddenly all I wanted to do was to sleep again.

Chapter III

In which Payton Edgar's mind wanders

Dear Mr Edgar,

Unfortunately you have missed this week's deadline for Friday's Clarion. This is clearly unacceptable. We shall run a "Best of Margaret Blythe" piece this week. Please contact me directly as soon as possible to explain your extremely uncharacteristic omission and to reassure me that things will be back on track for next week.

Yours sincerely,
Temple Bilborough
Managing Director, The London Clarion

Hours passed by. Hours that stretched into long days.

The light outside the window seemed to last forever, and when darkness came it was over all too soon. I had been too long without food or water, and it was my headache and the dryness of my mouth that had forced me onto my knees, where I took the dog's bowl in both hands and, once resigned to such a degrading action, drank thirstily. The tepid fluid had the unpleasant metallic tang of long-standing water, but I drank vigorously all the same.

Later that day I kicked off my one remaining Standard Oxford and again lay grieving for the loss of its partner. My best shoes, gone! I could not bear to think how my beautiful suit looked amongst this dust and depravation.

I had been driven to kick off the shoe as the beginnings of an escape plan crept into my mind. Once trapped, it was only natural that one should dream of escape, and I had come to the conclusion that it would be easier to run with no shoes rather than hobble along with just the one. A few minutes later I had managed to crawl to the door, as if I were expecting it to open. I could barely pull on the door handle, I was so weak, and, of course, it didn't move an inch.

Would nobody come to my rescue?

And then a dreadful truth had laid itself before me; *nobody knew where I was.*

Nobody!

I cursed Irving silently, for it was his actions that had forced me to act with secrecy over this whole business. I cursed him for giving the cat my best fish and for forcing us to argue. He would no doubt be at home, splashing paint violently about, enjoying one of his sulks.

I cursed the whole of Potten Way for not realising that they harboured a deranged murderer within their stupid village. I cursed the man with the squealing pig and the lady with the floppy hat playing bowls on the green. Surely someone had noticed this stranger and would wonder why he had not been seen catching the bus home? Weren't these small villages supposed to be full of twitching curtains? Where were the nosy neighbours when you needed one?

And then there was my lost shoe. Would somebody find my shoe on the Mason's lawn and raise the alarm? I knew such hopes were improbable, but I exhausted myself further by damning the outside world for not noticing my absence. And then, of course, there were my newspaper columns. If nobody else cared, at least Temple Bilborough would have something to say about my missed deadlines, surely?

How long would normal life go on without me before the alarm bells rang?

Aunt Elizabeth would surely only celebrate my absence. The last words we had exchanged had been heated ones. A television set in her bedroom indeed! But then there was Grace - surely she would be concerned about my disappearance? I recalled our last few conversations, and cursed myself for being cryptic about taking a trip away, for this is surely the conclusion at which she would arrive.

My penchant for maintaining a dignified secrecy around my affairs would perhaps be my downfall.

Again my thoughts returned to Irving, holed up in his studio, awaiting my knock at the door, an olive branch at the ready. After our spat, he would be expecting me to come crawling back on my knees, no doubt. Irving hadn't a clue about all I had been through in the past few weeks. He knew nothing of what I had been doing. He did not even know what had happened to the poor young man on Hyde Park Square in the first place. He had no reason to be concerned over my welfare.

He would be left waiting for this particular olive branch.

And then suddenly in the silence, like a deep clanging bell, I could hear my Aunt Elizabeth's low cackle. It sent a shiver through to my toes. I pictured her sitting up in bed, those gnarled claws running through the ginger cat's fur as she chewed on her dentures, her heart full of scorn. I saw her face, a skeletal mask with sunken eyes and cheeks, and that snarl of judgment fixed over a jutting jaw. The anniversary of my mother's death.

Had it really been a year?

I had last seen Mother in her hospital bed. Persistent visits by Enid Smith, Mother's dowdy friend from church, had forced me to attend. Enid had assured me that Mother was at death's door, and I had indignantly set out to disprove this.

Hospitals are grim places, the stench of bleach and vomit alone is unbearable enough. I had used my handkerchief as a posy as I passed through the gloomy lobby where, to one side, nurses's capes were hung on iron pegs, awaiting the changeover of each shift. I had been greeted efficiently by a young nurse upon entering the ward and was directed to the far corner of the long, imposing space to behind a pale-blue flowered curtain. Beds were placed side-by-side along each wall, each precisely positioned, rather like graves. Beside almost every bed sat a shadowy, silent man, reluctantly going through the conventional procedure of *visiting*.

Feeling the eyes of the sick on me I passed along the ward with some discomfort, hearing the occasional patient mutter as I headed to my mother's bed.

I had not expected what I found.

Sunken into the bed amongst the crisp white sheets lay a woman deflated. Her chins slid from beneath pale blue lips, with tiny eyes closed under folds of loose skin. Around her head, faded orange curls laced the pillow. Her once heaving bosom was practically concave, above which three or four ribs jutted out under taut skin. A puffy arm lay outside the sheet, extending along the bed and I was appalled, as she herself would surely have been, at the condition of her fingernails. What had once been painstakingly smoothed and shaped and polished were now chipped and brown.

For a moment I had thought the patient before me was dead, and then Mother took a breath. It was a noise like no other, as if she were being strangled by her own weakness.

Weakness.

This was not a concept I had ever associated with Mother. Winifred Lily Edgar had always been strong. Fiery even. One day at school, after one of the many miserable summer fetes that came around all too quickly, my teacher had casually referred to her as "*your formidable mother*". From that day on she remained, in my mind, formidable.

My formidable mother.

The formidable Winifred Lily Edgar lay defeated.

I had sat beside Winifred Edgar for a good half an hour, listening to the woman catching an occasional breath, before deciding that it was time for me to leave. Although each second had been uncomfortable and somewhat surreal, it was perhaps the calmest and nicest thirty minutes I had ever spent in my mother's company. I did not speak, having nothing to say.

And, in the end, she had only one thing to say to me.

I had shaken away a chill that had settled on my shoulders, collected my hat and stick and was about to leave. Noticing my movement, Mother's eye opened and for a moment she lay glaring up at me.

Her dry cracked lips moved, but no sound came out. I looked around me for assistance but we were sheltered by the foul blue-flowered curtain.

'Payton,' she said, faintly.

For a moment I had felt a swell of emotion as she said my name, a comforting, reassuring warmth within that had brought a smile to my lips. She had said my name.

Her lips moved again.

'Payton,' she said.

I waited. Words came out slowly, as if each syllable took considerable conscious effort.

'You are…no son of mine.'

Her eyelid flickered and her pupil rolled upwards to rest underneath, leaving only the yellow-white of the eye exposed. Mother passed away later that night, leaving the memory of those last words lingering in my ears forever.

You are no son of mine.

I had demanded that Aunt Elizabeth tell me exactly what Mother had meant by this, only to be pooh-poohed. The ramblings of a dying woman, Aunt Elizabeth had replied dismissively. Mother's death had upset her greatly, and I soon learned not to talk of it.

The sisters had been insufferably close throughout their lives, and so it was no surprise that Aunt Elizabeth had been quick to judge me after reminding me of the macabre anniversary. A year since mother's death, she had said. A year since the funeral. It was as fresh in my mind as my fall-out with Irving.

In the days leading up to the ceremony I had vowed loudly and proudly to anyone who would listen that I would not be attending. I have never been a dedicated attendee of funerals, and Mother had known this. I was not too proud to admit to myself that those final words she had chosen to say to me played a part in it, too. And yet curiosity, or something close to it, had gotten the better of me and had I found myself standing amongst the trees of Highgate Cemetery, watching as only a small handful of mourners gathered graveside.

There was something quite sinister about standing in the shadows of great, looming chestnut trees and watching a funeral, and I have to admit that in some ways it appealed to the dramatist in me. I had stood for some time watching the few people alive who knew Mother drag themselves along after the coffin.

I recognised only two of the black shapes with some certainty. One was the tiny pinheaded form of Enid Smith, Mother's mousey friend who followed slowly and hesitantly behind the group like some straggling ant on a paving stone. The other, of course, was Aunt Elizabeth.

Despite being bent double with arthritis, Aunt Elizabeth still managed to lead the procession as they moved through the church yard. Leaning down on her two sticks and cloaked in black, she had resembled some horrific beast of gothic fiction as she pushed onwards, with two spindly legs creeping out front and two thicker, twisted hind legs following on. Her crooked head was encased in a dark veil. This malevolent form was a chilling apparition even from a distance, and I would have been apoplectic if somebody had even suggested that the woman should be sharing my house within a matter of months.

I had beaten a hasty retreat through the gravestones whilst sucking on a lemon sherbet, and on the tube ride home I had commended myself at how unmoved I had been when watching the funeral. I had watched the box with tearless eyes as it was carried along, and I told myself that a chapter of my life had closed, and that was that.

And now here I was, one year later. The fear I had once felt for my Aunt had been replaced by something else. What was Aunt Elizabeth now? Nothing more than a bed-ridden, decrepit old woman.

And I was all the family she had left.

I turned myself onto my back and glared up at the dark ceiling of my prison, my quiet contemplation being quickly vanquished by the familiar warmth of anger with had welled up at the thought of Mother's deathbed impudence.

Suddenly I caught myself. What was all this? Why was I flying through the miserable moments of my life, wasting precious energy on sour memories? The four walls seemed to close in around me.

I pictured Aunt Elizabeth in her room, bedridden, staring at the wall, the four walls closing in around her. *Poor Aunt Elizabeth!* Suddenly I understood just how horrible it can be to find yourself confined to one room, day in, day out. I found myself drifting again into uneven sleep.

The last thing I heard was the distant squealing of a petrified pig.

Chapter IV

In which Payton Edgar learns of a plot

Dear Margaret,
I have had a terrible row with a dear friend of mine and I fear I have lost his friendship. My problem is that I just don't understand what it was we had argued about. I would be able to apologise if I were at fault, although I am sure I am not. I am never wrong. And now I have been kidnapped and imprisoned and forced to drink from a dog bowl. Any advice?
P. Edgar, Pimlico

Margaret replies; you will die tonight.

I awoke with a start, my heart pounding in my chest.

Shaken, I blinked the dust from my eyes and gathered myself, recalling exactly where I lay by the aching of my bones. My throat was terribly dry, and I noticed that the water bowl had been refilled during my slumber. Across the room the rubber figure had reappeared and was sat hunched in the corner, watching me. Outside the filthy window the clouds had receded, scattering rays of sunlight through the blades of grass and across the stone floor. The creature shuffled back into the shadows, careful to avoid the light.

I did not speak. The last thing I wanted to do was converse with the thing, even if it was indeed Mildred Mason. I rolled from my blanket onto my front where I supped from the dog bowl, savouring each mouthful of the unsavoury water within. It had the nasty tang of raw potatoes.

Then, once I was sat upright with my back against the cool brick, the rubber creature moved. I noticed for the first time how the eyes were pulled tight through the holes in the mask, and how a sealed zip formed the metal teeth of the mouth. The creature, so spindly and flat chested, bore no resemblance to the flowery housewife I had been introduced to, and I struggled to believe that it was her.

There was a rustle, and I could make out white bony fingers working at something familiar on the ground. My hand went to my jacket pocket, which lay flat.

My lemon sherbets!

The creature pulled at the paper a little more, but in the heat it had stuck to the boiled sweets. She gave up and tossed the clump of sherbets to the far corner of the room. My mouth ached - how I longed for the sour tang of one of my lemon sherbets! I would have happily sucked the paper from them.

And then she made a sudden swift movement, taking something from an upturned wicker basket beside her and tossing it onto the stone floor between us. It bounced twice, showering white crumbs across the floor before coming to a halt at my feet. A rock bun. This was indeed Mildred Mason.

Without a thought I took it, and ate it.

She watched me as I chewed at the stale, dry dough. I was under no illusion that this gift was no act of kindness on her part, she was merely showing me where I stood in the pecking order. She had the power to feed or to starve me, whichever she desired.

Once again, as darkness crept in outside, the door was unlocked and Mason took his wife away. Mason was very heavy handed as he dragged her away. I tried to call out this time, suddenly anxious at being left alone, but my shouts fell on deaf ears. I stopped only as waves of nausea passed through me, withering me to silence.

After they were gone I sat for a while, alone in the dim light, and thought about my miserable position. After some time I drew in a deep breath in attempt to pull myself together and then felt across the stone floor for any large crumbs or sultanas from the rock bun that I had missed.

The following morning, Mason surprised me by enquiring sharply what I would like for my lunch. The cruel irony of this question was not lost on me, and I did not honour the question with a reply, even though my stomach groaned inside.

Nevertheless, not long afterwards, he returned holding a large tray.

He pulled a wooden box along to rest at my to my feet and laid out a bowl of steaming tomato soup, some crusty bread, a fat round soup spoon and a small yellow angel cake. This he placed carefully on the corner of the box for my dessert. I restrained myself.

'What am I doing here, Mason?' I croaked wearily.

'Penance.' he replied, simply.

'But I have done nothing!'

'Oh, you would, if you could, Mr Edgar. You would if you could.'

'Will you let me go?'

'Never.'

He moved over to the darkness of the curious corridor to the right, and returned dragging an old dining chair. He positioned this by the door and sat with his arms folded. I was far too hungry to refuse the food set before me, much as I would have liked to. Mason sat and watched as I tore apart the bread and ate like some wild animal. After a minute or so, he cackled grimly.

'You like my wife's soup, I take it?' he said. I remained mute.

'Well then, Mr Edgar, culinary expert, restaurant critic, give me your review. Is the bread crusty enough? Is the broth a soupçon too peppery? What?'

Despite my weakness a pounding strength was brewing within me. The man certainly knew how to irritate. I knew that I would maintain my dignity in silence, but his jibes were so very tempting. However, I surprised myself. Upon finishing the soup I merely lay back quietly and turned my face to the wall.

'Mr Edgar,' said Mason in a calm authoritative tone, 'please sit up and look at me.'

I did not move.

'Do as I say, Mr Edgar. I have to talk with you.'

I smiled at the brickwork. 'And what will you do if I don't?'

Mason cut in quickly. 'I am not a violent man, Edgar, I-'

'Pah!' I turned to glare at the man over my shoulder. 'I've seen what you do to your wife. Locking her up, treating her like an animal. You are a devil, Mason, a-'

'Now look here!' he said, his face reddening as he sat forward in his chair. 'I do exactly what she tells me to do. My wife, Mr Edgar, is an exceedingly strong woman.'

'Pah!' I said again.

'You really don't have the size of Mildred at all, Edgar. Looks can be deceptive. She has ways…ways you could never imagine.'

He looked to the door as if checking we were alone, before turning his eyes back on me.

'Yes, she makes a perfect wife for the newspapers, a fine figure of domesticity. She stands beside me at rallies. She whips up scones and rock cakes for the jumble sales. But at home, behind closed doors, she is… someone else. *A devil*. She has…dark desires.

'She asks me to do things - and when I don't, she forces me to do them. I am to lock her up, to treat her like a dog. She loves it. She-'

'Oh, come on, Mason-' I began, exasperated.

'I am not a violent man, Edgar. At least not by choice. I am the brains of our little twosome, whereas she is the...the force. She is a very persuasive.'

I stared at the man, confused by the whole situation. It was so absurd, it had to be true. He hesitated, as if deciding how much to reveal. Finally he spoke, and with something of a whisper.

'She finds murder - how can I say it? Very easy. It comes naturally to her. She lives for the kill.'

'What nonsense!' I spat with all the strength I could muster. Mason cleared his throat.

'Mr Edgar, I believe there are three types of people in life; the fox, the hound and the huntsman. I am a huntsman. Quite literally, too. I have been known to don my pinks and to even have heralded a horn in my time. I am a natural leader, you see. You, Mr Edgar, are the fox - a perpetual victim, doomed to failure, despite what he may think of himself. And Mildred...Mildred is our hound. She leads the pack, as a savage and relentless killing machine.'

'Rubbish!'

Mason clicked his fingers and pointed to the discoloured bricks that formed the floor.

'You see these stains?' he asked, his voice cracking a little, 'I can tell you where they came from. We keep chickens out back. Or we used to. Mildred became fascinated by the eggs discarded by broody hens. She would take tweezers and pick them open, to see the poor dead chicks inside, some barely an hour from hatching. But it wasn't enough. We stopped getting any chicks, because she would pull apart all the eggs - she began taking them warm from their broody mothers. And then, when bored of the eggs, she wanted the hens and went after them with a knife. The yard is empty now. All of our hens have gone, dead at her hands. And so I have to buy her livestock, to satisfy her bloodlust. Roosters, chickens, mice. Sometimes a rabbit. And she toys with them. She likes to-' he struggled with his words, '-she, she kills things, Mr Edgar. With her bare hands. You saw in the summerhouse, I think, that she likes to collect the heads.'

I looked at the deep brown marks across the floor, nauseated, and recalled the smell of the summerhouse, where I had looked down on the large bucket of rotting chicken heads. A dozen dark glassy eyes staring up at me.

'I tell you, Edgar, she lives for the kill. She relishes it.'

Despite his apparent fear of Mildred, there was still a twist of pride in his voice.

Suddenly I could hear a muffled chorus of high pitched laughter from somewhere. It seemed to come from deep in the house above us. Mason looked up to the ceiling.

'What's that?' I asked. It was the first noise from the house above that I had heard since my incarceration.

Mason swallowed, sitting back on the floor.

'The Potten Way Women's Institute. It's Mildred's turn with the meeting today.'

I paused for a minute in silence. There I was, shoeless and disheveled - not to mention tired and hungry - a prisoner in the cellar, while one of my captors entertained the Women's Institute with scones and tea above me. I was almost as surprised as Mason when I let out a rasping laugh, tickled momentarily by the sheer absurdity of it all.

Mason was watching me suspiciously and all of a sudden, looking at his wrinkled pale face above that horrible floppy polo-necked jumper, I realised that beyond his bullying façade the man was pathetic. Vulnerable to his wife's whims, if what he had been saying was true. And I had no reason to disbelieve him. This defenceless man was pitiful, and for a fleeting moment I did indeed pity him. And then I spoke my thoughts.

'You are so very pathetic, Mason, you really are!'

'What?'

'I heard of men being *"under the thumb"*, but you? A man petrified of his own wife, locking her in the cellar! It's revolting.'

It was refreshing to goad the man, and I instantly felt stronger in spirit.

'You don't know what she can be like!'

'You are spineless, Mason!' I was satisfied to see that my words were disturbing him. He hissed like a snake.

'Spineless, am I? Spineless? There is so much more happening here than you could ever imagine, Mr Edgar. In a few days, everyone will know the name of Ercot Mason! I am almost sad that you, arrogant Mr Edgar, won't be alive to see it!'

It was the first I had heard of this. So I was to die.

I kept my cool. 'You don't want to hurt me, Mason-'

'Oh, killing you means nothing. Mildred simply cannot wait. You are nothing but a trifling annoyance in our grand plan. And so was Pouche. Small fry! Squash-able!'

I had grown tired of his bravado. 'So what is this great plan?' I asked lazily.

'Oh, I'd love to tell you, I really would. It has meant years and years of preparation, and now, in just a matter of days, it will finally happen.'

'Planning to be Prime Minister, Mason?'

He glared at me, chewing his tongue, and I was delighted to see the frustration on his face. 'You saw what was in the summer house, did you not?'

I would never forget the summer house. I nodded grimly.

'Well so did Pouche. Mildred had taken a fancy to the young man, for many reasons. She has an insatiable appetite for presentable young men. In a moment of lust after dinner with the Raqs Sharqi, she invited the dirty foreigner to tend to our garden. She is terribly impulsive, as you found out to your cost while you were nosying about the summer-house. And so pouche came. He needed the cash. I had to restrain her, of course, to stop her doing anything to the lad. And, on his third visit, just like you, the nosy foreigner saw what was in the summer house. He saw our blueprints and equipment for our grand plan.'

Mason shook his head. 'The fool tried to blackmail us.'

'You gave him money?'

'Oh, yes indeed. That was whole point of our rendezvous at that ridiculous guest house. Somewhere neutral, somewhere *anonymous.* I have used it before, for…private meetings. But this was more than a pay off. It was money for him to enjoy his last days. I had no choice. We had to get him out of the way, the blackmailing little runt. Mildred was in her element. She was overjoyed, like a cat with a spider. I dropped her off at his flat, but that was all I could bear to do. She made her own way home. God knows what she did, but the man was dead, our secret safe. You see, Edgar, how important this whole thing is. We will kill to keep this secret, to stick to the plan.'

I pictured Pouche, young and healthy, opening the door to find Mildred Mason, nothing more than a dowdy housewife, standing before him. What would she do? Tell him that she had more money? He would let her in, of course, with Mildred no doubt salivating at being allowed in to the young man's flat. Then, once inside, what would she do? Change into the beast. The very idea of it was incredible. Had she caught him unawares, or had he run? I pictured her pelting through the flat in hot pursuit, screaming in delight, grabbing the rolling pin as they passed through the kitchen. She would have cornered the poor man. And then it was over for Fabien Pouche as she battered the poor man's skull to pieces in the bathroom.

'Your wife is a murderer,' I said with surprising calm.

Mason sneered. 'More than you can imagine. Our friend from Belarus learned that the hard way, too.'

'Belarus?'

'Victor Lutrova.'

It took a moment for me to make the link.

'The doctor? The seventh member of the Raqs Sharqi?'

Mason nodded.

'The man was an idiot. He didn't deserve the title *"doctor"*, and never would have had it if the authorities had bothered to question the man's credentials. He most certainly never deserved to be a member of the Raqs Sharqi either. He was a fraud and an anarchist back in his home country, and about as good a doctor as I am a ballet dancer. What he was, however was a very good physicist. A technical marvel. We spent some wonderful afternoons tinkering in the summerhouse. Yes, he was curiously good company for such a bad, bad person. If you think what we are doing is appalling, he'd done some truly terrible deeds in his time, I tell you.

'He was a marvel with timed ignition systems, and created something very special right here. And we paid him well. Only too happy to help with constructing the device, he was, until he found out what it was for. So often, when it comes to the pass, a man reveals his true strength. Victor was weak. The man was scared when it came to attacking the government. It transpired that he liked the English way of life too much to risk anything. A factor which we had overlooked.'

Mason stroked his chin.

'We agreed to talk about it, to come to an agreement over a game of golf. My dear caddy Mildred slipped digitoxin into the tea flask and that was that - dead of a heart attack in minutes and nobody any the wiser. He had helped me with all that I needed. As you saw in the summerhouse, I had all the equipment ready.'

'To make a bomb?' I said with disbelief.

Mason thinned his eyes and sat back. 'I dislike your childish terminology, Edgar. I prefer to call it a device. A device for freedom.' He sniffed. 'You are privilege to some very confidential information, Edgar. I think you know enough. You can only pray that Mildred will be quick, and not play with you when the time comes. Quick and relatively painless.'

'So full of words, aren't you, Mason? Typical of a politician, full of plans and promises, when underneath it all there is simply no substance whatsoever. You are nothing but a bully.'

'Rather the hammer than the nail, Mr Edgar. Rather the hammer than the nail.'

'Words, Mason! Nothing but words!'

'Mr Edgar-'

'Planning and plotting won't get you into the House of Lords, Mason, believe me.' I said, suddenly doubting my words. Planning and plotting was perhaps the most common way to get appointed.

'Damn the House of Lords!' shouted my captor, his fists clenching. He lowered his voice, mindful of the ladies party upstairs.

'Damn them all! For twenty-five years I have struggled on my soapbox, trying to convince the band of ignorant fools in parliament that they are taking the country down the drain. Bloody St John Townsend! A Home Secretary entirely unworthy of the title! What's happened to our country because of him? Ship-loads of foreigners at our shores! Blacks on every corner! Nothing is English anymore! They are killing our England, slowly and surely. I have tried for years to make them see, and what do I get in return? Treated like a leper, that's what! They write that I am the fool, that I am the one without policy! What rot! Well they will see!'

I could not suppress a smile.

'And what exactly is your plan, Mason?'

He moved his face closer to mine, his expression was deadly serious.

'Do you really, really want to know?'

Reluctantly, I nodded, however for all his ranting I was still not prepared for his reply.

'I'm going to blow up the Houses of Parliament.' He stated proudly.

Chapter V

In which Payton Edgar attempts to save the day minus his shoes

The Best Of Margaret Blythe

Dear Margaret,
My neighbour is always so rude to me. She seems to do every-
thing so perfectly; her whites are whiter than white, her children
scrubbed and dutiful and her house is immaculate. She takes every
opportunity to point out my shortcomings, and often I find myself
crying over her sly comments at my expense. I try and keep my
temper, and have tried to tell her how she makes me feel, but to no
avail.
Any advice?
Doreen, Chelsea

Margaret replies; Charles Dickens once wrote "have a heart that
never hardens, and a temper that never tires, and a touch that never
hurts". This is a piece of flimsy advice that I urge you to ignore in its
entirety. Roll up your sleeves and punch her lights out.
Sometimes it is right to put up a fight.

Sometimes it is right to put up a fight.

I am a well travelled and experienced gentleman, however being
held captive by a pair of maniacs who were orchestrating a plot to bring
down our government was an entirely new and unwelcome position to
find oneself in. And so, I concluded, I must put up a fight.

My public needed me.

There was, however, one thought that really crushed my spirit; the absence of my column from the pages of The Clarion. It was more than just a newspaper column, it was a public service! I felt for my poor, poor deprived readership who had relied on my every written word. Those poor people who would now stumble through life at a loss without my wise, wise words.

How would they know where to eat?

I remained petrified of Mildred Mason.

The morning after Mason's terrifying disclosure, she had entered the cellar, her body encased in the rubber she so enjoyed, but this time without the mask. Seeing her shiny form, with her greying tufts of hair sprouting wildly from her pale head, her face a picture of grim serenity, was the most terrifying apparition imaginable. A strange, long thin smile was fixed on her wretched face. She was alone, and did not resume her usual position on the opposite wall. Instead, she chose to stand unnervingly still against the closed door where she stared at me coldly.

After a while I spoke, as calmly as I could.

'Go away, Mildred.' I croaked.

The woman didn't flinch, speak nor move in any way, but instead continued to simply watch me, her thin arms folded. I dared not turn away from the woman in fear of what she could do. I could almost read her thoughts as she appraised me in what must have been calculated contemplation. What was it Mason had said? She lives to kill. Like a cat with a spider.

Eventually, much to my relief, she slipped away, locking the door behind her.

Mason fed me with bits and bobs.

Since his confession he appeared to have warmed to my company. As if he had nothing to lose, he unlocked the floodgates on stories of his life and I was forced to sit through his nonsense as I nibbled hungrily on Mildred Mason's horribly wet cucumber sandwiches and stale rock buns.

Some of what he said was curiously engaging, titbits of gossip from Westminster that would have kept Beryl Baxter's society column in raptures for some time. However just when his words were getting interesting he would flip from calm discussion to ranting endlessly about the treatment he had received at the hands of other political parties, and how the government was weakening its military grip for fear of another war.

He truly believed that the war had been a missed opportunity to unite with the Fuhrer and share in world domination, and sat for some time in the little alcove behind me, ruffling though papers under a desk lamp which cast light on the swastikas decorating the walls and ceiling.

The sight made my stomach lurch with a fresh wave of nausea.

He revealed much more about his ridiculous plot to bomb parliament, and had learned from mistakes made by his predecessor in this plot Mr Fawkes by having anybody linked to the plan murdered. The man was certainly insane enough to go through with such an absurd idea . The determination and conviction in his voice told me as much. He had his plans clearly laid out. The explosive device had been designed to be small enough to fit in a briefcase. Mason had asked me, with pride in his voice, what right minded person would suspect a member of parliament carrying a briefcase?

Once inside the building he had access to the Commons Chamber, where the device would rest, forgotten, beneath a bench until detonation. The force from the blast would destroy the very heart of the building, and the resulting fire bring the whole government to its knees.

The timing of this had been carefully considered, as the Home Secretary was Mason's target. St John Townsend was scheduled to deliver his report on immigration.

'It's perfect timing,' Mason had explained. 'The fat fool is due to present his nonsense before the close of day. The place will burn to its foundations. People will recall the spectacle for centuries to come!'

'But the people inside-' I began.

'They will have the privilege of expiring at an historic moment.'

'And what about me?' I said, attempting to be brave despite the odds. 'I could stop you, you know.'

The man chuckled irritatingly lightly, snatching the empty plate from my lap and gliding to the door.

'I don't think so. I have Mildred, my secret weapon. She will… dispose of you, and meet me by the river. We have contingency plans at the ready. Plan A is to mourn the loss of our country's leaders and publicly condemn the violence, while preparing myself for some deft political manoeuvring. I shall introduce a new leadership with a fresh vision for our country.'

'And Plan B?' I had enquired.

'We have bookings for a flight, should we be incriminated in any way.'

Mason then moved closer, leaning in on me.

'Don't worry, Mr Edgar, I like you. Because I like you I have eased Mildred off, just a little. It will be the chains for you.'

The chains?

'A much more dignified exit for such a perfect house guest. Bound with heavy chains and then a quick plunge into the cold river. All over very quickly, I assure you. Mildred was a little put out, but as I have told you before, I have the final say in this house.'

The heavy door swung shut behind him, leaving me alone to ponder my fate.

The following evening Mildred Mason came at me in the cellar.

She set at me with tough ropes, deftly binding my wrists and ankles before shoving me up the stairs and out into the cool night air. I stumbled most of the way, my legs unused to the weight of my body, and practically fell into the boot of the car that sat just outside the front doorway. Thick, heavy chains were tied around my ankles. Heaven knows what the rough rusty metal was doing to my trouser legs.

It was all very undignified.

At first I struggled, but it was no use, the jerking movements only exacerbated my exhaustion. I lay powerlessly on my side, my cheek pressed against the coarse material of the car's interior, as the car boot slammed shut leaving me in a petrol-stinking darkness. I found myself cursing silently in frustration.

No self-respecting connoisseur of fine dining should be treated in such a manner.

The Masons had treated me like just another piece of luggage, and I felt the weight of the car shift as they heaved several suitcases into the backseats, in case they needed to flee the country should anything go wrong. I was to remain in the boot for some time before I felt the car shake a little as they seated themselves up front. I assumed that Mildred Mason would be driving, to drop off her husband near Westminster before moving on to dispose of me.

The chains were surprisingly heavy, pulling at my ankles. I was barely able to shift my feet an inch. Although my hands had been bound, I was pleased to find that I was able to pick at each wrist with my fingers, which I continued to do as the car swung out of the driveway and headed into town.

In the darkness I mulled over how I was to die. Weak and unwashed, bound like a wild animal and left to sink to the depths of the stinking Thames, where I would rest forever in its current. I never could swim, even as a child. Curiously, as I lay there picking at my bindings, I felt a wave of calmness overpower my fear. I would not die. I would simply not allow it!

We drove onwards for some time.

Anxiety bubbled up again as we came to a bumpy stop and I felt Ercot Mason vacate the vehicle after a few words to his wife. He would be setting off for parliament, a bowler-hatted public servant with briefcase and umbrella, on a mission of murder, and I was left alone with his accomplice, the dreadful Mildred.

I had no doubt that she intended to kill me, and was most certainly going to enjoy it too.

It felt as though the binds on my wrists were loosening a little, and my heart leapt with the first feelings of success. I picked ceaselessly at the rope with my nails as the car ploughed onwards through the city. It was as we slowed a little on an uneven road and then reversed, nearing our destination, that the ropes at my wrist gave way. The relief I felt while pulling them away from my sore wrists was strong, but I did not pause before pulling wildly at the chains around my ankles. They were bound tight.

Suddenly the car stopped with a jolt.

For a minute we were still, and then again we reversed slowly, the car bumping over uneven ground before coming to a complete halt. I heard the driver's door slam shut, as Mildred Mason made her way around the vehicle to dispose of me.

The chains would not move, so tight and unwilling were the knots. I was too late, I would never get them off in time. The sharp sting of the metal rubbed at my ankles. There was only one thing I could do. With barely a thought I shuffled down to the very end of the boot and brought up my knees. This proved difficult, as the weight pulled down on my ankles, but I summoned up all my strength. Now was my only chance to act, or I would be dead.

It felt like an age before the car boot was opened. I lay there wondering what Mildred was up to. Perhaps scanning the area for safety, or waiting for a potential witness to move along, even.

And then, the car boot was raised.

With a roar that seemed to burst from deep within me, and despite feeling incredible resistance, I lifted the dead weight of my bound feet and thrust my legs out of the car towards the sky. I must have hit Mildred Mason straight on, for there was a cry and for just a second I saw surprise on her pale face as my feet and the chains pushed against her chest. She disappeared. The car had been backed immediately onto the river, and her scream faded and then was swallowed by a splash.

I had done it!

I found myself cursing down into the darkness.

'And your rock buns are most unpleasant!' I hollered, dizzy with victory.

The weight at my ankles allowed me to sit up with ease, and I found myself with my bound feet dangling over the side of the car boot. I looked up and around in a moment of glory. It was an overcast evening, and much cooler than in recent weeks, and there was precious little moonlight to aid my plight. The car had come to a stop with the boot just inches from the descent, where the black swelling river moved a good ten feet beneath me. I was suddenly aware of my position, with barely a foothold of land before the ground gave way sharply down into the water. I could hear fierce gasps and angered splashes coming from the darkness below.

I eased myself gently forwards until I could feel the crumbling earth beneath my socks, and was careful not to let go of the car. One slip, and I would fall, joining Mildred Mason in the dark water below. If I did fall I had no doubt that the weights on my legs would inevitably drag me down to my death. As it was, the chains seemed to be pulling me down towards the edge as I eased myself, inch by inch, towards the side of the car. For a while I sat, hugging the sides of the vehicle and summing up all the strength I could muster.

And then I stood with a grunt, both hands clasping the car tightly as I swung around, dangling perilously over the water for a second before pushing myself aside. I felt the earth crumble and give way beneath my feet as I fell in a rather undignified heap onto the grassy bank at the side of the car. I lay panting in relief, safe from the pull of my chains.

There was, however, no time for resting. At any moment Mildred Mason could find a way up and out of the river, and that she would be determined to make me pay for my attack. And then there was Mason himself, heading to Westminster with his deadly briefcase.

There was no doubt that the man must be stopped.

After a number of shambling hops over the uneven embankment, and with something of a burst of joy, I felt the chains loosening. I tugged relentlessly, lifting one leg after another as best as I possibly could, the jagged edges of metal scratching along and, in places, cutting deep into my flesh.

Suddenly one leg was out, the chains slipped away and I was free.

I cantered for a few steps, my calves feeling lighter than ever, and then forced myself to stop and take in my surroundings. A number of warehouses spread out across the riverside to my left, each standing dark and empty. A long brick wall curled around to my right. Ahead of me, through a gap in the wall, I caught a fleeting sight of a passing car, and forged ahead towards the road. The rocky ground tore at my socks, but by this point I was well past caring for the sanctity of my apparel.

As I approached the wall, the rumble of distant traffic sounded like a gift from heaven. Civilisation! I made the mistake of looking back as I was clambering over the brickwork. Besides the car, silhouetted by the shimmering river, stood the skeletal form of Mildred Mason, watching me from afar. She was not running, merely standing erect, her dripping fists clenched at her side. My stomach churned with fear at the sight of the woman, and I ploughed on desperately, only coming to a halt as I reached the roadside.

The road was perilously empty.

My eyes scanned furiously for a car or even a bike to wave down.

It seemed, for a moment, that everyone had vanished leaving me alone in the darkness with Mildred Mason once more. I would have run, but could not see in which direction I should head.

I jumped at the sight of two beams of light in the distance, and took uncertain steps towards the headlights, waving my weary arms as much as I could. It was as it approached that my heart gave a leap - it was a police car! What divine luck had sent this my way? Finally, something was happening in my favour!

The car slowed and stopped just yards from where I stood, and I nearly cried out wildly. Instead I swallowed my sobs. As the driver got out I shook myself, there was no time for tears, no matter how relieved I was to see the man approach.

The officer was young, far too young to be on the force, but nevertheless he sported a neat uniform and was holding his helmet underarm as a headless ghost might hold it's head. Looking at me with careful suspicion, he stepped up with a practiced air of formality. His hair was red and a little wavy, his skin pale and spotless.

'Good evening, Sir-' he began.

'There's no time to talk!' I snapped, grasping the young man's shoulders. 'We must move fast, we cannot waste a moment. There is danger! Grave danger!' The words that tumbled from my mouth felt more confused and garbled than I intended, and I had to concentrate to speak with as much clarity and urgency as possible.

'Sir-'

'People will die if we don't go immediately. Do you have a radio?' I glanced over my shoulder, half expecting to see Mildred Mason gaining on us, but there was nothing there except the darkness of shadows.

'Sir, I am off duty, on my way back-'

'There will be no off-duty tonight, Constable! Are we near Westminster?'

'Well, not far, but-'

'We must go, immediately, in the car - to Parliament!'

The young officer eyed my ragged clothes with an infuriating calmness before pulling out his pocket book with a sigh.

'May I take your name, Sir?' he said steadily.

'Payton,' I said, 'Payton Edgar. Now we must go!'

'Peter...'

'Payton! Payton Edgar!'

'And where do you live, Mr Edgar?' He had conjured up a little pencil and begun to scribble in his little white book. I moved around him and made for his car. At my sudden movement he called after me.

'Now wait just a minute, Sir. You are behaving very oddly. I'm sorry - I will have to take you in.'

I stopped in the car doorway and eyed the officer, who clearly had no time for the ranting of this disheveled stranger. There had been no sign of other cars on the road. Had there been, I would happily have dismissed the policeman and seized another, less argumentative, ride.

I left the doorway and stepped up close to him.

'What is your name, young man?' I asked with a careful superiority.

He hesitated.

'Constable Woodcock.'

'Now Woodcock, you must listen to me. I am Payton Edgar of Clarendon Street, Pimlico. Don't write this down! Just listen! I am a journalist for the London Evening Clarion. I move in social circles that a young lad like you has only read about in print. Now, every word I am telling you is true. I have been kidnapped by a pair of revolutionaries who at this very moment are making their way through London with a bomb - yes, a bomb - and a plan to blow up the Palace of Westminster. Their plan is to assassinate the Home Secretary, Townsend! If we do nothing, people will certainly die. All I ask is that you take me to Westminster, immediately. If I am right, we could stop this terrible thing from happening. If I am wrong, you can arrest me for wasting your time - but not until we have tried to stop the very heart of our government from destruction and innocent people from being murdered!'

'Sir-'

'If you do not believe me, people will die. If you trust me and I am wrong, you will have lost nothing. It is your choice, Officer Woodcock. Your choice.'

I held in my breath for just a moment, but had to release it and pant a little, for this was my longest speech in days. Young Woodcock stood still for a while in contemplation.

'Get in the car,' he said sternly, and made his way to the driving seat.

I called to him over the warm bonnet.

'You will not regret this, I promise.'

Soon we were on our way, and I had watched the darkness of the docks disappearing behind me, eyes searching for Mildred Mason's dripping form in vain. I had convinced the young man to sound his siren, but still could not get him to go as fast as I desired. As it was, we were only about ten minutes ride from Parliament.

It was the longest ten minutes of my life.

It was as we moved alongside the river just a short stroll from our destination that I caught sight of Mason, his bold, arrogant strides unmistakable as he made his way through Victoria Tower Gardens. He head was high and he was swinging the briefcase slightly as if all it held were pens and paper.

'Stop the car!' I screamed, and a startled Woodcock did just as he was told.

I leapt out and bounded in Mason's direction, shoeless.

Chapter VI

In which Payton Edgar fights alone

Young Woodcock followed after me as I tottered towards the Thames.

Ercot Mason was looking out over the river as I approached, and did not spot me until I was on top of him. Without a thought my hands reached out for the briefcase, and, just as the man pulled back, I seized the handle and his wrist and pulled hard. We entered into a rather nasty struggle.

Mason, it turns out, was a consummate actor. Years of political fibs and insincerities can do that to a man.

'What the devil?' he cried out as we tussled. My fingers had woven firmly around the case's handle and I refused to let go. The idea that the contraption could perhaps detonate at any moment did not cross my mind as perhaps it should have. As Mason pulled the briefcase in close to his chest, I yanked it back in my direction. We circled for a minute, rather like street dancers on the pavement. I could sense Woodcock standing, perplexed, out of the corner of my eye.

Mason addressed the young officer.

'For God's sake, man, help me!' he cried. 'This person is insane!'

Poor Woodcock was at a loss, baffled at the sight of two grown men struggling like children over a chocolate bar in front of him, and he didn't move at first. Finding a strength I had never known before I gave the case a few good hard tugs and saw Mason's eyes open wide in fear, his teeth grinding.

With one final tug, the case flew from his grasp - it was mine!

I wasted no time. I circled on the spot once, twice, and then tossed it with all my might into the air. The three of us stood motionless and watched the briefcase fly up over the river and then plummet down with a muted splash some way from where we stood. I struggled to catch my breath as the case bobbed calmly in the waters. The relief!

A curious silence had fallen, broken only as Mason approached Woodcock in fury, his face crimson and a vein on his temple bulging.

'What the devil are you playing at, Officer? I have just been assaulted! Arrest this man, *immediately*!'

The pale constable looked over to me, speechless. A small crowd had gathered and amongst them were two more police officers in domed helmets, one of which, clearly an older and more experienced officer than Woodcock, pushed forwards.

'Do you know who I am?' my foe spat at the onlookers, rather like a street performer. 'I am The Right Honourable Ercot Mason, Member of Parliament, and I have just been attacked - assaulted - by this, this... vagrant here.' He pointed a finger of accusation in my direction. Breathless and exhausted, I could barely speak in my defence. I felt the eyes of our onlookers examining my shoddy attire.

'Woodcock!' I panted, and said pleadingly, '-what did I tell you?'

'A plethora of lies by the look of it!' blurted Mason, his nostrils flaring. 'Officers, I insist this drunken madman be arrested immediately!' The larger of the policemen moved over to my side as Mason continued to rant. 'I have never been so savagely attacked in all my life!' He pointed out to the river wildly. 'This lunatic threw my briefcase - government property - into the Thames! Top government papers were in that case, lost forever thanks to this... this senseless maniac!'

'In that briefcase was a bomb! This man is dangerous!' I growled, myself pointing a finger. I was so tired, and so very weak, it was hard to get my words out. I may have slurred a little. 'Dangerous! In that case is an explosive, to destroy Parliament! I was kidnapped! Locked up in a cellar! Fed with stale buns and soggy cucumber sandwiches!' I looked from face to face, the officer's expressions changing from confusion, concern and then to pity.

'Alright then, Sir,' the officer said in a sing-song tone as he rested his hand on my shoulder. 'Suppose you come with us and tell us all about it.'

I nodded but then stopped myself. They didn't believe me!

'It is the truth!' I said. 'Ask young Woodcock here!'

The senior officer looked over at his young colleague, his eyebrows raised. Woodcock swallowed, and shrugged. 'I picked him up over near the water works, Sir, talking about an assassination attempt. He seems to think... well, he is a bit confused, it seems to me.'

'Woodcock!' I gasped, betrayed. 'There is a bomb in that case! Please believe me! Look, it will explode at any minute!'

For a short while we all looked to the water, but there was no sound except for the gentle lapping of waves against the bank. The case was out of sight. Before I knew it the crowd was dispersing, and I was being led away in shame. I was surely on my way to being bundled in a police box like some common criminal. I stole a look over my shoulder to where Mason was playing the part of victim for all he was worth, dusting off his clothes unnecessarily and shaking his head in mock distress. The smug look on his face gave me a fresh spurt of rage, and I tore free from the policeman's grasp.

The man started as I approached and grabbed his lapel tightly.

'I will stop you Mason!' I grunted, holding my pose for a second. And then I stood aside, once again pointing an accusatory finger.

'This man is a murderer!' I called out.

'Get this unstable vagabond out of my sight!' Mason called, playing the exasperated victim with aplomb. I was hauled away.

In the darkness, Mason's briefcase sank into the murky waters of the Thames.

PART FOUR

Chapter I

In which Payton Edgar receives some suspicious news

London Evening Clarion (late edition)
'COMMONS COMMOTION: M.P. ATTACKED BY LUNATIC'
A man has been charged following a brutal attack on Sir Ercot Mason,
Member of Parliament for the Hemel Hempstead constituency. The inci-
dent occurred yesterday evening as Mr Mason was arriving for an
evening session at parliament. The politician, a former Grenadier
Guardsman, required medical attention at the site but did not require
hospitalisation. It is thought that the assailant has a history of mental
instability and is currently being held at Scotland Yard.

Scotland Yard.

I had been offered no additional clothing to cover my rags, not even shoes or slippers for my feet. I must have looked a sorry character, wrapped in an itchy blanket and locked away like a petty criminal. My new cell was almost as uncomfortable as the dungeon back at the Mason house, and the irony of the situation I found myself in would have been amusing were it not so disagreeable.

After some time, I was taken to a stuffy interview room where, to my horror, a familiar figure plonked himself before me, a smirk on his fat face.

I had seen enough of Chief Inspector Standing earlier that year, and the man had done little to endear me towards him. Indeed, he had proven himself to be something of an imbecile, with no talent for investigation whatsoever. I had, however, got one over on him by thwarting a

167

particularly nasty murderer. Unfortunately for me, I was certain that the officer would never forget it. His attitude was as ugly as his wiry moustache, through which he was openly smirking as he drummed an irritating tattoo on the tabletop with disgustingly unkempt fingers.

'Good evening, Mr Edgar,' he grumbled.

'Standing,' I grunted, pointedly dropping his title. 'I have to say that I'm surprised to see you. A lunatic vagabond? Bit of a petty case for a man of your rank, surely?'

'I saw your name and couldn't resist, Edgar. Been getting yourself into a bit of a fluster, I hear. Some very peculiar behaviour indeed!'

I mulled over my options; to remain silent and risk false judgement, or to explain myself and risk sounding at best delusional, at worst, insane?

I opted for the latter.

The story, when blurted out in its entirety, was indeed a strange tale, and were it not for the evidence of my filthy, tattered clothing I would forgive any savvy officer for disbelieving at first. But Standing was having none of it.

'Double murders? Kidnapping? A gunpowder plot?' he mused, an infuriating twinkle in his eye. 'The ramblings of a madman!'

'It's the truth, Standing. The Masons-'

'Mr Edgar, you have said your piece, now please allow me a response.' His tired, pitying eyes blinked with barely concealed impatience. 'It may interest you to know that I am well acquainted with Mr and Mrs Mason, for they hold Summer cocktails in their rear garden every year, all in aid of the constabulary. I have seen their beautiful country cottage and admired their plush and plump soft furnishings. I too have sampled Mrs Mason's delightful scones. A very pleasant afternoon was had by all, and there was absolutely no evidence of murder, devilment or foul play of any kind. Mason has also been instrumental in the funding of a project to recruit delinquent youngsters to The Force-'

'Search the house!' I spat. 'Ask to see the cellar!'

'We will do no such thing! The mere act alone would cause a sensation of the worst kind! Besides, having a cellar isn't an offence, Mr Edgar. You seem to forget that Ercot Mason, the man *you* attacked, is the victim in all this. And poor Officer Woodcock. You made a prize fool out of a promising young officer, you know. Well I won't let you make a fool out of me. Drop the nonsense. You have no evidence whatsoever to substantiate your tall story.'

'They were planning to escape to South America, if they were caught out! There must be-'

'The Masons have absolutely no intention of going anywhere, Edgar. Ercot Mason will, no doubt, have a full diary after this incident, as you can imagine. Your woeful attack will only raise his public profile, of course.'

'Then what about the briefcase? The bomb was in the briefcase!'

'Sank without trace, I'm afraid. But then it would, wouldn't it? Laden down with top government papers. You are in a great deal of trouble, Edgar. Violent assault carries a heavy sentence - you do know that?'

His words were chilling, and yet that unbearable smirk was still there under the moustache. I inspected it with distaste. It was the most unkempt moustache I had ever seen, more suited to accompany a dustpan than an upper lip. Standing's words, *a heavy sentence*, echoed in my mind.

Payton Edgar in prison? My heart stopped at the very thought of it. How would I possibly survive?

I hadn't asked Irving to stump up the cash for my bail, nor would I thank him.

Even the trauma I had suffered at the hands of Ercot Mason couldn't distract me from the way my so-called friend had spoken to me after his exhibition. In some ways, somewhere in my heart, I blamed him for picking at me and forcing me to act with secrecy over the whole Pouche affair. He was suspiciously calm when collecting me from the station, adopting an air of quiet confusion as we left Scotland Yard to hail a black cab.

We sat in the back of the cab in silence, and it was only as we neared Pimlico that he spoke.

'The exhibition's been pretty successful, all in all.'

I gave no reply. I hadn't asked.

'The portrait *"Pomposity"* was a particular favourite.'

I felt that I had to answer this, but was careful to keep any warmth from my reply.

'That's good, I suppose.'

It was a minute or so before Irving spoke again, but when he did his words were ill-chosen and spoken with the hushed tones of a parent to a naughty child.

'Crikey, Payton! Brawling in the street! What on earth were you thinking?'

I studied his face for a moment. That questioning look was all too familiar, but there was something else, something new. There was a look in his eyes that I had never witnessed before; an abhorrent, unwelcome trace of pity.

Having laid myself bare to the Inspector with terrible results, I was not of a mind to repeat myself, and so I said nothing in reply. I simply turned my head back to the window. It was clear that I was to be disbelieved by all, even those closest to me, and could only benefit from holding my tongue. We arrived outside my house, and I was over the threshold by the time Irving had finished paying the driver. As I closed the front door with a slam behind me, I caught his cry.

'Payton wait-!'

I made it to the bathroom without stirring Miss Kemp or Aunt Elizabeth, where I quickly shed my ruined clothes and bathed, letting the warm water wash away my tears.

The days grumbled on and I remained behind closed doors.

Grace Kemp tentatively knocked at my bedroom door and asked if there was anything she could do, and I sent her away sharply. Despite this, she brought food and drink to my door with a sweet, silent efficiency. Miss Kemp was a proficient cook, and I ate what I could dutifully, despite feeling an overwhelming lack of appetite.

I wondered what she understood about the trauma I had been through, and on top of that, what she had told Aunt Elizabeth about it all. I wondered, but didn't ask. That look of pity so unwelcome in Irving had also been detectable in her clear blue eyes.

I have always kept a secret cache of savings hidden in the old hoover bag at the back of my wardrobe. Over the years it had become habit to stash away the odd note, and the bag was stuffed. One morning, I raided this and handed over a bundle of notes to a surprised Miss Kemp. I requested that she purchase a television set for my Aunt's bedroom.

She was indifferent to the notes in her hand, but expressed surprise at the request.

'For her bedroom? A television set?' she coughed in disbelief. 'What's brought this on?'

'I need not elaborate!' I replied dismissively. 'There should be enough cash there for a good model and the license it requires.'

As Miss Kemp had put it, what had *"brought this on"* was day after day trapped in a miserable cell at the Mason's place. I had then been similarly trapped at Scotland Yard, and now here I was again, trapped in my own bedroom. I understood my Aunt's boredom only too well.

Miss Kemp had been careful to hide the Clarion on the day after my arrest. I had been expecting a report of my shenanigans, however, and insisted that I see the edition. She had handed the paper over with reluctance.

Commons commotion indeed!

And so I was branded a lunatic in print. What was it Inspector Standing had said? *The ramblings of a madman.* I stared down at the article for some time, my heart broken.

They would all be laughing at me, the whole sorry tribe that formed the Raqs Sharqi gang. I could picture Lord and Lady Follett taking breakfast with toast and marmalade, nodding down at the newspaper and telling each other how disgracefully I had acted. I pictured Sir Maurice sipping at a whisky in his dressing room and chuckling over my downfall.

No doubt Ercot Mason had told them first-hand how ridiculously I had behaved.

The only saving grace was that I had not been named in the piece, a fact I noted with some gratitude. Whether Bilborough did not believe that I was guilty or whether he was only trying to preserve the good name of his newspaper, it didn't matter to me. I know very well how mud sticks, and how many a fine career in the press has been ruined by gossip or scandal.

Any warm feelings I might have had towards my employer evaporated, however, when I received a typed letter in the post one morning. Due to recent circumstances, it said indifferently, my association with the newspaper was to cease immediately, my contract terminated. There were no words of support or concern, and no thanks for my years of fine work. It was signed simply "T. Bilborough".

And so, *"Payton's Plate"* and *"Dear Margaret"* were to be no more. This was a move the young manager would surely come to regret. His shortsightedness would only mean a drop in sales, that much was clear. I angrily filed Bilborough's cruel words in the waste paper basket and sat for a long time in silent contemplation. My anger eventually subsided, only to be replaced by a far worse feeling; *loneliness*.

The doorbell rang, and I jumped.

Miss Kemp was out shopping and I challenged myself to answer it. What was I afraid of? That Ercot Mason would come calling? Or, worse still, Mildred Mason, wielding a blood stained rolling pin? Was that at all likely?

I made myself go to the door after the second ring of the bell.

On the doorstep was a squat, bespectacled, rabbit-like lady in a drab brown mac, peddling some charitable nonsense. An unusual sense of relief had washed over me at the sight of the stranger's buck teeth, and I stood for some time as she told me all about unwanted dogs, cats and rabbits. I felt a curious sense of achievement upon answering the door, but soon snapped out of my reverie and sent her on her way.

The fact I had been brave enough to face the outside world gave me a new strength, and soon I shook off my loneliness, gathered my things and took myself around to Irving's house. He would surely have had time to reflect on those badly chosen words he had said after rescuing me from the police station, and I rapped on his door ready for the apology I was bound to receive.

The door opened surprisingly quickly, for he was already showing two young gentlemen out of his house. Both wore strange fitted suits, too tight at the waist and too short in the leg. Both had unruly hair, and both were smoking thin papers of tobacco. I stood aside.

Irving made no introductions, but waved the men on their way.

'Hello, Payton!' was all he had to say once they had skipped off down the street. I stood still, rooted to the pavement.

'And who were they?'

'A couple of friends, from the academy.'

I drew in breath. 'Must you associate with beatniks and trendsetters, Irving? Fraternising with lank-haired youths? I cannot imagine what you have to talk about-'

'We have been debating the legacy of Expressionism on the contemporary art scene,' came the swift reply.

'Really?'

'Indeed. It's invigorating to debate things, Payton. You should join us, make friends-'

'I don't need friends,' I snapped.

'Everybody needs friends, Payton!'

'I have you,' I pointed out, archly.

'You need more than just me and your plants to talk to, Payton.'

I swallowed. He knew that I had been known to chat to my begonias, but had never used it as an insult before. Must we fight again?

'Grace popped in earlier,' he went on.

'Oh really? To debate the legacy of Expressionism on modern art?'

Irving ignored my jibe, but wasn't about to invite me in.

'She tells me you are buying Aunt Elizabeth a television set for her room! What brought that on?'

'That's no business of yours,' I soberly replied. He bit his lip.

'Mmm. You are behaving very oddly, Payton. I'm concerned, worried that you have...'

He let his words trail away.

'Worried that I have *what*?'

Irving thinned his eyes and I gave him time to think. And then, as if he couldn't have made matters worse, he went on in a highhanded, patronising tone.

'Have you calmed down, Payton?'

'Calmed down?'

'Dropped the whole Mason nonsense?'

'What?'

'You know what you get like-'

'Tell me!'

'Come inside, have a cup of tea.'

'No! I don't want a cup of tea, Irving. I want you to tell me what you mean!' I had balled my fists at my side.

Irving went on, mentioning Ercot Mason and my penchant for becoming obsessed - obsessed! - with people of whom I didn't approve. I couldn't believe what I was hearing. I held out a wide palm to break his speech.

'That's quite enough, Irving! You clearly haven't time for my take on things, for the truth! Don't bother to call on me anymore. I'm going home to talk to my begonias! At least they don't question my sanity!'

I turned on my heel, but my dramatic exit was ruined somewhat.

A patrol car had slid up to the pavement, and it stopped with a clank of the brake. The door opened and Constable Woodcock got out, fixing his helmet to his head with a frown. I bit my lip as he approached, and said nothing. I hadn't expected to see the man again so soon, and certainly hadn't prepared any words by way of apology or explanation for my behaviour.

To his credit, Woodcock remained stiff and professional.

'Good morning, Mr Edgar. I was just on my way to see you. Not interrupting, I hope?'

'No, Constable. I was just heading home, if you'd like to come in for a cup of tea?' Irving heard my words but made no move to close his door. Instead he addressed the officer.

'Is anything wrong, Constable?'

'Quite the opposite,' Woodcock replied before lifting his chin to address me. 'Thank you for the offer of tea, Mr Edgar, but I have to get on. I just wanted to inform you that Ercot Mason has dropped all of the charges against you.'

For a second I was stupefied.

'I beg your pardon?'

'A charitable move,' Woodcock continued with some care. 'I believe he's hoping that we can all move on from... the unfortunate incident. To set it to rest.'

'Well, that's good news!' Irving chirped behind of me.

Woodcock was looking at me with a thoughtful gaze. He clearly thought he was addressing the lunatic mentioned in the Clarion, a madman who needed soothing before he struck again. Fury bubbled within, and I struggled to find the words I'd need to make my escape. A sigh escaped my lips.

'Thank you very much for informing me, Constable Woodcock,' I uttered woodenly before turning my back on both Irving and the policeman. I sauntered as casually as I could along the street, and let myself in

173

as quick as I could.

Once inside, I leaned heavily against the door and mulled over what I had just learned.

Why would Mason wish to drop the charges against me? The man must be desperate to brand me a violent madman, and what better way than to have me charged? And yet he was letting me go, without fanfare. *Why?* I should perhaps have felt relieved, pleased even. And yet I didn't. I felt suspicious. Suspicious and fearful.

Something was very wrong.

Chapter II

In which Payton Edgar enjoys his elevenses

The London Evening Clarion (early edition)
NO FATALITIES IN TUGBOAT EXPLOSION
An inquest has begun into a large explosion on a Tugboat on Monday morning. The vessel was travelling west, just along from the Putney Bridge when the incident occurred, resulting in minor injuries for the skipper. The blast could have been much worse as a number of small gas canisters had been a part of the cargo. The cause is yet unknown, however it is suspected that a pipe or cigarette is to blame. There have been similar reports of cigarette-related incidents on vessels in recent months, a spokesman from Scotland Yard has pointed out.

Something reported in the pages of the Clarion the following Tuesday would have caused me to sit up, had the reporter been less inept and more detailed in their report. As it was, I passed my eyes over it mindlessly and then moved on to mourn the absence of my columns.

Unbeknownst to the incompetent reporter, the blast was absolutely nothing to do with a pipe or cigarette. What had actually caused the explosion was a small briefcase, bobbing in the pull of the tide.

The days passed and the summer gave way to autumn.

This has always been a favourite season of mine, yet I was in no mood to admire the yellows and browns of the trees, nor to kick at the leaves in St James's Park. In fact, I found myself steering clear of any wide open spaces, as if away from the city crowds I was in some way more open and vulnerable. But to what? The whole ridiculous chapter with the Raqs Sharqi Club was over, just like the hot Summer itself.

I went through those first few weeks of September in something of a dream. Without the rhythm and routine that producing my columns provided, I felt more than a little lost. I had no dining experiences to anticipate, and no reason to put pen to paper. Irving and I remained estranged, and I didn't even bother talking to my plants.

I had nothing to say.

It was Beryl Baxter who pulled me from the doldrums and she did so with an invitation to a function. Beryl didn't care what I had or hadn't done - all she wanted was an arm to hold and someone to fetch her drinks.

She had pushed a note, hastily written, through my letterbox. I almost declined, but then had a little talk with myself and decided that it was about time I stepped out and at least tried to enjoy myself. Besides, one does not lightly dismiss an offer of champagne flowing gratis in the comfort of the Mayvere Hotel. Having been given a number of days notice, I confirmed my appointment with a similarly brief note which I left with Cockney Guy at the front desk of the Clarion. Following my abrupt dismissal, I wasn't about to enter the miserable place.

These first steps towards normality motivated me to scratch an itch, and I arranged to meet the young French girl from Sebastien Ferrier's restaurant at Mario's Café. I felt that I owed her something of an explanation.

The day was a bright one, the air crisp, and, for the first time in a while, I had set out in relatively good spirits. I sauntered happily along Bond Street then through to Saville Row, however - most unlike me - I failed to purchase a single item. My favourite tailors, Cromley's, was closed, a note at the window announcing a family bereavement. I cursed my bad luck, and could only hope that it wasn't Cromley senior who had popped his clogs, as very few tailors had his deft eye for bespoke fittings.

I ploughed on through a number of establishments, my high spirits steadily ebbing with each bristly sales assistant. After leaving one particular shop in a funk, I collided against an unseen telephone box and bashed my left knee painfully against it's side.

Where were all the blasted boxes coming from? It seemed that with every year the gigantic telephone kiosks multiplied, littering the streets with their shining red ridiculousness. What were they needed for anyway? Should I wish to make a call, I would return home and dial accordingly. Very few calls had to be made there and then, so why ruin the streets with giant upended red coffins?

'What if you forgot your shopping list?' Irving had once dared to ask, in praise of the kiosks.

'Then I should use my imagination, Irving!' came my swift reply.

'And what if you were running late for a meeting?'

'Then I would be late!'

'And what if you were feeling unwell? Or had been the victim of a pickpocket?'

'Then I would signal a passing bobby! We survived quite well without telephone boxes before, Irving! You won't win this argument!'

There simply was no reason to be by a telephone at all hours of the day. And yet kiosks were sprouting up like weeds through the cracks in the pavements. I kicked at the structure angrily before moving on.

Soon I arrived at Mario's Café.

As usual, the windows of the eatery were thick with steam. It was a little after eleven, and the place was lively enough. Therese was there already, seated in a spot that I wouldn't have chosen, rather too close to the serving hatch. She looked nervous, and I did my best to put her at ease. She had a mug of coffee in between her hands, and I encouraged her to order something sweet.

'No thank you,' was her timid reply.

'Oh, but you must, Therese. It's time for elevenses! When did you last eat? What time was breakfast?'

'Oh, at eight or eight thirty…'

'Then I insist!' I gesticulated in Mario's direction and ordered a pot of tea for one and two slices of the Victoria sponge. As usual, it was a long time coming and we had almost finished our chat by the time our cakes arrived.

'I do hope that you didn't mind my calling?' I asked gently. 'I felt that I owed it to you, to explain a little about what happened…to Fabien Pouche.'

'You know what happened?' she asked, her face brightening, and I began to tell her all about my misadventures. I left out some of the more unsavoury notes, and only stopped for a moment as a rather grim little teapot pot was placed before me, with equally unimpressive cup, saucer and milk jug. This was eventually followed by two generous slices of the Victoria sponge. Therese pushed hers about her plate after having only a few meagre mouthfuls. I polished mine off, along with my story.

'Thank you so much, Mr Edgar, for thinking of me,' she said with her sweet gallic lilt. 'I must go now.'

'But you haven't told me how things are for you - what's the latest on that rat Ferrier?'

'Rat is the right word! I have left, I have no job. He touch me, I say *no*, he say *yes*, I go.' She put all this very simply when in fact it must have been anything but. 'I look for another job.'

'Allow me to recommend you for a position - Harvey's Restaurant, just off The Strand. I hear they are hiring. Have you heard of it? No matter, I can put in a good word for you, if you like?'

'That would be wonderful!' she chimed, and when she left she was still smiling. It was nice to be able to do something for the girl, and I only hoped I could butter up the Maître-d' at Harvey's sufficiently on my next visit.

I was left alone at the table, and took a moment to contemplate certain things. I had the evening edition of the Clarion on my lap but was not of a mind to read. Instead I drained the pot and gazed at the swirls of milk I had produced in my teacup.

Suddenly I felt the hairs on my neck bristle, and I was immediately on edge.

Just what had set this off was unclear, and my eyes scanned the room. A tall figure had entered the café, draped in shawl and hood. There was a new coolness in the air. The hood covered the face, and I watched the figure move hesitantly over to the counter. Mario said a few words and the figure nodded under the hood. And then painted fingers reached up and slid the hood back to reveal long grey locks of hair. The woman turned, searching for a table. She had a kindly face, with ruddy cheeks, and I instantly relaxed.

Calm down, Payton, I told myself firmly. It had been days since I had felt this way, and I must snap out of it!

As the newcomer passed by my table my gaze rested on another customer sipping tea against the far wall.

I was being watched!

Watery green eyes glared at me over a steaming cup. Above the cold eyes, the messy cropped grey hair of Mildred Mason was all too familiar. Long white fingers held a teacup to her mouth, yet she did not drink. Her gaze pierced the room as she stared so very coldly in my direction. Very slowly, she lowered the cup, to reveal a thin, predatory smile.

My heart immediately began to race, and I may have uttered something to myself in dismay.

I was being hunted.

Chapter III
In which Payton Edgar actually runs

I left my tea untouched.

All I could think of was to grab my hat and run, and run far. Unfortunately, I hadn't actually moved my legs any quicker than a gentle trot in as long as I could remember. Not even, perhaps, since I was placed (very much against my will, I might add) on the hockey team at St. Augustine's. However, once I was out on the street I found myself actually running, if only a little. I wanted to put as much distance between myself and the apparition in Mario's Café as I could.

What was Mildred Mason doing there? There was only one possible answer - and it chilled me right through to the bone.

She was there for me.

I had not gone far before I felt a little out of puff and slowed from a canter to a quick walk. A few steps later, I steadied myself and turned, half expecting to find the dreaded Mildred bearing down on me with murder in her eyes. She was indeed behind me - at least, I thought it was her - that impossibly familiar skeleton stood way back outside the tea room. A narrow form draped in a drab pastel green trench coat. She made no move, but stood and watched me from afar. It was as if she knew that she didn't need to chase after me. What was her game? To frighten me half to death?

If so, then it was very nearly working.

I carried onwards, walking briskly now, and could not resist another look over my shoulder. The skeleton in a trench coat had gone.

Where to go? I asked myself, coming rather speedily to the conclusion that I needed to keep near to people, to stay in public where no harm could possibly come to me. I was heading in the direction of Victo-

179

ria Station, and so that became my destination.

Any astute Londoner dislikes Victoria. One expects many places in the capital to be bustling with activity and even at times to be a little chaotic or haphazard, but few places have the air of disorganisation that Victoria enjoys. Normally sensible travellers find themselves spun around in ever-changing directions, rather like numerous herds of cattle all trapped within one impossible meadow. I cannot abide the hustle and bustle of it all, that sense of hundreds of people, each with somewhere different to go, all jostling about together like flies in a bottle.

I felt sick, and ploughed onwards into the rabble.

It was, however, surprisingly soothing to be amongst a crowd. Suddenly, the place seemed inviting and, more importantly, *safe*. Once I was in the centre of the concourse I found a bench and sat stiffly.

I was to remain there for some time, furtively watching passers by, without a skeleton in a trench coat in sight. I told myself that if I sat it out, Mildred Mason would give up her ridiculous game of cat and mouse. What on earth did she hope to achieve?

A pale-faced bobby passed by, and for a moment I dared myself to go up to him and inform him of my fears. But what could I say? The minute I mentioned persecution at the hand of the Masons, any bobby worth his salt would recall that lunatic from the papers and there would be egg on my face yet again.

I certainly didn't want to play into that trap.

Of course, I couldn't stay sitting amongst the crowds of Victoria forever. Countless people had caught their trains, and many more arrived in the time I sat on that bench, but I was quite, quite happy to sit and wait. What could have been hours passed by, and there was still no sign of Mildred Mason or her vile husband, and eventually I decided that it was safe to move on.

If I left through a lesser known exit at the far end of the concourse, hailed a cab and headed straight for home, then I would be alright. Back on Clarendon Street I would knock at Irving's door and tell him everything. I had kept the man in the dark for too long.

He would know what to do, and would surely guide me with a sensible and logical approach.

A train had just rolled in on the Brighton Line, and I took this opportunity to engulf myself in the ensuing crowd, following them through the passageway to the cool air outside, where it had started to spot with rain. Two large red buses were parked immediately in front of me, and I passed these hurriedly, finally arriving at an empty taxi rank. I badly needed to hail a cab and to get myself home as quickly as possible. Standing still did not appeal, and I moved on along the pavement.

Mercifully, two taxis rolled along. I hailed the first, and bundled myself into the rear seat. The driver, bug-eyed and grey in pallor, grunted a question.

'Clarendon Street, Pimlico!' I panted. 'And step on it!'

He made no effort to use the most sensible and direct route, or to nudge against the speed limit, however it didn't matter. Once I was in the moving car, having seen neither hide nor hair of Mildred Mason for a good hour or so, I relaxed and told myself that everything would all be alright.

In fact, there was no reason to worry Irving with this news. What had Mildred Mason actually done? Sat near to me in a tea shop, that was all. He would surely only say that I had scared myself. Suddenly I felt unsure of myself. *It was her I had seen, wasn't it?*

No, I wouldn't tell anyone about Mildred's appearance. I had to put the whole ridiculous affair as far behind me as possible.

Chapter IV

In which Payton Edgar finds himself in a sticky situation

The Royal Mayvere Hotel
Admit One
"Policy and peregrination: a potted history"
A lecture by the Home Secretary
5pm
Tuesday 18th September 1962

Beryl Baxter and I arrived at the Mayvere fashionably late.

This was down to the fruitless search for a hairpin back in Beryl's office. We had agreed to meet in her office at Thistle House and that Beryl would lay on a car for us. I had tried to tell my ex-colleague that I would wait outside for her, but she was having none of it. After reluctantly entering the building I made a point of wavering outside Bilborough's office with a scowl, but the man was nowhere in sight. It was disheartening to be back in my workplace. I could not fail to notice that nobody approached me with a kind word or expression of dismay at my dismissal.

I found Beryl in an unusual position on her office floor. She had, as expected, hit the whisky already, and was cowering on all fours, searching for the missing hairpin while uttering expletives under her breath. I studied my watch.

'I'm here, Beryl, bang on time. Now, I have seen no invite, and could barely read your note. What exactly is on our plate this evening?' I enquired to her backside.

'You should know!' she sang from the floor.

182

A somewhat strange thing to say.

'Beg pardon? I thought you would have the lowdown on the head-liners, Beryl!'

'Lecture and dinner, Payton, so it's the usual mob,' she replied to the floor. 'Although it's a mildly political affair, the whole thing's laid on by the Van Deusens, so they'll be an element of glamour about the whole thing. I want to catch the senior Van Deusen with a query about the Spring collection. Where is that damn pin?'

'Do you really need it?' I put in pointedly. 'Surely you have other hairpins!'

'I have hundreds of pins, Payton, and many of them on my head. I just don't want anyone getting stuck by this rogue. I think it rolled off the side there-'

'Let the cleaner find it, Beryl,' I grizzled, and she caught my tone.

'I'll have to! Though judging by the dirt on these floorboards behind the cabinet I'd say it would take an age. Help me up, then!'

I did as I was bid and she straightened her wig. Tonight's choice was rather like a stack of currant buns in a teashop window. She dusted down her dress, a fashionable cut with a plunging neckline that would have been indecent on someone of Beryl's age were it not for the stole that she then draped over her shoulders. She took a final swig of her drink and I escorted her out.

A political affair, Beryl had said.

These words should perhaps have set alarm bells ringing, however Mildred Mason's fleeting appearance at the tea shop had had a strange effect on me. One might say it was the opposite of what one would expect. Suddenly, I wasn't afraid of the Masons. Suddenly, I told myself I was ready for anything, that I couldn't - and wouldn't - be hurt. I most certainly wouldn't be hounded out of High Society to become a well-dressed recluse. I had vowed to forget all things Mason-related.

I had, rather, buried my head in the sand.

The Mayvere Hotel was busier than I had ever seen it, the foyer stuffed with cigar-smoking gents in well-worn dinner jackets, and a lesser number of female guests dotted about. It was certainly a man's affair, and I instantly felt out of place. Gentlemanly pursuits such as talking politics or sports while choking on stinking cigar smoke was never my thing. Still, I fetched our drinks and with shoulders up and chest out I plunged in to the crowd with Beryl at my side.

A sizeable platform and hundreds of chairs had turned the Mayvere dance floor from a ballroom to a bustling lecture theatre. At the far end stood a towering lectern. A number of people were seated, but the majority gathered around the bar and foyer. Suddenly I realised my mistake.

'Beryl, did you say that this was a mildly political affair...'

She snorted. 'Yes, rather fusty in here, isn't it? I feel like a pot plant in a gentleman's club! It's all rather thrilling! Can't see a Van Deusen in sight, though.'

'We might as well be at Westminster!' I spat, feeling the first tinges of concern. And then, suddenly, I saw the face I had been dreading. Ercot Mason was propped against the far wall and laughing in his exaggerated, high-handed way. He had not spotted me, and for a minute I weighed up my options.

'Will you excuse me, Beryl. Please stay here, I will return in just a minute!'

I summoned all the strength I had, and headed over to Mason.

He was irritatingly unbothered by my appearance.

Before I could say a word he had greeted me in the way one does with a tolerated colleague, a quick word and a dry handshake. My mouth was dry and I struggled to speak.

'Strange to see you here, Edgar. Wouldn't have thought a legislative lecture was your bag. Here for the free champagne, I presume?'

'I just wanted to say hello, and now I have!' I found myself saying. Mason chuckled.

'Don't look so frightened, Edgar. I've left Mildred at home, you know, baking some more of her delicious rock buns.'

I found some sly words from somewhere.

'Any delusional grand plans to overthrow the authorities, Mason?'

The man laughed as if what I had said was an extremely amusing joke.

'If I had, Edgar, I'm sure you would be ready to thwart them!' He drew on his cigar and fixed his eyes on mine. 'As it happens, there is something.'

'You have a new plan?' I scoffed. 'It'll be just as good as the last one, I'm sure.'

My adversary issued an elongated sigh tinged with an irritating lightness. He lowered his voice carefully.

'Even better than the last one, Edgar. I realise now that my original plan to silence St John was something of a folly - at best a dream, at worst a childish act of vandalism. I freely admit that I had not thought it through. If the finger of suspicion pointed my way, as it would have in time, I would have been done for, despite our plans to flee. I would be incriminating myself, besmirching my good name. However, thanks to your actions, Mr Edgar, I have received nothing but accolades and good wishes. Everybody loves a victim, it turns out. You have rather raised my standing. I should thank you, I really should.'

His gloating was intolerable, setting that heat bubbling in my chest.

'So then, it stands to reason that I should take the opportunity you have presented me with. You, Mr Edgar, are nothing but a lunatic and a fanatic, at least as far as our press and constabulary believe. A lunatic with a mind to attack those in power. So, we ask ourselves- what would such a lunatic do next?'

'I think the question, Mason, is what would a lunatic such as Ercot Mason do next? More dud explosives?'

'There was nothing dud about that device! Anyhow, contrary to what he looks like on the outside, Payton Edgar is a very resourceful lunatic. He employs the machine of both defence and attack.'

'What the Dickens are you on about, Mason? You sound like a rambling madman!'

'And yet that's exactly what they thought of you, wasn't it? You were, Mr Edgar, a fairly well respected member of London society, until your embarrassing display at Westminster.'

He leaned in, with a wry smile.

'I do indeed have a new plan, Mr Edgar. And you are it!'

'I will be no such thing!' I snapped immediately, engaging all the defences I could. My head began to spin. Was he really threatening me? With all these people around us, and without his bloodhound of a wife? The man had a hide thicker than a rhino in lederhosen.

'You try anything, Mason, anything at all, and I report my findings to the police-'

He interrupted with an explosive guffaw.

'Oh, yes! And that went so well last time, didn't it? Mr Edgar, you have already lost your job, your prospects and the respect of all those around you. What more is there to lose?' He answered his own question. 'Your freedom, I suppose. Locking you away for everyone's safety is the next obvious step. I guarantee, Edgar, that if you carry on with your wild accusations and queer behaviour you will indeed be put away.'

Mason rested his tongue on his top lip for a second before withdrawing it suddenly, rather like a slithering snake.

'I hate you, Mason!' I grumbled, finding nothing more substantial to say.

'The feeling is mutual, my dear friend! Enjoy the lecture!'

And so I backed away from the man, more than just a little bit shaken. Beryl must have noticed my ashen look.

'Payton, Good Lord, what on earth are you doing? That was Ercot Mason you were talking to? I'd have thought you'd never go near him with a barge pole!'

'Why didn't you tell me what this night was all about, Beryl? A constitutional lecture? You should've known Mason would be here! And what is the lecture, anyway?'

Beryl was glaring at me with a dark look. I have never crossed the queen of the society pages, and based on that look she was giving me, prayed that I never would. Her look was icy to say the least.

'You wanted to come tonight, Payton. It was your friend who suggested it!'

'My f-friend?' I stammered in confusion.

'Townsend. Townsend sent me the invitation, and had scrawled on it…wait I have it here!' She fumbled in her handbag and brought out a tattered card. Below the printed details was a hand-written note.

"Please bring my old friend, Payton Edgar."

'St John Townsend? But I've never met the man, Beryl!'

'Then why-?'

The crowd around us began to disperse as people took to their seats. By the stage, St John Townsend stood at the far left, awaiting his cue. He clutched lecture notes to his chest as his eyes scanned the crowd. I had read a lot about the man, but had never seen him in person. Townsend was a portly gentleman with flushed ruddy cheeks and the bearing of a scholar. He had been, no doubt, born into his position, as he held the air of the aristocrat. He looked bored.

Suddenly, a familiar face loomed out of the crowd and made straight for Beryl and I.

'Mr Edgar! What are you doing here?'

It was young Constable Woodcock, out of uniform and looking dapper in a shirt and tie. His expression was one of grave concern, and he spoke in urgent, hushed tones.

' An invitation,' I uttered by way of reply. I went to introduce Beryl, but Woodcock cut in.

'Something's afoot, Mr Edgar, and I am extremely worried. The Mason's are up to something!'

A wave of relief passed over me and I leaned in closer to the young man.

'You - you believe me?'

'Something just didn't feel right about the whole thing, Mr Edgar. I've kept an eye on things ever since that palaver at Westminster. And then a boat was sunk on the Thames! I checked in on the investigation and it was something of a mystery, the only possible solution being the most unusual - a stray explosive in the waters-'

'The briefcase!' I sang.

'Exactly! Couldn't prove it, though. Skipper got the blame, and that was that. But it set me onto watching the Mason household a bit closer, like. The man has a particular fixation on old St John Townsend-'

'He does indeed!'

186

'And they are here tonight, it's no coincidence!'

'*They?*' I parroted.

'I think they're up to something. I've called on Standing, he should be here anytime. I think tonight's the night. Whatever it is, they're definitely up to something.'

'*They?*'

'*Woodcock!* What's the meaning of this?'

I recognised that disavowing tone immediately, and turned to see Inspector Standing. He wore an ill-fitting dinner jacket, and was clearly unhappy to find his subordinate chatting with the lunatic Payton Edgar. Woodcock went to speak, but was silenced before he could utter a word.

'I thought you were talking nonsense when you called, Woodcock, and seeing you with this cretin only proves it! You've fallen for this idiot's gobbledegook!'

'Sir, I'm so glad you got here so quickly! There-'

'I was here anyway, you fool. St John is a fine speaker and a good friend of The Yard. He's on the board of our membership committee, Woodcock, you should know that. I am here for the lecture.'

'But Sir, we have to stop the lecture immediately!'

'Out of the question! I shall enjoy the lecture, and you should too. You're welcome to join me at the side,' Standing turned and wagged a finger in my direction. 'And no funny business from you, Edgar!'

Once he was gone I issued an observation.

'That man is an irritant of the highest order!'

'Never mind!' said Woodcock with some urgency. He looked over the ballroom where almost everyone had taken to their seats. 'Mason's up front, but where is his Missus...' His eyes searched the room.

'Mildred is here?' I said faintly, fear tightening my throat. 'Mason said she was at home.'

'He lied. She is most definitely here, somewhere,' said Woodcock. 'I followed her in. And there's Townsend!'

At the other end of the ballroom St John Townsend and a number of his lackeys were mounting the stage. We watched them for a minute, until I put my hands in my pockets. My right hand rested on something alien.

'What is this?'

Beryl and Woodcock turned and watched as I slid a pistol from my pocket.

'How did that get there?' I asked weakly.

'Oh, Mr Edgar!' Woodcock gasped. 'We have to get that man off the stage!' He darted away.

Beryl was looking at me with wide eyes as I fingered the gun.

'I am the plan!' I muttered helplessly, as the trap was sprung around me.

Chapter V

In which Payton Edgar brandishes a firearm

I have always disliked guns and muskets, and distrust those who hold such a licence. In my opinion, our leaders should strip the land of all firearms, and now there I stood, wielding a gun in some confusion. I gripped the weapon in my hand and stared at it fearfully.

'What's going on, Payton?' Beryl asked briskly, and not without excitement.

The lights around us dimmed, and polite applause scattered the room. I looked frantically around, desperately searching for Mildred Mason, however the rear corners of the ballroom were shadowy, and she could have been lurking anywhere. There was a balcony at the far wall that was set in the shadows, a perfect place for Mildred to shelter. It was a horrifying thought.

'Payton! What's happening? Why have you brought that gun, for giddy's sake?'

'I have never seen this gun in my life, Beryl! It must have been slipped into my pocket! Someone somewhere is about to shoot Townsend - leaving me in the frame!'

I looked to the front. Woodcock was pushing through the stiff-suited men who loitered at the side, but he was still some way from the stage. Up at the front, to the left of the platform, Inspector Standing had appeared and was peering up at Townsend and clapping like a seal. The man had no idea what was going on.

Up on the stage a lanky academic type had been fiddling with a microphone. He pushed round spectacles up the bridge of his nose and spoke gingerly.

'Good evening- ah!' an electronic squeal flew from the machine.

189

'Sorry, sorry all. Now, testing! Yes, good...good evening gentlemen. Good evening! Welcome to the Mayvere ballroom, and to our annual Autumn Lecture. Transcripts will be available in the lobby after the session...'

'Good grief!' I exclaimed helplessly. 'We can't just stand here!'

'What do we do?' Beryl trilled.

'What do we do?' I repeated her words helplessly.

'We have to do something!' said Beryl.

And then the applause around us picked up as St John Townsend mounted the stage. He accepted the applause with a casual air and took his position at centre stage. My heart was pounding in my chest.

'We have to warn Townsend!' I found myself saying. 'We have to warn him!'

'Fire the gun!' said Beryl excitedly.

'I beg your-'

'Fire the gun!' she repeated.

'Are you insane?'

'You want Townsend off the stage? Fire - into the air - a warning shot!'

'That, Beryl, is exactly what they'd want me to do! If I fire this thing I'll be done for! Do you want to make it look like-'

'Oh, give it here!' Beryl growled, and she snatched the pistol from my grasp. In an instant she raised it into the air and fired. The bang of the gun was unbelievably loud and she was lucky that she hadn't sent a chandelier crashing down upon us. For a split second the room froze, and then there was pandemonium, both on stage and off. Some of the audience ducked and some fled. Many were shrieking and fussing. I searched and searched among the clamouring crowd for Mildred Mason.

A second shot pierced the air, this from somewhere behind us - our invisible assassin had struck!

Instinctively Beryl and I ducked wildly. Firing the gun had had an odd effect on Beryl, who was was cackling and grinning as though this was all a fabulous jape. Over on the stage I could see St John Townsend being ushered away, unscathed. Inspector Standing, however, had not been so lucky. He was clutching his thigh with blood stained hands as he slowly sank to the floor. Woodcock jumped over to his side.

The whole room was in chaos with people rushing for various exits, some screams ringing out over the general hubbub.

I was searching the mass of people, and caught sight of Ercot Mason just in time. He was pushing through the throng, making his getaway. I plummeted through the tumbling crowd and stood firm in his path.

'Hold on there, Mason!'

One could not help but smile as he stopped in his tracks, a grim look on his pale face.

'Get out of my way, Edgar!' he growled.

I allowed a victorious laugh to escape my lips. Around us, people were fleeing in all directions.

'It's all gone a bit wrong, hasn't it? Townsend will be fine, and I have a number of witnesses to your scheme!'

'Shut up, Edgar!'

'No! I will not shut up! I will not be silenced again! You're for it, Mason!' It was a wonderful feeling to be saying these words.

Mason grimaced, his phizog fixed in fury.

'Oh, how I despise you, Edgar!' he wailed.

Suddenly, he lifted both hands, shaking and claw-like, and then dived in my direction. The last thing I remember were shouts all around me as I was propelled sharply backwards into the wall. I met the wall with some force, feeling a sharp crack of pain at my side and an explosion inside my head. All I could see was Ercot Mason's furious gaze.

Despite the pain, I was smiling contentedly as I slid down to hit the cold hard floor.

Chapter VI
In which Payton Edgar receives some visitors

Dear Margaret,
My wife is mutton dressed as lamb. We have been married for
twenty years now, and she has always thought of herself as a snappy
dresser, but I wish she would dress in clothes appropriate to her age.
While other men obviously have a fancy for such looseness, I cannot
bear to be seen with her. What should I do?
George, Croydon

Margaret replies; *George, you begin your letter with the words*
"my wife is mutton". Clearly you have great consideration and venera-
tion for the woman. I would like to know why you find it easier to write
to a stranger than to discuss this with her? Indeed, rather than advise
you, I would rather advise her; my dear lady, you wear what you feel
comfortable wearing, never mind what your petty minded, uncharitable
husband thinks. If he has a problem with your apparel, simply leave the
man and go play the field and frolic with some other sheep.

Hospital.
I am sure that I looked like a prize idiot, my head bandaged like
Jack after his fall from the hill, and yet I was quite past caring. I had,
ever since waking in my hospital bed for the first time, been silently con-
gratulating myself for my sweet victory over Ercot Mason. After his display at the Mayvere, everyone would see him for what he really was, and
my name would be cleared. It would only be a matter of time before
Bilborough saw his error and reinstated my columns.

My good spirits, however, were severely tested by the very atmosphere of the ward in which I lay. Everything about it put me in a foul mood.

I overheard the nurses telling Irving that I was concussed, that I would be back to my "*normal self*" in "*no time at all.*"

What rubbish!

Confine a man to his bedside and feed him boiled cabbage and dry anaemic lamb or poorly rendered joints of beef each day and you will get nothing from him but a lack of motivation and a foul disposition.

'Ignore his grumps!' one particularly irritating nurse was telling my friend in an irritatingly cheery tone. 'Mr Edgar is just a little concussed.'

'Believe me, this is perfectly normal behaviour,' was Irving's dry reply. I kept my eyes firmly shut but filed the remark away in my memory for the time being. I was too beleaguered by the rush of hospital life to comment or argue. The place was ridiculous. I was shipped out of a nice warm bed at a preposterous hour, despite the agony of my hip and my head, and then ushered back into crisp cool white sheets where I would lie helplessly and painfully until visiting time.

On Irving's first visit I had begged him to take me home, to release me from the clinical prison that held me captive. He had said nothing, merely furrowing his brow and issuing a deep sigh.

'Please, tell me they got Mason?' I asked desperately. Irving nodded.

'After he'd clobbered you he tried to get away, apparently, but Beryl got in his way. He was no match for Mrs Baxter, by all accounts.'

For a moment I was annoyed. Trust Beryl to get in on the action and to steal my glory. I calmed myself. We were then interrupted by a bossy nurse - Nurse Maskell, the very worst of them all, and she fussed around me and tutted relentlessly. It was from her that I learned that I was proclaimed to be '*a poor confused soul*'. She had then ushered Irving away as a bell rang out from somewhere.

For a good day or two I was too weak to kick up any kind of fuss.

My knock on the head had been a rather bad one. For most of the time I had slept, only waking for each disappointing meal that was plonked before me. I thanked the Heavens for the fat bag of lemon sherbets Irving had left aside my fruit bowl. Across the ward from me lay the Invisible Man, a figure of plaster and bandage who lay motionless, almost white from head to foot, the only hint of humanity being the pink nose which poked through where his face should have been. That and the occasional wretched sobs of pain that came in the night.

On what may have been my second or even my third day in hospital, Irving arrived baring an unwanted gift. It was a new walking stick. I did not stop to admire the craftsmanship of the carvings or the ornate rams horn handle, and instead insisted that my own beloved stick be brought in if I was to rehabilitate successfully. I wanted my own stick, my beautiful stick, the fine dark mahogany stick with the beautiful brass owl perched atop, its smooth head revealing dark, wise eyes. A truly noble bird.

I dropped the unwanted stick aside with a clatter and lay back in my sick bed, demanding my own stick, my owl.

Irving had remained only for an unsatisfactorily short period on that particular afternoon.

Constable Woodcock paid a brief visit one morning after tea, accompanied by his superior officer, a Detective Inspector Wilson. Woodcock said very little, but his colleague only added to my discontented disposition by issuing a rather stern command. The Mason affair was to be kept top secret. This part was apparently worth repeating. *Top secret!* Under no circumstances should I discuss what had occurred in Westminster or at the Mayvere ballroom. It was to be a matter of public protection, young Woodcock had added with fervent importance.

'You have an excellent constable here,' I said, pointing at Woodcock. 'He saw what was happening better than any of you. He is a credit to Scotland Yard.'

'You'll get no argument from me there,' said Wilson casually. Woodcock beamed.

'It won't be easy to keep an assassination attempt on a top politician under wraps,' I told them. The senior officer glanced around him.

'The cover story is that Inspector Standing was the intended victim of some disgruntled lowlife. A person with a grudge-'

'Mmm. An entirely believable scenario,' I put in pointedly. 'And how is the dear old Inspector?'

'Only a flesh wound,' Woodcock piped up. 'He'll pull through. He's on the next ward along, incidentally.'

'No permanent damage that might push him from the force?'

'None,' replied Woodcock.

Shame, I thought to myself coldly.

And so I had been silenced. My keen investigations, my deductions, not to mention my suffering, were to be spoken of no more. As if this were not enough, there was one more alarming piece of news they had for me. A piece of news that I really did not wish to hear.

'I'm afraid to say that we have failed to locate Mildred Mason. She was lost in the crowd at the Mayvere, and hasn't been seen since. It seems she must have slipped the country. Her luggage and passport are gone. Our best guess is that she will be far away by now.'

A cold hand gripped my heart.

'Where do you think she could be?' I asked fearfully.

'Not a clue,' said Woodcock. 'The trail ends in the direction of South America, though.'

Not far enough, I thought to myself. *Not far enough.*

Later that evening I woke myself by cursing the Raqs Sharqi club and all its miserable members. In my dream, Charles and Bunny Follett had been laughing and eating stale rock buns as Sir Maurice Williams rehearsed, holding a skull aloft on the Mayvere ballroom stage.

It took me a minute to remember where I was before that tang of bleach in the air snapped me back to reality.

I had been stirred from my slumber by raised voices at the nurse's station. Despite the fact that visiting hours had long since passed, Beryl Baxter won her argument with the nurses and stomped over to visit me. She spoke loudly, quite unaware that everybody in the place was listening to her high tones, and only lowered her voice to a whisper when she surreptitiously passed over a shining silver hip-flask.

'For medicinal purposes!' she chuckled. I slipped the flask into my pyjama pocket appreciatively. It was not the alcohol that appealed so much as the act of rebellion. That grim nurse would be apoplectic if she so much as caught a whiff of liquor.

I congratulated Beryl on her apprehension of Ercot Mason, and she shook off my praise with a shrug, as if attacking mischievous politicians was merely second nature.

'Nobody hurts my dear Mr Edgar and gets away with it!' she cackled. She informed me that she too had received a visit from the constabulary and had been officially censored.

However, if I were not allowed to speak of the Masons and their murderous plots, nobody had said anything about the other members of the Raqs Sharqi Club. While in my bed I had mulled over the things I had learned over the Summer. I knew that any news about the Folletts was worth reporting, and I had a humdinger of a story. I also had some prime tittle tattle on Sir Maurice Williams.

It was time to release it.

I told Beryl everything I knew, allowing her to make a few notes on her pad as she licked her lips in delight. She would need to dig a little further elsewhere, but I set her on the right path.

The following afternoon I purchased a copy of The Clarion from the tea trolley. There was no mention of Mason's downfall, of course, but the society page held a number of interesting titbits. Titbits that had been most gratefully received by my colleague Beryl Baxter.

Beautiful, delicious titbits!

I sat upright in bed and read her column with growing satisfaction.

I had finally triumphed over the Raqs Sharqi rabble!

Chapter VII

In which Payton Edgar discharges himself

The London Clarion
Beryl Baxter's Society
September 1962

RSC actor in failed audition shame

Beryl Baxter has been reliably informed that ageing thespian Sir Maurice Williams has been snubbed by television after failing to successfully audition for a screen part. As regular readers will recall, the stage legend has often voiced his disregard for screen acting, but we can reveal that Sir Maurice unsuccessfully auditioned for a BBC television drama just last week. Beryl Baxter has it on good authority that Sir Maurice does not have a face that is considered comfortable for televisual viewing. Cheeky!

Divorce for Art Gallery Millionaire

As eagle-eyed gossip-mongers will know, Lord Charles Follett yesterday announced his divorce from Lady Barbara Follett, née Baggott. Further details remained undisclosed by the formal channels, yet we can now exclusively reveal the grounds behind this divorce. Beryl Baxter has it on good authority that the split comes following Lord Charles's steamy affair with the Follett gallery curator. The young lady in question has since fled to New York. Why should the guilty party cite the divorce and not the other way around, I hear you ask? Regular readers will recall my account of Lady Follett's notorious comments and shameful inebriated behaviour at the Palace Gardens Gala Ball in South Kensington, as reported last weekend. Lord Follett yesterday cited unreasonable behaviour as his grounds for divorce.

197

I read these articles a number of times with pleasure.

I pictured rancid Sir Maurice Williams in his dressing room, tossing the paper aside with anger. I pictured Charles Follett, alone in his vast dining room, grumbling over the details of the scandal he had created with his own infidelity. And, best of all, I pictured horse-face Lady Follett reading the Clarion on a bench in St James's Park, clutching a claw to her be-jewelled bosom and gasping in horror and shame.

When Irving arrived I was still smiling to myself.

'You look better.' he said in earnest, handing me my stick at last.

'I feel better.' I said, grasping my owl and swinging my legs out of bed. 'I want you to do something else for me.'

'Mmm. That depends what it is,' said Irving wisely.

'Take me home.'

Irving frowned. 'But the nurse said-'

'Nurses talk a lot of tripe, Irving. I cannot stand any more clucking and fussing. I am tickety-boo, and I am going home.' I retrieved my bag, already packed, from my bedside locker, and began to pull my jacket over my pyjamas.

'You can't go out like that!' said Irving.

'Pish-tosh! It's hardly the dead of winter out there, is it? Please! I have to get out of here, Irving. I would run out into the streets naked if I had to. Besides, I've got my stick to help me!' I tapped the owl stick sharply on the cold floor before leaning in and touching his hand briefly.

'Now take me home.'

The man had no choice.

Thankfully the taxi driver did not comment on my unsatisfactory get-up, and we rode through London in silence. I have to confess that my hip and my neck still ached, but I would have rather suffered the pain alone at home. I closed my eyes for much of the journey, resting my fingers on the smooth surface of the owl's head. As we neared Pimlico, Irving turned to face me, his expression stern and serious.

'Payton, before we get home, there are a few things I have to say.' I cast my eyes to him lazily as he went on.

'I want to apologise for not having believed you about Mason.'

I nodded and waited. Was that all? It had been a long time coming, and I had expected a long, more heartfelt apology. Irving went on.

'My next point, and I'm not quite sure how to put it-'

'Then don't bother!'

'Payton, all I ask is that you never keep secrets from me again.'

'Oh, please-'

'No, I mean it, Payton. If you had told me what you were doing, where you were going right at the start, none of this would have happened, would it?'

'Perhaps,' I said lightly, 'and perhaps not.'

I mulled this over to myself. True, if Irving knew where I was when visiting Mason's cottage then he could have acted upon my abduction. However, if I had shared my plans it could have been even worse. There was no predicting the animal that was Mildred Mason. Perhaps she would have killed Irving, and enjoyed it too.

We were nearly home. I mindlessly ran my hands over the cool metal of my owl stick, finding some pleasure in its soft curves. Irving wisely remained mute for the rest of the journey, and it was only once we were home that he spoke again.

'There is a gift here for you,' he declared softly as we entered the living room.

The gift was the first thing I saw - the portrait on the wall, above my mantelpiece. He had removed my old sketch of Westminster Cathedral and replaced it with a more contemporary piece. A dozen shades of blue swirled over the canvas.

"*Pomposity"* by Irving Spence.

The colours were vivid, beautiful even. Irving had said how popular the piece was, and yet he had saved it for me. Rather overwhelmed, I spoke without reservation.

'It's beautiful! It really is. I shall never tire of looking at it. Thank you, Irving.'

Grace Kemp appeared from the hallway, set down some dirty cups and threw a kiss past my cheek. She smelt of talcum powder, and had a mischievous glint in her eye.

'Wonderful to have you home, Payton,' she sang. 'Sit yourself down, I'll brew you both some tea.'

I did as I was bid. Miss Kemp busied herself in the kitchenette, and approached me once the kettle was set on the gas.

'I did as you said, and bought your Aunt that television set…'

I sensed hesitation in her tone.

'And?'

'Well, at first it was fine, a perfect distraction for her. But she's gone right off it now. The set's been off these past few days, I'm afraid, she's not at all happy with it.'

'I gave you plenty of money to buy a good model!'

'Yes, and I did, I did. It's not the picture or anything. It's the programmes. She says she'd like a different set with better programmes.'

I growled a low growl, but made no reply. Even Aunt Elizabeth couldn't put a damper on my victorious return home.

'Irving,' I said, contentedly. 'Let's go out for dinner soon. I suspect the Clarion will be pining for the return of Payton's Plate.'

My friend agreed firmly. Unfortunately it was not long before he resumed his mantle of worrywart and began to nick-pick once more. Miss Kemp had passed us steaming cups of tea and was busying herself at the sink.

I should be wary, Irving informed me, of involving myself in dangerous situations. I should stay away from gangs and groups and places where I perhaps don't belong. And I should simply be myself, not strive to integrate myself in exclusive clubs with avaricious motivations. On and on he went. To achieve notoriety is an unfavourable goal. Prestige is not everything. And then, he ended his ridiculous mumblings with a hideous cliché.

'Pride,' he said, 'comes before a fall.'

I simply nodded at this, for I was tired of arguing.

'Did you hear me, Payton?' Irving pressed relentlessly.

'Indeed,' I replied wearily, 'Pride comes before a fall and prestige is not everything.'

I was still only half attending, for my eye had caught the glint of a golden envelope atop my mantelpiece propped alongside my chipped antique singing bowl. I issued a small enquiry and made for the fireplace.

'What's this?'

'Oh, that came the other day,' Miss Kemp said without much care. 'I put it there to remind me. It looks interesting.'

'It looks *expensive*!' I corrected her enthusiastically. The gold-embossed envelope was evidently not of standard manufacture. I deftly slid open the envelope with my crocodile tail letter-opener. Inside was a similarly glamorous card, crimson with shining gold holly leaves and berries decorating each corner. The words upon the card were carefully considered and the handwriting displayed a good schooling behind the pen.

'How wonderful!' I exclaimed.

'What is it, Payton? An invitation?' asked Irving.

I clutched the missive to my chest with pleasure, my eyes gleaming with hope and anticipation.

'An invitation, Irving! An invitation of some import!' I announced with joy, and then continued in a hushed tone. 'A prestigious invitation, summoning Payton Edgar himself!'

'Payton...' my friend growled wearily. I inspected the card once more, with glee.

'A most prestigious invitation indeed!'

THE END

Thanks...

I would like to thank Becky, Judith and Sally for their time and effort in helping me polish and shape this book. Thanks also to Chris... for being perfect.

MJT Seal